PICCOLO MONDO

Piccolo Mondo

*a novel of youth in 1961
as seen somewhat later by*

Angela Bowering

George Bowering

David Bromige &

Michael Matthews

Coach House Books

Copyright © Angela Bowering, George Bowering, David Bromige & Michael Matthews 1998

ALL RIGHTS RESERVED

First edition

CANADIAN CATALOGING IN PUBLICATION DATA

Main entry under title:

Piccolo Mondo

ISBN 1-55245-014-7 (bound)   ISBN 1-55245-024-7 (pbk.)

I. Bowering, George, 1935

PS8550.P52 1997   C813'.54   C97-932408-4
PR9199.3.P52 1997

Dedications:

Thanks to Cecelia Belle for seeing that the name of the restaurant where we first cooked up this novel was the title we were looking for. It's a terrific restaurant, too.

We dedicate this book to Ian Dunn, Ian Currie, Barrie Hale, Bob Thomson, Jessie Webb, Carolyn Friedson, Warren Tallman, Robert Duncan, Red Lane, Charles Olson, Roy Kiyooka, Dave Berg, Toby Oldfield, Fred Hill, Paddy Manzer, Martin Bartlett, Sam Perry, and those other friends our ailing memories cannot now call to mind, or of whose deaths we have yet to hear. We might have been you. Sometimes we thought we were. You helped make the little world we loved, and we hated to see you go. Some days you are realler than what's left!

And to Thea Bowering, Chris Bromige, Margaret Belle Bromige, and Alison Matthews, who have had a different world to grow up in, small thanks to us, and might have preferred the one between these covers. Here it is, not exactly as it was (ahem), but close enough. Learn by our mistakes – grow up! And you have grown up. We love you for it, and we loved you anyway. Read and forgive!

Finally, hello, Earle, in your particular Valhalla.

Any resemblance between these characters and persons living or dead is purely coincidental.

"It is in the future that they must see their history."

—Henri Michaux

CHAPTER ONE

The first thing you need to keep in mind if you're going to write a novel about the 1950s, which began in 1951 and ended in 1962, is the multitude of stuff that hasn't happened yet. I mean no Sixties (1963-73), no Seventies (1974-79), no Eighties (1980-1992). We're sitting in The Georgia, and as far as the mini goes we're *tabulae rasae*. John, Paul, George are in Hamburg but we're in the cellar in Vancouver – and what is Vancouver? An overgrown small town, more wood than brick, more brick than concrete, the laws are so blue we can't be sitting there on a Sunday, and unless we've found a female over twenty-one to get us into the Ladies & Escorts side of the beer parlour, to meet other females, why, we're sitting in a space that's strictly men only. The expectation is frontier town, words like rugged and twofisted float, definitely not MCP or MADD. Mind you we're college eggheads, and other such are present, but some of the patrons are loggers or off the boats or psychos from Saskatchewan seeking a new love or an old grudge to be settled by punching some egghead and they're getting drunk fast. Though, being Canadian, even this rough trade has training in a certain mild-mannered benevolence, but only up to a point. You have to remember that they're not packing guns, and, seeing it's The Georgia, probably not carrying knives, either. But they're not without prejudices and they're paying taxes to keep us in school doing fuck all while they're bustin' their butts – and tonight they're getting *drunk*. We want to joke intelligently and sing our silly songs of sophomore humour so we have to negotiate the terrain, it isn't goddammit ours alone. Sooner or later some chump will ask to join our table and he won't be taking no for an answer. Sooner or later he'll want to argue in a language game we're not playing. The table is crowded with glasses full of beer because one can only order up to two glasses at a time so naturally everyone does. Then there are splashes of colour: the glasses of tomato juice. Sooner or later, but for sure, someone is going to knock one of these glasses over. It's 1961, two more years to go till the sixties begin, no-one has stopped smoking so the air is blue with fumes. We're smoking Chesterfields, Black Cats, Buckinghams, Cameos, Craven As, Players, Export As, Marlboros, you name it if you're fifty or over: never without a lit one. And what are we saying?

Before we say what we think we were saying we have to remember that it sounded utterly different then than those same words and phrases do today because today they willy nilly refer to major public or minor personal events of the past thirty-five years. Listening to us talk, talking back then, is like listening to a foreign tongue. It's akin to Pound's difficulty writing in American slang from the 1890s and the 1900s, in the 1920s and 1930s and 1940s – moving further and further away from its currency. After all, we're persons, and that's strictly an architectural affair. You live there a while and then the big iron ball comes through the wall and you move to someplace else. There I sit, never having smoked a joint. Haven't dropped acid. Jerussi hasn't invented the pill yet. I haven't met Jack Spicer. I haven't raised a kid. I eat without forethought. In fact I only eat when the person or persons I'm with eat; in that way I'm completely undifferentiated, a member of the herd. They shut down the beer parlour for an hour at 6:30, the other people at the table either go home for dinner or to Hudson's Bay Company where there's a snack bar or somesuch, eat, return for the evening's stint. If someone takes me home for dinner, I go, I maybe eat. Or I go to HBC and do eat. I have no notion what I'm eating. Eat, someone says. You'll be able to drink longer and not get so drunk. So I eat.

I never noticed stuff like that. There's a whole lot of stuff I simply don't notice, back then. I don't monitor my own behavior very closely. Well, I haven't had psychotherapy yet, I know I have problems of that order but I believe they make me who I am, and although it's evident even to me at times that that's a pretty desperate configuration of drives and impulses, I'm witlessly attached to my momentum and its baffles, wouldn't trade 'em whatever the offer or the cost. And ghoddamit I'm right, McGee.

So what is it I do notice? What you say, how you say it, how your face looks as you say it, things you do with your body because of what gets said. The power of the spoken word. And how our speech rings the bells of reference… Movies, books, people we know, want to know more of. And wordplay, slips, puns, or a word I can only guess the meaning of from its context. Sex – still a bigger mystery than the irreducible-minimum mystery it must ever be.

Peeking into the Ladies and Escorts side at the beauty and allure gathered there, boozing and smoking just like us guys. The people I know like movies where the hero triumphs over unbearable obstacles then fucks up and is killed. I don't know about you but I expect to die shortly. And don't let's forget we all expect to die shortly, atomized by The Bomb. The Cuban Crisis hasn't occurred to demonstrate that maybe It won't get detonated. No, the hourglass cloud has already been inverted, the sand is trickling quickly down. Drink, get drunk, have fun, get laid. Yet that's oddly only a partial imperative. Meanwhile, also, read books, wrangle over ideas, obey many of the laws we could probably get away with breaking, beads on a cultural string drawn pointlessly on. We worry about grades, finals, though I don't recall much worry about careers. I'm already an elementary school teacher anyway; somehow I had it together enough (definitely an anachronism there) to cause that to happen. At the same time I expect to be famous. I'm marking time till that happens. Actually I'm driven, writing through my hangovers, bad stuff about characters with fashionable hangups, weird poems about people turned to stone on the beach.

I would really like to do a lot of fucking. Being young can't have changed in some respects. So in that way, too, no longer young, it's impossible to inhabit that person sitting across the table with you. That I gets hardons two, three times a day, without apparent provocation. No wonder the gals look so glamorous. You college fellas are attractive too, though I hasten to add, etc. Some of you are thoroughly middleclass in training and I like your assurance, you expect, expect to be bright, intellectual, well-read. We give the middleclass a lot of flak, squares, dullsville, all that, no doubt this general dismissal can find many points of application, but the middleclass, being such, made you the way you are and I think it's wonderful. From time to time, as a college intellectual who's loads of fun, I get to see inside your houses (your parents' houses) and I like it there. It's tedium to you but exotic to me. And you're all exotic, just about everyone in this pub is exotic, simply by my being here with you – and simply by my being drunk.

But too, simply by your being Canadian. Because I'm British. And that's one more fact to remember, the aura of being British in Vancouver back then. Power. British voices on CBC. Brits permeating the theatre. You're either for 'em or agin 'em. The guy who has joined us at our table either wants to tell me about how great the Limeys were to him in the war, or he wants to smash my face in for being one of the oppressor race. Or he wants to get my goat until I smash *him*. Pick up a bottle and crack it over his thick skull. *Then* the shit will hit. Cece won't be standin' for any of that. Shit, Cece won't be puttin' up with anyone standing for anything: you have to drink sitting down. No singing, either – though we do.

So – Brits, the English in particular – voices modulated but loud, speaking out – saying how it should be done. Showing the rest the reasonable way. And then the Ozzies. Escaping my fellowcunts, I seek out the Ozzies. There's a hotel, the Gifford, in the West End, where a couple of lads from Melbin take me to dinner one day when the pub shuts. Everyone in the below-street-level restaurant must be Ozzie. Everyone knows everyone. They've met in a score of cities strung round the world. Here, they meet again. A bread fight commences – they know how to have fun. The women are just like guys. Easy come, easy go. Now that I've seen southern California, Ozzies don't strike me as so distinctive. But they were the first people I met who lived in their bodies that way.

But there's a plot to be planted here, if a novel's to be written. Three of us are walking a long way to our various basement suites, having no car, and a good thing too! The only people I know with cars are my sister, who lives almost in Burnaby, Eduardo Viejo Pink-Meadow-Pink, the Anglo-Portuguese-Canadian strawberry farmer from Saanich, who might have been along tonight in his classic 1934 Oldsmobile, but isn't, was probably singing something dainty, even ecclesiastical, in some well-connected mansion on the Endowment Lands, Fee McMannic, who drives a Morris Minor or a vw Bug, some vehicle, anyway, that causes his knees to touch his chin when he's behind the wheel, and who we understand on this particular evening was porking Iowa's finest, the sexually perspicacious Mary Beth "Thanks for the Mammaries" Hansen, and last but not least, driving a sobriquet bestowed upon him by Sally Hillcoot, Tommy Pavlow, aka Barfly, aka Tommy P, so that one might, in referring to the exploits of the drunkest drunk at the latest Hillcoot party, not get him confused with Tommy Deadwood, the Shakespearean, who, once Pavlow had been taken into the circle, became known as Tommy D. Tommy P had been known to D (second in the alphabet that constitutes our four protagonists) years back in Gopher Hole, Alberta, and D was the only one of our trio who was likely to wonder where Tommy was at this moment, or to come up with guesses as accurate as (a) boosting booze from (1) a neighbor (2) the LCB, (b) reading *Voyage au bout de nuit* while sucking on a six pack and mistaking a streetlight for the moon, (c) driving said car with an impressive deliberation into a concrete lamp standard.

We three – this three, G, D and M – are more than halfway across the Burrard Street Bridge. D was looking out to sea, and to see the few lights still burning behind the drawn drapes of the West End's tallest building, the Hotel Sylvia, just now heaving into view. Heaving, and having so heaved, had hoved. And D was turning back to speak to his companions, G (Delsing, the poet) and M. When there was the most almighty white flash.

Yes, that's what they behold, that's it, it is the most Gigantic White Flash. G sees it first, because of his exceptional peripheral vision. Then D and M together see it too. It lights up the whole sky north behind the mountains. It lights up the West End – not a collection of high-rises at this time, remember. Three, four-storey wooden houses. But they don't burst into flame, although that glare looks hot. White hot.

"¡Shock wave next!" G says. (G has spent time in Mexico).

"It's pleasant to recall that there's nothing one can do about it," M puts in. "It's neither seemly nor comfortable to curl up into a tight ball on a city sidewalk at midnight."

D says nothing. He's having *deja vu*. Trying to recall what comes next. But nothing more occurs. So they walk on. They pass by Sick's Brewery. And on its blank walls they see some letters – as though burned into the stone. Hieroglyphs. D has a pen, G has a wrinkled envelope. And says so.

"¡Hey you guys, I have a wrinkled antelope we can use!" he tells them. They copy down the symbols. M clicks his tongue impatiently.

"It probably says something like 'You only have 24 hours to live.'"

They put away the envelope, stumble ahead. They discuss this strange event, strange twin events, no doubt. They say pretty much what anyone would say, within the constraints of what we know of these three – precious little, from a reader's point of view. They allow as how it might have been a group hallucination – but M takes out the envelope and there's the hieroglyphs.

"¡Careful with that wrinkled antelope, M!" G chortles. He always clowns when terrified.

They point out to each other that there is no necessary connection between flash and wall-writing.

By now they have reached the region where the likes of them get to live. They're wired but tired, so say g'night in front of the basement suite of G. His gangly form, much like Buddy Holly's, vanishes between the camellia bushes.

"Astounding," comments M, "How calmly he took that."

"I expect we're in shock," D offers cheerfully.

"Did it occur to you that we might all be dead?"

A pause. Then, "If so, it's distressingly like being alive… I've got to piss," and D whips it out and pisses on the wall of G's landlord.

"This could just be the illusion of pissing," M says, joining him.

CHAPTER TWO

In those days G was always looking for the writing on the wall, and he usually connected it with death. He was in his twenties somehow and expected to die when he was twenty nine, dramatically and without pain. Like a movie or the Old Testament, at a distance, completely alone, his friends or the people who went to classes with him telling each other later that they should have been at his bedside, but now here he was at the side of the bed, trying to get up, a hangover without romance holding him down. But he does get up, finds a Black Cat cigarette on the backless wooden chair beside the bed, sits, white bare feet on the cakey jeans on the dirty brown carpet on the basement concrete floor. It is the late 1950s, Jack Kerouac is as glamorous as his name, ACK ACK ACK the reverberation through G's head. Oh to be in Vancouver, so much more romantic than to be in the air force on the prairie, end of the runway, aluminum jets taking off in groups of four all night and he not hearing a thing till his Newfy roommate wakes him to get to the mess in the last minute before it is closed, get coffee, tastes like the metal it is kept in, eat some bananas, good for the ulcer, 19 years old has an ulcer. More romantic than working in the "plant" in Lawrence in the Okanagan no one has ever heard of, deep winter, counting bolts with frozen fingers. Always wants to be on the road, and Greyhounds it from time to time, smoking in the back seats, holding the newspaper upside down because that is funny, sucking on the rye whiskey or if you are really unlucky some underage Okanagan Indian guy, has some lemon gin, doesn't matter. And he never did find out whether you are supposed to mix something with lemon gin, or is the lemon something mixed already. Lemon Hart is so pretty, and the lemon gin is sweet, but the fruit of the poor lemon is impossible to eat.

G was trying to get D to eat last night. Eat, eat, he said,

you might wish you had later on. What? Like midnight, says D, no like say 1985, says G. We won't live that long says D, and they both agree. What are you going to do, get shot, die in a fiery crash, puke blood and die at a hundred and eight pounds? I am going to be shot by a jealous common law husband, says M. Then he doesn't say anything in any language other than Horse for the next hour. D goes to the can and doesn't come back, we suspect him of having slipped into the Ladies and Escorts side, give him another fifteen minutes. Maybe some guy in a plaid shirt banged his head against the porcelain in the can. I will go and see, volunteers M, and off he goes. This is eleven p.m., you are in your twenties but you have to have a leak every half hour. But you are drinking a glass every fifteen minutes. Building tissue. Building a past to look back at fondly, not a narcotic in sight. Beer was still pretty romantic.

Right after the air force he had taken Trombone into the Devonshire and bought him a Zombie, something he had learned from the nurses in Quebec. Now that too was effete. As far as G was concerned these college types were effete, especially the ones who had ridden in any car driven by someone in a fraternity, especially all the Christophers and Anthonys from England. He was in love with a Wendy from England, but he had no idea where she was. She had never been in The Georgia, upstairs or down.

He was sitting on the side of the bed, a narrow iron thing, really a kind of cot, with a thin mattress on it, with a dirty sheet on the mattress. Last year he had lived in a place where the landlady changed the sheets every week, whether there were stains on them or not. Now he was living two blocks from a laundromat, good place for love, and fifty blocks from his landlady, in a basement under a lot of other people living in wallpapered rooms that contained the smell of leaking stove gas. What was that flash in the sky last night? Did the military, their military or ours, who, have some secret installation behind the north shore mountains? The prime minister, a three piece suit lawyer with a bad haircut, from the prairies, was ready to start an election campaign, his platform to keep U.S. nuclear weapons out of Canada. In the air force a few years ago G knew casually that there were nuclear weapons already sitting under a tin roof on Vancouver Island. What was that flash in the sky? G had seen northern lights, he had *heard* northern lights. He had been *north* of the northern lights. He was not even a patriotic Canadian yet, but he knew from northern lights. M was born in the North West Territories – he was probably born in a flash and coil of northern lights. Those weren't the northern lights last night. They were not a mass hallucination, they hadn't had a Zombie all night. Twenty-five trolley buses came loose from their connections all at once within five blocks of Stanley Park?

The worst kind of explosion is a silent explosion. He started to stand up. He pitched forward, landed on the elbow that was flexed as he reached toward his mouth for his Black Cat. Fell on his elbow and his other wrist on the painted concrete floor. The floor was a kind of dark purplish red dirt colour, it looked like plasticene gorged with very old blood. He got up and found his piss jar. This was an old marmalade jar he pissed into, then carried to the laundry drain in the floor, where he poured it down. Either the smell went away in an hour or one got used to living there with the smell of piss in the laundry drain. He imagined D in his mansion up the hill, sipping French coffee, D draped in a silk dressing gown, gazing out the window through a well-managed headache at the black squirrels. In G's seventeen years in the Okanagan he had never seen a squirrel. They scampered in England and in boys' books, and in leaf-strewn yards in weary old colonialist Vancouver.

We have been, unwillingly perhaps, looking at this skinny nearsighted person for fifteen minutes or so, and we have strewn a number of pages, depending on the impecuniosity of the publisher, and have not heard much about what these people are studying. They, each of them in his own way, think of what they are supposed to study as impedimenta, or as necessary weight, something to encumber oneself with as the price of pursuing fame at a west coast Canadian university, the best there is in the immediate area, totally unknown in, say, Rottinghurst. G could not shake the impression that his friends were getting a lot more sex than he was, and that they knew a lot more than he did. M could, for instance, speak pages of *Antony & Cleopatra*. He would often do such a thing, loudly, in the basement of The Georgia.

"Shut up and sit down," Cece would suggest.

We would concur, mainly to indicate to Cece that we could control this person, M, the bearded humanization of all our worst impulses. Our Canadian libido. Years later we would have waxed comic about our rights, about the terrible cost of puritanism, about M's stifled talent. As it was we did not want to be cast out of the bar. We wanted to be romantic, till about eight p.m. After that we just wanted our friends to save our seat in case some thin logger might want to drag it over to his table.

"What the hell was that?" asked some thin logger.

"Dwight D. Eisenhower, you dolt," said M.

We indicated to the logger and his eleven friends that this was a local matter, an academic matter. G felt as if he had a special seat and a special problem. He thought that he had not yet been assimilated into the society represented by these effete college kids. He was never a logger, but he knew how to feel like them, that these phonies with their dramatic scarves and foreign beards needed a Leckie in the upper jaw from time to time.

A reader might be excused for thinking that this narrator, one among a number, was planning to asseverate about university syllabus, about courses, about Psychology 101. I imagine the grown up D looking at this chapter and considering it too linear already, the author not dead but still filled with the apprehension that the reader might be alive in the middle of the 21st century, wiping his eyes over the beauty of these fifties youth, sleeping in their overcoats, eating spaghetti with warmed Campbell's tomato soup poured over top, piss poured down the drain. There's a sandwich in every glass, some would-be literatus had said last night, before being banished to the stairwell, the worst place to drink in The Georgia.

Peripheral vision: D would never have heard of Lou Boudreau, but even though Lou Boudreau had been a young playing manager of the Cleveland Indians, and beaten his boyhood Red Sox in the playoff, G liked Lou Boudreau. They said that he wouldn't have been such a good ballplayer if he hadn't had amazing peripheral vision. G can hear M scoffing in Horse right now, that idiot G and his baseball, harrumph. He would actually say "harrumph" in those days, like the equally American Major Hoople, equally American as Lou Boudreau was American; M would say harrumph rather than harrumphing harrumph, in the way that people who had read more strangers than they had heard them say, say things such as "Oh Pshaw!" Baseball and the comics, when G listened to lonely Okanagan radio stations from D's California back in the forties (we do get to go back to the forties when we were not three people on a too-narrow bridge ready to fall with the heat and blast into False Creek, we get to go back to the forties when G for instance would listen to the sixty four dollar question and hope that the category would be the comics). In case you are bored enough to be interested, G can still remember Denny Dimwit's going-to-school, ambling-through-the-wildflowers-to-school song:

> Ah, 'tis spring,
> De boid is on de wing.
> Dat's absoid,
> Everybody's hoid,
> De wing is on de boid.

In fact, G was probably singing it quite loudly outside the pub that night. He was frankly too scared to sing inside the pub, too scared to rise with a glass of beer in his hand, too timid to stand plaintively at the door of the Ladies & Escorts side, because not only did he think himself too inconsequential in their lives for the coeds inside to welcome, but he included them in the legion of the effete. Instead, he would intone in an almost-singing voice: "Scram gravy ain't wavy." Boid boid, kid from the Okanagan with what he presumes is a Brooklyn accent, don't even know the layout of Gotham, don't know Brooklyn's on the end of Long Island, don't even know that KerouACK lives farther up Long Island with his fat mother, writing books fast with a hangover, romance gone long ago.

Vancouver is not an overgrown small town to this kid, G, going to get famous. He was in Montreal in the air force, his ears sticking out, a virgin in a pink teeshirt because he is colourblind, catching shit for that from the Phys Ed corporal, scared again, abashed is the best word. This guy is abashed as his friends from England and the big Vancouver city are suave. They know what Swedish movies mean, they have been to a fraternity party, they have read Schopenhauer, they know what is meant by non-U, and he had a sneaking horror that he was non-U as U can get. He was in the big city, and he expected to see big flashes in the sky and not know what they meant. He did not know how to use a transfer on the bus for the first six months he was in town. D had snuck free onto the subway in London. M knew how to get into the knickers of rich girls. G didn't even know what knickers were. Is this an exaggeration? Was The Georgia really a little bit of an Olde English Pub?

G lit another cigarette and remembered the flash he had seen behind him and then beside him and then in front of him when he turned. Then he took a deep drag on the cigarette and as he went to pull it from his mouth it stuck to his lips, and his fingers slid down to the business end, to be burned and initiated into a day long pain that alternated for attention with the pain behind the bone of his forehead. He remembered the strange writing on the walls, walls that have still these decades later not fallen, hieroglyphs, fifties space ship writing, fingers long passed on, fingers free forever of pain. Flash and glyph. He looked for the crinkled envelope. It was not in or under any of his clothes. It was not on any of the lamentable furniture, it was not in the mud outside. He came back inside and put on his pants and shirt and white silk scarf. D must have the envelope. If not D, M would have it. It might be in the gutter, marked by tire tracks, at the curve of street next to the brewery. He put on his shoes.

Retracing their precipitate steps of the night before, he kept his eyes to the ground. His glasses were smeared badly but he was afraid he would drop them on the sidewalk if he tried to wipe them. He saw five crinkled envelopes between his grotto and the home of Sick's Lager or was it Molson's already. People were dropping envelopes all the time, apparently, addresses gone with the wind and rain, gone in a flash. One of the envelopes looked just like his and his heart leaped and so did his stomach as he bent over to pick it up. It did have handscrawling on it. The words, though, were in simple French, and this is what they were:

> Les gestes et les mouvements sont rendus pénibles par la pluie (porter un carton à gâteaux, traîner un cabas à roulettes, marcher en tenant un enfant par la main).

Pretty tentative. So he walked until he arrived at the near end of the bridge to the beer belt. There was a scaffold where the night before there had been only the wash of reflected light. There were three men on the scaffold, and they were not drunken students, not avatars. They were serious people in Bapco outfits, white coveralls and hats. They were painting the wall of the brewery, vandals with brushes. They were nearly finished their thoughtless task, wiping creamy yellow paint where last night's interstellar graffiti was now almost totally unreadable.

Oh yeah, like last night it was readable.

Last night he could not have read a flashcard held by a grinning grade one teacher.

Last night none of the three of them could have read the card called TO-DAY.

CHAPTER THREE

Drinking in The Georgia meant letting a wonderful warm buzz accumulate near the floor until it rose gradually up over your elbows, came over your table and up your arms and crawled up over your ears, leaving you honking happily in a brown sea of possibility and friendliness. Maybe even romance, either finding or losing the mysterious M. Likely enough, though, it would just be suds and song, something from the shiny tin Reddi-Hot oven behind the bar, then off hiking and babbling across the bridge with those old standbys, rudeboys, and walkhomewiths, D and G. Nothing special had happened to M this night in The Georgia, nothing except something on the bridge that looked like it might be the beginning of the end of the world seen at a very slight distance.

In M's night of dreams, two episodes clamoured with special resonance. The first was a hockey forum, The Forum (Vancouver? Montreal?), more likely the Kerrisdale Arena or just a generic hockey forum. Dreams won't quibble; they want to flow. It was between periods, and it was most likely Montreal and Toronto, the NHL teams whose games he heard on the radio in the forties when he was half asleep nearing nine o'clock bedtime, not yet asleep, not dreaming. In this dream there was a star with an unpronounceable and unspellable Czech or Hungarian surname. The star played for M's team, which meant, surely, the Canadiens. The prospect was to see this star lead his team back onto the ice from the tunnel leading to the dressing room. The star, then his teammates would burst from this darkness to subdued or racketing cheers, depending on whether the game was at home or away. M had the impression that the Canadiens were in their red road sweaters, the same red sweater that he himself wore for ankle-wobbling hockey on the pond behind his house.

Yet somehow it was not to the Canadiens' tunnel that M directed his attention, but to that of the visiting team. For it was realized, as in dreams things are ever only realized, never spoken, only announced by ghostly presences, realizers, announcers of the psychic world where pictures, words, plans, feelings, and philosophies are all one thing, that this was to be the final game ever in the NHL of Syl Apps, the legendary centre of the Maple Leafs. He was, it seemed, retiring, and at the height of his career. That was the only way M, who followed hockey but very slenderly, knew Apps, who'd finished his pro career in the forties, so it was natural that in his dream Apps would be at the top of his powers and fame. The arena was filled with expectancy and drama that M felt pushing down on his shoulders and neck; in fact he felt almost that he shared the pressure of these moments with the great Apps himself, felt that most intimate bond of fervid fandom. M understood that he was extraordinarily lucky to be present, and to be seated directly across the ice, opposite the tunnel, three or four rows up. He stared into the darkness of the tunnel and saw only men in dark pants and light shirts.

Then Apps skated out, with strong thrusts, but loose and easy. He dipped his shoulder to the left (he was carrying his stick on that side, M perhaps making Apps, of whom he'd seen few photographs, a southpaw). His face was pale and he shared with Mandrake the Magician and with Rip Kirby that single curling lick of black hair up and back over his probably brilliantined pate, and his blue eyes were down. There was just the slightest modest little grin of acknowledgment to the cheers. He knew that this was a great moment of adulation, one in which he was more a privileged participant than he was the subject of the commotion. Apps skated off in a businesslike way, and after a pause, the other team members spilled from the tunnel.

The mind's film did a quick fade here, and there was a feeling of conclusion and finish. It was a satisfying episode, rare in dreams, where too often he'd found he could hardly hook one vivid moment to the next one.

Later in that session of sweet silent unthinking came the flash, fully as sudden and vivid as it had been in actuality. The three of them were about in the middle of the bridge, and the flash threw light over the shoulders of the mountains and on parts of the city, casting the BC Electric building, for one, into monstrous silhouette. M, D, and G registered the event, but so did a fourth presence, though that presence seemed to be no definite person. This fourth was alarmed, and he spread alarm or he wanted to spread alarm. He at any rate wanted the three friends to take full and concerned note of the phenomenon, and not to try to shrug it off. "If you try to ignore this," the fourth presence said, "you will put yourselves, and everyone else, in even more danger than we are in from the nuclear blast itself." M was impressed by this statement, and suspected it to be a truth delivered from a moral realm frighteningly beyond his comprehension or his alteration. He felt silly and unhappy, and he knew that the message of light and menace was meant for him more than for any other person in the city.

Next day, though, there he was, pubbound again, this time in the passenger seat, ripped and squamous, of the Hillman convertible of the Gallant and Evil McMannic, Lord in Languishment of the Liquor Control Board, student sempiternal, lout, lothario, and honest lover. Teacher-in-training and actor in reserve. Unreserved bad actor and champion mocker.

"Fee!" cried M. "Last night they tried to blow me and D and G off the Burrard Bridge with an atomic bomb detonated somewhere up beyond and behind Lynn Valley! And then they projected Assyrian – ancient Assyrian, mind you – gibberish on the wall of the Capilano brewery! D thinks that it's a message of doom!"

A giggling gurgle from McMannic. Followed by a snorting, aspirated laugh which somehow fed on itself as a source of humour, a condensation or distillation of humour, a turbo version of standard humour whereby McMannic indicated that yes, the world is turning out to be just as funny as he thought it was. Or that the world is turning out to be even more richly ridiculous than he thought it was.

"Not Assyrians, M!" he shouts. "It's the tribes of Israel! They're after our young D, all in an unholy lather to get him, grind him up, bones and cartilage! They know him," Fee continued more quietly, "for an enemy of the hook-nosed race, for a Church-of-England man." At this point McMannic turned from Hastings into Carrall Street and pretty much transported a man in a khaki gabardine overcoat carrying a bottle-shaped bag the same colour into a nicer world. But not quite. McMannic's head spun in his neck-socket as he darted back over his shoulder a glance of savagely businesslike and curt inquiry. The effect, with the narrowed eyes and the long face and the hair swept back behind the ears in a sort of side-pompadour, was of an osprey or a kingfisher checking for prey. Then McMannic directed at M a more human glance.

"Now look here, M," he hissed in one of his many patented stagy voices, "we've all got to face up to some ugly truths. And I know more than I've hitherto let on in these matters." The stagey utterance was not really conscious, but purely habitual. McMannic simply found words too pallid without quotation marks around them. G did this too, but less obviously, and perhaps there was a hint of quotation in the speech of all M's friends.

McMannic continued, "The fact is I've made a little sortie past the brewery already this A.M., and I caught sight of these curious characters. They were not made by Christian hand, M! Nor did he who grasps the curved steel of Islam inscribe the fateful sign! It is the fell forces of Judah that we have to thank for this work! Who do ya think," he croaked a little lower and softer, "ordered those letters plastered over, anyway?"

Interpretation of the letters on the brewery wall continued in the West Hotel beer parlour, Ladies and Escorts section. McMannic was not the only one of M's acquaintance to see the words that morning, and not the craziest to interpret them. Janey the Red and Bora Dora were hostages to their presence on the ladies' side of the pub, or rather all were invited in there so that jangling Janey, grinding away in her monstrous monotone, could give her conspiracy theories. She also conducted some small hand operations. She kept her beer hand raised, though she seldom drank. The forefinger of her left hand went up the back of the beer glass like a small spine, and there seemed to be something important about to be found in that glass, though that important thing was never her mouth. With her other hand she smoked, though no more often than she sipped her beer. Her Salem menthol was kept in her fingers, it seemed, for the sake of the growing of an ever-threatening ash which it inexorably produced, an ash as long and grey and deadly and maddening and stupid as her mishmush Marxist diatribe. Her other job, given to either hand as available, was to plink or plonk on the table one or several fingers to emphasize… well, not emphasize. Accent, a little counter-strike, to keep attention and ears to the revolving grindstone drone of her theories. It's all goofy. And the goofier it is the more Janey seems pleased with it. She has heard all about the white flash in the night, and she knows who is behind it, who is in front of it, who is trying to cover it up, and where in the U.S. it is being financed from. She knows who and how the connections are in the Bennett government, where the nuclear device was triggered from (a mile-deep mineshaft near Shalalth). She knows the end of all endeavours (insurrection, planned, pieced, plotted, plausible) and the origin of species (Our kind comes with twisted brain/ Thus subterfuge it must contain. Saith Jane.)

M huddles briefly with the redoubtable Peaches Dobell, a sometimes partner in verse, and they compose lines to celebrate the recent independence of Ceylon, which has become Sri Lanka:

A Sestina for Sri Lanka

The sestina began
Uncomfortably dark
about Sri Lanka, green

and slow, the water
idling away
and red at the finish

How to finish
something so dark,
so far away,
disappearing like water
although it began
so new, so green.

The lizards in the grass are green
and bring poisons from far away
poisons to make a complete finish,
a throat gurgling in the dark,
seeking air, as when the world began,
and finding only water.

The solution is water,
where we all began,
millennia ago and away
where the world was green
from start to finish
and the water shone light on the dark

But it was all water in the dark.
Dark was always fighting green,
ever since we came across the water
from Sri Lanka where it perhaps began
with no thought ever of a finish
in bird-filled waters far away.

How shall we fare away?
In a world that is no more green,
in Sri Lanka, where the world grows dark?
Away across the water?
Knowing how the dark will finish,

remembering how the green began.

In a corner of the Men's side of the West, hidden but audible, someone is softly warping "Sinner Man" on a mouth organ:

> Oh, sinner man
> Where you gonna run to
> All on that day?

Larry Koerner, boy pornographer, sits in another corner on the Men's side. He too can be heard but not seen. He is planning and boasting about making another movie, a further exploration of middle-class liberal *angst*. He learned this word in a creative writing class, and he learned to underline it. In truth, though, he's German enough, an Afrikaaner, so he might use it plain. He doesn't do anything plain, though; it's all fancy for this boy except for the actual work with the camera, which Larry uses as a blunt instrument. His second movie will be an unholy compound of gritty realism (rainy city streets, a boy actor wearing what looks like G's Air Force trench coat – probably borrowed from G; it was always too short for him anyway – cigarette in the corner of the mouth, James Dean hardly cold in his grave), sentimentality (simulated sex, tears on the girl's face), and social meaning (tears on the boy's face). Like his first movie.

> Run to the sun
> Sun won't you hide me?
> Sun won't you hide me
> All on that day?

CHAPTER FOUR

She didn't really know them at first. At first, she just saw them sitting in The Georgia, spilling their beer and tomato juice all over the girls they had conned into accompanying them into the Ladies and Escorts so they could look at and impress other girls, steal them from the tables of the fraternity boys, gather glory for "not fitting in" – and they did; they gathered glory and girls, stole the women, robbers, outlaws, bandidos – still operating out of the cowboy ethic. They imagined they were rescuing. And they were – those who wanted to be rescued. They gave a focus for the need to be rescued from the bland boredom of buttoned-down Brooks Brothers' shirts, though Elvis had the idea first. In the Fifties it was important to choose between Elvis, the Bad Boy, and Pat Boone and his white buck. She balanced one on each shoulder for a while, but when A was fourteen, the choice was made for her.

A was in love with a boy on the highschool basketball team because he had the eyes of Rupert Brooke – whose eyes, for A, were archetypal poet's eyes. And so, one night, after one of those basketball tournaments which cause the players to cry in the showers and the cheerleaders to be given the job of comforting them, A went to a party that she was much too young to go to. She went with another boy to be near to David-with-the-poet's-eyes. Her first drink put her out until she was awakened, along with three remaining team members who had also passed out, by two police constables called by her mother who'd thought A must be dead in a ditch somewhere. During the police interview, in hot defense of the respectability of the boys and herself, A answered the red-faced young constable's questions about whether or not she'd had sexual intercourse with anyone during the evening with "Of course not! What kind of girl do you think I am?" (A had read *True Confessions* and knew that she wasn't that kind of girl). Protesting the innocence of the basketball players in intellectual and artistic terms, A proclaimed, "He reads Pogo!" "He plays trumpet in the band!"

It didn't help. There was a trial anyway. The boys were charged with contributing to the delinquency of a juvenile. A was on their side, not on the side of a righteous community, not on the side of the cops, but that meant A had to lie for them. She was terrified, not morally (A had her moral priorities straight), but by the formality of the proceedings. Standing in the witness box, clothed in coat and scarf – A had some idea it was like church and you had to cover your head in court – she perjured herself in a small voice in response to the judge's questions until she heard him say, "Will the witness please remove her outer clothes." Appalled by her ignorance of court protocol, A hastily stripped off her coat and scarf as a young constable moved the witness box (which was on wheels) nearer to the judge's bench. Her mother, mystified by A's inappropriate striptease, told her later that what the judge had actually said was, "Will you please move the witness box closer."

Well, A's mind was made up for her, not only by these events, but by what followed. A was the high school intellectual – not the best student, but the smartest, and had learned long, long before, in the poverty of her childhood, that what saves one from disgrace is being smart. For that reason, A was the darling of her highschool English teacher, Miss Yule, who also happened to be the girls' counsellor. Unmarried though she was, she had street smarts that A's mother, a girl brought up in Victoria by a domineering and protective Scottish mother, did not have. Miss Yule got right down to business when she called A into her office: she advised her to shed her tight skirts and sweaters and adopt puffy sleeved dresses with full skirts. A felt bad about that. She had a morning ritual that involved bath, teeth, make-up and hair curling, ironing sweater, skirt, bra, panties, slip, white bobby socks, brown paper lunch bag, and putting white shoe polish on her white bucks and their laces. A had ironed her black skirt until it was shiny. That was the uniform. There was more. Miss Yule (who smoked) also advised A to run for a position on the student's council, try out for cheerleaders, and take part in the high school operetta – and so A did, though her tastes ran more to blues and torch songs and country music. She was a kid who listened to San Francisco jazz stations, radio pressed to her ear in bed, late at night when all the local stations had gone off the air: Ella Fitzgerald, Peggy Lee, Frank Sinatra, Carmen McRae, Chris Conner, Dave Brubeck, Charlie Parker, Mingus and Monk. Magical names, magical songs: *Night in Tunisia, Lover Man, The Man I Love, 'Round Midnight, Love For Sale, Ten Cents a Dance* – A went to T*he Ruth Etting Story* and loved it. A always figured if university didn't work out, she could be a torch singer, sang up and down the streets to keep in practice, always in a minor key. Thirty years later, A's sister told her that one of the neighbours still remembers A with fondness, singing down the night streets of that small town. She was European, and A found out many years later, rush of remembrance in 1985 Berlin as two girls rode by on their bikes, kids sing in the streets in Europe. Her sister and A sang while they did the dishes–harmony Les Paul and Mary Ford (*The World Is Waiting For The Sunrise*), Got along without ya before I met ya, gonna get along without ya now (Who did that?); happily they sang:

> Lord help the mister
> Who comes between me and my sister
> And Lord help the sister
> Who comes between me and my man

learning the words from *The Hit Parader*. Daytime was for pop music and country and western – The Sons of the Pioneers. Jazz made mother nervous. So did the hit parade, especially Elvis Presley. And she was too snobbish to admit that she liked country and western music, though sometimes she sang *Be Nobody's Darling But Mine, Dear*. She listened to

Saturday Afternoon at the Met with Rudolph Byng and sighed a lot. For years A could not listen to opera without associating it with the smell of damp washing, the Saturday pot roast cooking and the sound of her mother sighing (she had recently ended an unhappy marriage). Later, A loved it, and even then, singing Handel's *Messiah* in music classes and choir was pretty good. Music was taught by a wonderful little Mennonite man with corrugated hair who wore a white sports coat and a black bow tie over pink, white, or blue shirts and shiny black unfashionable pants. His name was Albert Wedel, and he lived outside of town in the Mennonite community nearby. He sure gave that highschool class some terrific music to sing. He ran the operettas, and so A became Miss Rowena and learned to sew, though she'd failed sewing in Home Ec, and made puffy sleeved dresses. "It's a matter of camouflage," Miss Yule said. She was right, too. It worked. But A knew, and was cynical about its working.

So A was on the Elvis side, and A learned deceit-as-camouflage. And dreamed for years of walking down the upper hall of the high school with the whole population of the place lined up on either side pointing at her and whispering about that court case and what a bad girl A was. And waited for the walls to fall, walking the gamut in slow motion. They did whisper too. A had "a reputation." She learned to mask her intelligence by becoming (publicly) what we now call a bimbo. She had two friends who knew her; one became an actor and singer; the other became a television news director. They knew they were weird and had to hang onto each other. A was always an opinionated lecturer on every subject under the sun, but hid her real intelligence except in the papers she wrote for her English courses. She was in love with T.S. Eliot's *The Waste-Land* and Baudelaire. All that gloom flashed with brilliant images, the twist of the writing hand inscribed in heart, brain; felt thought, the good of the intellect, all that taking her through her own dark ages–fourteen to eighteen. The only time A was ever ashamed of Miss Yule was when she mockingly read out e. e. cummings's poems in class and laughed at them. A wrote a paper on *The Waste-Land* to avenge herself on this betrayal of art to a class she knew were mostly yahoos. As, much later at university, she would likewise do in defense of William Carlos Williams's *Paterson*. So A became a secret outlaw. The writing was on the walls, inside her skull. It was a matter of interpretation and camouflage.

When she was living in the dorms at the university among the sorority girls and their fraternity boyfriends and brothers, adopting their camouflage, going out with those camouflaged boys pretending to be young in the recommended way, the one that would prepare them to be the businessmen they would become, A watched the others, the outlaws, closely. First she shed the engineers and the boys from the forestry department, then she ferreted out from among the fraternity boys the ones who formed a group that imitated the Hi Los, and then she began to hang around a jazz club called The Black Spot, listening to crazy (even then) Al Neil and Scott somebody play piano with the various saxophonists, bassists, drummers and trumpet players who wandered in and out, sometimes bringing in whores from the notorious Penthouse – beautiful blonde baby-faced newly transformed Cinderellas – all pink and white fluff. A fell in love with Cary, a nineteen-year-old alto saxophonist because the first thing she heard him play was "Night in Tunisia." And then "Lover Man." And so on. After a while, the saxophonist couldn't be bothered with this little hick from the sticks of Vancouver Island who was going to hang onto her cherry until she was married, so he dumped her. A lay on her bed in the dormitory staring at a spot on the ceiling for the whole exam period. Nothing moved.

Finally, A's best friend, a sensible girl from Toronto, dragged her down the cliffs to the Point Grey beach to get her drunk, snap her out of it. Six cases of beer, something A never drank, and six bottles of Manor St. David's Bright's White Table Wine (85 cents a bottle) later, they managed it. The last thing A remembered in the black hole of that two-day drunk was trying unsuccessfully to do up her pants after peeing on the beach and falling flat, laughing, into a mouthful of sand. A was no help to the others hauling empty beer cases and bottles up the cliff, except in the way of entertainment. She recited for those labouring others (evidently) the whole of *The Waste-Land*, which she punctuated randomly with Gregory Corso's phrase "Fried Shoes!" at the top of her lungs. She went straight up the hill, collapsed when they told her to stop, got up when they had caught up with her, and resumed her recitation where she'd left off. Keeping her quiet proved to be as difficult as it was necessary – those were the days before coeducational university residences, when girls were expelled for abusing the curfew, for drinking, for sneaking their boyfriends into the dorms, the days when scandal was still possible. A remembers clusters of girls gathered outside Mary Bollert Hall to look at the dirty foot marks up the whitewashed wall under the window of a girl who was expelled, hushed stories of lesbian activities, the friend of one of the senior girls who used to sneak into the dorms at night after sleeping with her boyfriend in the men's residence who told us wonderful sophisticated stories about her sex life. As far as A knew, none of the other girls had one. Her daring in talking about it was more impressive than what she told them. One of the dons had been stripped naked and tied to her chair all night; Chester the Molester was on the prowl around the campus and on the beaches; various exhibitionists paraded their wares for the titillation of sunbathing girls studying on the grassy cliffs overlooking the beach. There were notices all over campus about these ominous threats to virginity. None of A's acquaintances took them seriously.

Suicides in the dorms were hushed up – no one knew about them until much later. G's girlfriend Trudy was the don of the dorm next to A's. She was known to be very strict. When Vicky Hunter's friend snuck out with the pseudo-writer Liam Chutney (composer of "Poem of a Man With A Puce Clarinet") the girls delayed getting help when she cut the tendon in her knee climbing out a basement of Trudy's dorm.

The tourniquet, fashioned of scarf and coat hanger, may have saved her leg, but A never did find out. Dissolving forms, disappearing into mist, outlined briefly like the rock islands in the seamless sea and sky of the West Coast. Blotches on a personal landscape. Hamish. Perhaps it was Hamish Redfen she was sneaking out with, whom Vicky loved, though *he* loved her older sister Alex. Everybody loved Alex – Thadeus Young pursued her relentlessly, helplessly, poor woman-mad Thadeus, saved A's friend's epileptic son from a swimming pool death at school and died of AIDS thirty years later. Or was it Snowy, Alice Spireia's older sister, Hamish loved? Eight-pound roast beef dinners were provided by the wealthier parents; it kept the poorer ones fed. Their places in Shaughnessy were bright spots for warm dinners and wine, parties and gorgeous boys, 4:00 o'clock tea parties with the light falling, the girls' heads bent, talking, talking, Snowy's pale blonde head lifted, up, back, withholding, intent on separation; Alice's defiant red hair, her Katherine Hepburn voice and gawky manner. What became of that appalling innocence of that Great Gatsby world, the shine of hair, the shimmer and strain of possibility, of those elegant boys and girls?

Alex married her fraternity boy, Alan McNeil, fired from his position as principal of a boy's private school in a scandal that surfaced thirty years later. A sat opposite her in a hair-cutting place while she bragged to the assembled ladies and stylists about how many times they'd been robbed, twisting enormous diamond rings on her fingers, her blue eyes straining wildly out of their sockets. Vicky began saving trees in the Carmanah Valley. A sees her on television sometimes. Those girls whose fathers went to college with A's mother got caught in social fictions. A was determined not to be caught in fictions made up by others.

So A watched those boys at The Georgia and eased her way into their world slowly. That summer, she worked at the main branch of the Bank of Nova Scotia during the day and went every night to the jazz clubs around the city: The Cellar,

The Harlem Nocturne, The Black Spot. In those days you had to be a member at some of the clubs, and you brought your bottle in a brown paper bag and kept it under the table. The Cellar stayed open until 4 a.m. some nights, if there were enough people. After they closed you went to the Harlem Nocturne on East Hastings where black musicians jammed until dawn. A spent the whole summer sleep-deprived: in at 7 am., up at 8, if she slept at all, to work by 8:30, on No-Doze pills until noon, sleep for the lunch hour, get someone to wake her up, work on No-Doze for the afternoon, then back to the apartment to sleep until 7:00 or so, then bath and hair and out at 8:00 until seven in the morning again. Her life and eyes and ears were full of music and the romance of being out in the "real" world, away from home, the blurred images of those sweating black musicians at the Harlem Nocturne; Tommy King playing *Harlem Nocturne* at her as dirty as he could (alto sax, same as Cary, trying to get A away from him), Art Pepper at The Cellar, feet tangled in the stage wires, so stoned, high on heroin, playing badly; the skinny Scandinavian bassist kid, Bob Neilberg, in his brown business suit, straight from the bank, shooting up in emulation, thought it would make him a great jazz bassist–short cut; one black woman at the Harlem Nocturne, so fat she couldn't dance, standing there moving her mountainous body with great subtlety, making it dance for her, all that flesh jiggling to the jazz, teaching A what "jelly roll" really meant, and the seventeen-year-old boy with acne dancing with her, in love with that flesh. When A went into the toilet, his girlfriend was vomiting her brains out into the sink. And seven o'clock in the morning coming home, kissing in the rain in the middle of the tree-lined summer street, umbrella rolling away behind her and who cared?

Joy and desolation. Finally giving up to it one night, ditching a date with the actor who did Shakespeare soliloquies for her, who had bought a bottle of gin for the party they were going to. But they went to The Black Spot first and there was Cary, arms around her, kissing A's neck, and she was gone with her paycheque and John Stark's bottle (A owes you an apology and a bottle of gin, John Stark, wherever you are), gone to make herself drunk so she could say yes, gone to Stanley Park where, sitting across Cary's lap in a car hidden under a weeping willow tree that hung to the ground (like the one called the kissing tree, which stood in A's mother's yard, where A used to neck, hidden from her gaze, ignoring her voice calling her daughter in) gone, A gave up, gone into God knows where, remembering nothing until halfway home hearing herself screaming at him not to tell, thinking "Maybe it doesn't count, maybe my hymen hasn't broken and it's OK.," but at home, when she saw her bloody underpants, A knew it counted – everything – the angel he saw in her face that arrived there after her conviction that it couldn't possibly go in dissolved into desire and wonder, the certainty about the foolish cheat of the taboos when she thought: "What are they talking about?" the soft voice, the gentle hands, the slow deliberation, the blood that came in the amnesia darkness, blotting out ecstasy, the re-emergence in hysteria. Everything counted. And when, next time, in Tommy King's mother's white lace bed, Cary's nose bled all over the white pillow, A thought how fitting it was that he was bleeding for her as she had bled for him. Years later, a man pleading with A, having lost all hope of success, was startled out of his humiliation by the arrival of a wet facecloth and her sudden acquiescence: his nose had begun to bleed. She cannot remember now the song that Cary gave her name to, but A remembers perfectly the silent moment, like the moment before fall birdflight, the gathered hush that precedes flight and absence, the beauty that was there, the heartbeat and the rush of wings. A cannot remember how it ended, only that it ended when A understood he didn't love her. That dizzy life had no focus, or its focus was revenge on women, clamour for them, for the lost child of his high school girlfriend's abortion. A didn't think, soft voice, soft hands, he knew A had shed her childhood skin. A mourned his loss for a year, going back to repeat the year she'd lost, weeping every night for him for a year – which is a long time when you are nineteen. A has always been devoted to her losses.

When A went back to The Georgia, they were still there, and A watched them, eavesdropped, listened to them talk about poetry (Baudelaire, Charles Olson, the Roberts–Creeley and Duncan, Ginsberg); about Marxism and philosophy (existentialism–Sartre and Camus–A had been hooked on Camus from the first), film-making (A had seen Raymond Radiguet's *Diable au corps* two years before when she had first come to UBC and fallen in love with Gerard Phillippe, even though he was only a tiny image on a television screen; they talked about Truffaut, Fellini, Antonioni, Bergman, Agnes Varda, Robbe-Grillet, Marguerite Duras, the French New Wave, and about the antinovelists – Nathalie Sarraute and Robbe-Grillet especially, and Ebbe Coutts gave up talking about Baudelaire after enduring and tenderly ministering to the suicidal attempts of a girl called Marie, and took up drugs instead; A endured Larry (later Laurence E.) Koerner's glib hype about his film-making when everyone knew it was the only way he could get girls to take off their clothes for him, endured his exposure of his fat white belly and his hairy black belly-button that looked like an asshole.

There they were, acting on stage in the Old Auditorium – Fee McMannic in his famous old flasher's raincoat with his brilliant smile that would stop a Mack truck, and he knew it and used it, especially on girls, drinking in the green room – acting at The Georgia, acting the lives they wanted to become, full of hope and frenzy, wearing their smiles and costumes, pretending, as were we all, trying out fictional lives. But they really knew it, did it with daring, insisting on more than most of us did. M was Jacobean in his black velvet jacket and skinny pants, made stylized gestures in an apparently self-possessed and restrained manner. D was the most intellectually intimidating of them all. He was elegant and British, and, good little indoctrinated colonial that she was, A knew that "they" were superior to "us." After all, it was their literature the Canadians studied – from Jerry and Jane in their 1920s style polka dot dresses with the ballooning skirts, their sailor suits and tams, the Arthur Rackham style illustrations, wind blowing tormented trees, to *Winnie the Pooh* and all the other pooh-generated stories and poems to *High Roads to Reading* to *Alice in Wonderland*, and *Through The Looking Glass*. *The Books of Knowledge* belonged to them. The red on the maps belonged to them. A's grandmother's photographs, especially the one she took of Victoria and Albert and the Romanovs with little Anastasia looking like a baby pig, reminding A of the sneezing pig in the Duchess's arms in *Alice* told her that "they" were the owners of the world, the standard by which and by whom Canadians were measured. Later, seeing the Albert Memorial for the first time, A laughed at its earnestness, felt sympathy for Oscar Wilde, was startled out of illusion by that preposterous vulgarity. But then, A believed. All the evidence was on their side; the British school teacher who taught her dressed in British tweeds, had been in "The Great War", had a glass eye and a wooden hand which he encased in a thin black kid glove and rapped the desk with to call his charges to order; "the lily, thistle, shamrock, rose" told A, even if it was supposed to be a song about "the maple leaf forever," that Canada forever belonged to them. They had "it" in their bone and blood cells forever. And so D was wrapped in all the power and authority of A's grade six teacher's wooden hand, of the British Empire, British intellectual and cultural superiority. And so, when A was in the Creative Writing class and finally met them, though she was still only watching, D was the one she was most afraid of. The others were like her, but he might find her out – find out about the illiterate Finnish grandfather, the schizoid father who only had a grade eight education, the childhood poverty in a B.C. mining town, owned by *his* people, Lord Dunsmuir, coal baron, making his money out of Japanese, Chinese, black laborers; lost in his mines, only their numbers, no names in the lists of the dead; only white men had names, and they were his people too, Welsh and Scottish, British and Irish; she had heard the accents of the people with names, though one of them – Ginger Goodwin – was killed by the police for trying to organize the miners; he was a hero, her mother said, persecuted, like her mother's brother, who was not called to the bar of the law association during the McCarthy era because he was a communist. A's mother went to college in Lord Dunsmuir's Castle, and was called "the Duchess" because of her manner; she looked and bore herself like Nadine Gordimer. She said she was shy and was mistaken for a snob, but A thinks her mother grew up, like herself, with her allegiances split. Nevertheless, she lived true to her ideals, sometimes excessive in her demands of herself, saving years worth of string and elastic bands, refusing to eat meat, or earn interest on her money, giving to charities all over the world until finally it became too much for her and she settled for the study of Gaelic and Lallans poetry, writing articles, political and literary, devoting herself to the cause of Scottish Nationalism in a world that was making common markets wherever it could. All this complexity lay back of A's feelings about D, and so, when he asked her out, she agreed and then stood him up, in part, for much the same reasons she stood up Robin Niederstrasser, the Physics professor with the German name and the Scottish accent who'd been so enchanted when, in response to a question about what character in fiction A would be if she could choose, she'd said "Gruschenka." She really meant it, but she'd read *The Brothers Karamazov* when she was seventeen, in the way that a seventeen-year old would read such a novel; a year or so later she'd been captivated by Maria Schell's film version of the holy whore, Gruschenka, by the passionate turmoil of the allegorical family, that psychomachia of the Russian soul with Lee J. Cobb as the drunken old Karamazov, Yul Brynner as the glamourous misfit, Dmitri, Richard Basehart as the atheist intellectual Ivan and William (Star Trek) Shatner as Alyosha, religious mystic, along with Albert Salmi, epileptic Smerdyakov, Lord of Misrule; when she saw it, A knew she did not know as much as she needed to know, and that what she needed to know went far beyond the simpler schisms of her life, exceeded the limitations of her small town's description of things, and she wanted it, what she didn't know – that larger world. A also knew that Robin Niederstrasser had an inflated idea of what she did know, and so, when she didn't respond for the third time to his knock at the door and found his note in the mailbox next day – "Fuck you, you bitch!" – A was much relieved; she had time to find out. D's invitation had something of the same effect on her, though by the time A was to have met him, she had met G and forgotten about anyone else. A remembers standing on the steps of the library at the university with G, dazed with love, seeing D coming across the quad in his British trench coat to keep their appointment; shocked as she remembered what she had forgotten, A thought, "He's washed his hair and brushed it so carefully." Shamed by his care, she pretended she'd just run into him, and elegant British D pretended too; it was just a casual encounter.

A and her associates were all trying out who to be and how to be – impostors, *poseurs*. But G,D,M and their peers knew it. Their posturing required character, discipline. Required that they do something remarkable. They were courageous liars, and A knew that's what she had to learn to be. So she watched them and graded them, she separated the real fakes from the false fakes. All that witty lovely masquerade, the first serious attempts at disguise. They were looking for credible fictions. A had been looking for the truth – as if she could ever hope to know it – so they became writers and actors, and she watched them, admiring or dismissing them on the basis of their style and the dreams behind their sometimes anxious eyes, trying to see the faces beneath those faces, the skin stretched taut with the reach of their minds, through the flesh, the tightened skin revealing mind-reach. She was waiting for the collision of truth and fiction. And so were they.

"And how *do* you like your blue-eyed, brown-eyed boys, your green-eyed girl now, mister, as they step through the watery mirror?" A might ask, and continue: "I am your echo. I remember you all. I dredge you up. Sea-bed, earth-cave, shattered glass."

CHAPTER FIVE

Wasn't that just like them or rather, in this respect, wasn't this one of them just like all the other ones who made up the rest of them, with all too few notable exceptions, keeping a fellow hanging around when he's straining at the leash, talking to him about feelings when the situation calls for action – and taking her sweet slow time to do it, looping back and forth, bringing up the distant past to account for the present, dwelling on incidents from the pre-D era to – oh, of course, it was all for his sake! – endeavor to clarify for D where she, Elizabeth, was, as we did not yet say, Coming From?

D identified with a goodly band of characters from literature – that was the past he preferred to have conjured – and the character he found had popped into his head, pooped and popped out again most recently was the Wedding Guest who beat his breast for he heard the loud bassoon.

D had been compelled to sit (or pace) in the coachhouse for what felt like two months (but was actually more like two hours) while Elizabeth (they were drinking Seagrams and ginger ale: Elizabeth had begun to stutter) sifted through the dust from one more chunk of her life story searching for some glinty flakes, bits of essence, nutty grit amid the yellow huskings of experience... D grew erratically poetic when drinking and made to wait. To the gods of Impatience a large portion of his young life had been dedicated – sacrificed really, for it was not to come again – and this tendency, with all the inertia of the uninspected, meant to exact further and continuous tribute from its acolyte.

Which made things tough for D, since he was, in the other half of his being, Patience personified, having in fact passed several years here and there as a virtual catatonic. His patient part resented the chivvying from his impatient part, dug in its heels, wasting, in the opinion of his impatient portion, even more time, a waste which required the hurry-up button to be leant on, long and hard. Or depressed in a series of sharp short jabs. So his was an inner conflict and of course, Elizabeth was a handy target for projection. "For Crissake, everyone'll be passed out by the time we get there – we're gonna miss the Party!" Elizabeth looked, probably was, genuinely startled. Why blame her? Other times, D enjoyed hearing her tales of the UR-Time, of the world of the University of British Columbia shortly after WWII, a time of nonconformity. "Those veterans weren't about to take orders from *anyone* any more," Beth was wont to say, "and they wanted to have *fun*!" And then she'd laugh the laugh that says "And they got it, too, *and* spread it around." Beth was just two years older than D, she had entered university at sixteen, a grade-skipper in high school who was thus suddenly plunged into the social-intellectual whirl of college amid demobbed thirty-year-olds aged further by close calls with violent death, kept immature (on the other hand) by the parenting of the armed forces and the weird irresponsibility of life at war. Their morals, too, were in flux. D could connect with this. He had used, during the war, when he was trying to stay alive in London, a series of Canuck soldiers as surrogate big brothers, and was drawn to the wilder among them, with their tales of "liberation" of this or that prized item... Later D was to find a like enchantment in the British phrase "Fell orf the back of a lorry." "Ere, mate, have some of these – fell orf the back of a lorry." D didn't seem to have any morals at all, except where phrasing was concerned. So it was some relief to his loneliness when he heard such lines. However, he did have ideals; in fact it was his true work at this time in his life to realize these; of course, being ideals, they refused to be realized, and so one might say that his true work at this time was to destroy his ideals and grow up. This mission was rendered complex by his association with Beth. She had done a lot of growing up; so much so that she quite easily mothered D, which hampered him in his quest for independence. But since D didn't know the name of his quest, their conflict always surprised him. He knew himself to mean well where this woman was concerned.

D thought his search was for himself – the old "Who am I?" pilgrimage. But lately he had heard that what he was actually doing was looking for roles to play. The woman who had told him this, A, was a cool blonde with a swan hairdo who dressed well, i.e., like Beth, who also wore a swan, and dressed like a sorority girl who happened to have good taste – dressed up rather than down. Until meeting up with these middle-class Canadians, D had known nothing about clothes, and had gone whole years during his agricultural practice wearing the same pair of pants; he had known nothing about laundering, and therefore these proved lonely years.

D's mother had not had the heart for this kind of education. He was a not-so-noble savage when he entered the University of British Columbia. At first he resisted all attempts to civilize him, but he realized he liked looking at offbeat elegance, and he let M pick out some of his clothes – pipestem cord suits still looked better on M, possibly thanks to M's perfect physique, but Beth found it some kind of an improvement. In the photo taken of D winning the CBC Playwriting Award, he sports as well a narrow, narrow tie, also courtesy of M's up-to-datedness. It had been purchased along with the suit at Frederick and Nelson's during a Seattle visit, of which more anon.

Now, therefore, four years into his college days, D began to have a rudimentary-my-dear-Delsing sense of what others used to disguise their nakedness. A wore skirt-suits, or tight pants on her elegant legs. In the matter of self-assurance, she was not yet quite Beth's match. Beth's was an assurance shared by her women friends from her college days. These came from money, more or less. D didn't think that A did. (Therefore, forty years later, Beth's group had lost their money, while A had acquired some). But that made for an interesting combination. D didn't come from money either; but his way with words meant that he never let money talk down to him. Right or wrong, he believed he could see through that shit, and he treasured the saying "Keep your thoughts to yourself – there's a rich man coming" for what it said about society, but not as advice he would ever heed – the snotnose scholarship boy.

D figured A was going to be at the party, and he hoped to talk with her some more. Of course she was going out with G, suddenly, so anything else was out of the question, but then "anything else," although uppermost in his consciousness sixteen hours a day, wasn't (little did D know) really what he was after. He wanted the woman to talk with, to talk with him. Even that was less than most of what he was after. For D really wanted to *be* the woman, he wanted, like all hero-worshipers, to become the object of his worship. What a burden, and for all concerned. And so, having met A, and spoken with her, D wanted to know more about her.

D had told Beth of the events the three had witnessed the night before. She had looked quizzical, as if he was trying to tell her a joke with no punchline. Then she had laughed anyway. Off and on throughout the day he had tuned in to CKIK, but no reports had surfaced – and yet it was impossible that just those three should have seen a flash that grand, equally impossible that if anyone else had, no news of it had reached the radio or TV stations. Very odd, they agreed, replenishing their drinks.

D had been looking out the window–not easy to do, had to stand on tiptoe – at twilight deepening over the millionaire plumage of the gardens of Shaughnessy, and now turned back to Beth, puzzled by her silence, to find (O no!) she had passed out on the couch. Just then a car pulled up and Tommy P stepped out. D watched him smooth his black hair down with the flat of one hand, then run a comb through it with the other, patting the small wave in front until he had it just so. Tommy was wearing pegged pants although it was now the sixties. He had worn them in Edmonton when he first got busted for boosting heaps, and they became forever part of his image, along with the dark glasses and the rat-tail comb.

He swaggered in at the door. "Same old scene I see," he

said, pouring a stiff one and stirring in the mix with the tail of his comb, which he then licked before smirking "how long she been bye-byes?"

"Just," D replied, picking up Tommy's glass and drinking.

"You want to make that party, man?"

"Sure," D said, "But we got to get Beth upstairs first."

"Fuck that," said the newcomer, adjusting his shades, "Let's just leave her where she is."

"Can't, man," D told him, "Remember? Axel is on the prowl. Got to erect the painting."

Axel is the European gambler Beth lived with for three years prior to D's coming into her life. She sat in all-nite joints watching him lose her inheritance while she knitted. Then she went to work the next day. Beth finally managed to leave Axel, with a little help from her friends. Axel had dropped from sight but had recently re-surfaced, reported as waving a pistol in a club and promising to use it on Beth when he found where she's living. From the outside, the coachhouse appeared to be one story; the tiny window of the bedroom might merely give onto attic space. So each night, when they went up to bed, Beth and D hung a painting, large enough to almost completely fill the doorway (but no door is there) at the foot of the –

[The painting was a genuine Gherkinczy, that is to say, a complete fake. Montgomery Incline, eager to spend more time with Joan Nevers, and having discovered that she painted, and being coincidentally the (unpaid) publicity person for the upcoming Little Theater production of *Private Lives* (starring, by the way, Georgia Littlewood, D's ex-wife), decided to stage an art hoax in the theater's lobby; came up with the notion that a Madame Gherkinczy, a Czech in exile, was to have her North American premiere there, then set Joan up with paint and canvas and gallon jugs of Regal Sherry until she came up with a Rouault-like series of portraits (the one D and Beth used to hide the stairway was a Regal Sherry-ish impression of D, Montgomery Incline, and noted Vancouver theater impresario Ian Newhouse, who had fucked more of the women D knew than any other single man (though Ian Newhouse was married)).

The hoax had fooled *The Vancouver Bun* reporter sent to cover it: a large pic of D had adorned the front cover of the arty section, with D ("noted UBC art critic") being quoted saying some nonsense about these wretched oils, and Joan Nevers (dark glasses, Italian scarf over red hair, cigarette holder) being quoted on the oppressive regimes in Prague and Ottawa. This all went missing from the later edition; an editor familiar with the name and MO of Montgomery Incline, master of a thousand hoaxes, had seen through the team's little ruse.]

– stairs, to disguise the upper story from Axel should he break in.

Therefore Tommy and D must now lug Beth, no mere slip of a thing, up the steep and narrow (and twisting) staircase, so that the painting could be put in place and the dwelling rendered Axel-proof. This manoeuvre struck both as very funny, and even Beth, in her happy state, smiled as if to go along with the lark. D tucked her in (still fully clothed) and, stopping only to install the painting and top off the Seagrams bottle with ginger ale, the lads slammed the doors of Tommy's Pontiac and slid off into the velvet night of a thousand eyes – D scanning the horizon for any further flashes while telling Tommy what he saw the night before… Tommy is naturally unbelieving.

"College kids go ga-ga on dago red."

D chortled. He had long since learned to live without Tommy's validation.

They glided along the tree-hung streets, broad and quiet in this part of town, D speaking while Tommy vented occasional snorts of disbelief. D hadn't meant to tell Tom until G and M were also present. That way, Tom would at least be impressed with the way these three had worked out an elaborate lie. Tom believed nothing – why would he believe this? Except, sometimes, Tommy believed D because he could get D to tell him all his secrets.

Five years ago on the prairie, working in a mental hospital, D had been looking for a brother-confessor. In return, he learnt about jazz: and about Tommy's secrets, about boosting cars and stripping them down, taking these items to a fence, getting caught, appearing in court, then, being given the choice of jail or a socially helpful job, choosing the latter (natch)... so for Tom this job was the next worst thing to being in the slammer. D framed it this way. To do so was tactless, but he wanted to see if he could nettle the guy.

"Yeah, same as it is for you," was the laconic response. D saw that this was true.

He saw that he didn't have to pretend with Tom that he believed in his job, that it was a great way of doing good, that the low pay was made up for by the spiritual benefits. He saw that it *was* a shit job, performed for the socially trapped by those only slightly less so. He recalled (for himself as much as for Tom) the circumstances that had forced him into this occupation – the string of jobs that had paid even less, his improvidence, his inability to resist the merest impulse... They got very drunk and became staggering friends. When they got kicked out of the dorms for having their chests-of-drawers filled with empties, they took an apartment together and D began to meet the delinquents Tom was no longer supposed to associate with. They would drive clear across Edmonton (not quite so far in the mid-Fifties) because there was a beer parlour that served cheese and onion sandwiches. There they would all play bullshit poker until it was time for the employed among them to go to work (D and Tom were on the afternoon shift).

One day, they followed a firetruck to the fire. It was their own apartment. Some of Tom's 33s had melted – it had been D's cigar that had fallen into the couch. They found another flat, a place where the floor sloped so decidedly that a bottle could roll from one end of the pad to the other (there was little furniture to stop it). Spring finally came, and D entrained for the Coast. One night six months later, Tom turned up on his doorstep. Tom's folks had moved out here, and he had come with them. They went over to Tom's place – he had the entire basement to himself – and tied one on. D told Tom about university, and Tom told D about hitting a concrete lamp standard with his father's chevy.

D glanced sideways at Tommy P, his carefully tended black hair with a wave in front, the shades, the Brando pout and hunch, the slightly zooty outfit, the faint but unwavering air of amusement his friend emanated… amusement and malice, slight, but there to be sniffed on the characterological breeze. It appeared to appeal to some of D's newer friends, too. Tom had become an attraction at their parties.

The Hillcoots especially loved him. They were a dramatic family in all senses – D had gone briefly with their daughter, Gloria, an actress – and Gloria's mother was given, 'round midnight, to manifesting at the top of the stairs, bare naked, declaring "I'm Norma!" then regally if unsteadily descending. While Norma did this and other party tricks, husband Archie would chat pleasantly on – quite uninterruptible – about his time spent panning in the Yukon. They liked it when Tommy sat on the round coffee table clutching flowers from various vases, wearing his shades and declaring that he must run out into the street with his hair down so. He showed no sign of actually carrying this out, but they liked this beatnik having memorized *The Waste-Land*. The other guests were intrigued, too. Among these was another Tom, surname beginning with D, and so it became necessary to have a Tommy D and a Tommy P. In one quick act of naming, Tom was put on a par with one of the Giant Esthetes on campus. (Oh, there were Giants in those days! Tommy D bestrode the campus like a colossus. D had stood agape, an attendant lord, as tears came to Tommy's eyes when he spoke the lines "Tomorrow and tomorrow and tomorrow/ Creeps on this petty pace from day to day…" He sounded like he knew whereof he spoke.

Those Hillcoot days were over now, alcohol having taken its toll (Norma was drying out at a clinic, and Gloria had married Nick, an Arty Major, and borne him twins) but Tommy P had made an easy transition alongside D to the next party crowd, crowds. He went everywhere with D and Beth, and several of their acquaintance believed them to be a *ménage a trois*. D liked this as long as it wasn't true.

They pulled into a driveway, semi-circular, behind a raft of other cars – those closest to the mansion parked neatly, the more recent arrivals at rakish angles over the lawn. As they got out they could hear screams from the grounds as well as from inside. Yelps, more like it. Squeals. Coarse, low laughter. D saw people he knew chasing and being chased by others he didn't. The anti-semite, Fee McMannic (if M was to be believed), was – was nailing someone to a cross against the east wall! And surely that was M, helping him? And it was G they were crucifying!

But no, coming closer D saw that the three of them were trying to repair some trellis work that had come down – because, he shortly learned, Ham Meatfist had decided to leave the living room via a window, that was further from the lawn than he'd realized. Ham lay motionless in a bed of rhododendrons. Fee scowled as D and Tommy came within scowling distance. This meant, D knew, that Fee was glad to see them. It counted, because this was Fee's place. Or rather, his parents' place. D hoped they had gone away for longer than a weekend. It was going to take time to put things back together. Glancing through the open door, he could spy further structural damage – it was going to take more than a hungover Sunday to fix all that. And the ruination was still going on. D elbowed his way through the Earl Grey kitchen crowd and hunted up the Lord Byng intellectuals ensconced in a small den lined with books. (These were books about real estate but at first glance resembled a professorial stash). Angus Carey had the floor, in fact was wiping it with Jackie Krock, the hopelessly inebriate (Dewars) editor of the local litmag *Smoking Carrion.*

"But look here old chep," Angus was purring, one hand twirling the waxed point of his left mustache. "Look here, read the depths of degradation to which your inertial humanism has brought you. High hopes, desperate crashes. Liberate yourself, my dear fellow, come to see yourself as a unit in a system, so much empirical evidence, an instance of a general disposition. After all, old chep, you are, simply put, a tiny part of an arc of tendency... Look, to what your enormous outlay of energy has reduced you, and why? What for? All in the name of inspiration! The novel of the future, I can tell you, will be written by a sociologist. Your intuitions are pimples on the face of the times."

Krock, supported by the bookcase, swayed forward, head down. His words could be caught intermittently: "...carried alive into the heart by pashun... fire of individu,um,al, jeenyus... what thought was oft, ne'er well so expressed... rell-wart urn... " – it didn't matter to D that Krock's phrases kept coming up short on verbs: D had heard this spiel before, while its utterer was stone sober.

D felt that drunkenness somewhat improved it, bringing it a little closer to Pound's *Cantos*, a little further away from the Hall-Pack-Simpson anthology *New Poets of England and America*. But Angus Carey was merciless. "Look at you, you poor, pathetic creature, you dribbling excuse for an argument, you stalwart appendage to the term nincompoop, how dare you presume upon our time with your shopworn verses and their enfeebled defense? The art of poetry has been studied systematically over the past half century by research scientists working in a variety of fields. Some of these – "

" – were cunning linguists," put in Dan Danielson, who didn't think that parties should be for anything but singing (them) and playing the ukulele (him).

Before Carey could conclude, Krock lunged towards him, screaming "I'm going to kill you! Refute this!" A coffee table was in his way, however, and it sent Krock sprawling. This allowed Carey enough time to exit with dignity, for all the world as though he had been about to leave in any case. D saw his opportunity and intercepted with "Angus, I've got something to tell you. But let's find G and M first – they want to tell you too. "

"Goodness gracious me," drawled Angus, fiddling with his mustache again, "Whatever can it be? Are you three laddies about to serenade me?"

As D and his companion became increasingly lost in the throng, Carey visibly relaxed. Krock would never find him now. D glimpsed Tommy P on a couch with Caroline Anthrax perched upon his knee. Turning a corner, they were confronted with the objects of their mission. They stood one on either side of A, practicing stichomythia.

"My stomach empty and happy," chanted M; then,
"Desire makes it impossible to eat anything," from G.
"She took my pork and put it in a tin," M continued;
"History is full of holes," responded G.

Seizing the chance, D cried "and no hole bigger than last night's!" thrusting Angus into the center of the group.

CHAPTER SIX

It was in such a setting that G could wrap around him the mantle of inchoate or rather uninformed class-consciousness, but he never would have used such a term. It was enough for him that he was a burning novelist from the Valley, a genuine, while these twits, half of them English boobs in tweeds and imperial accents, were College Types, parents probably all drove Jaguars, young men who had never got up at five in the morning in a tent up north and washed their faces in cold water from a creek. So all he wanted to do was wrap his nail-bitten fingers around a glass of rye and creme soda and slouch in a corner, maybe on a Queen Anne table, and not so much watch as be watched. Oh how mysterious, some young Green Room actress in first year, might say. Or what a pretentious looking young jerk, let's pass on, Rodney, was more like it.

But M always got him away from his best intentions. M had a way of talking at parties the way an educated whale might surface and spout. He might bellow Richard the Third's soliloquy, replacing horses with lawnmowers and French history with speculations about the sex life of Professor Joe Bobby Cottonbug, the rhetoric and composition teacher at the university on the hill. M was a delight, you had to give him that, the most animated short-term imagination in the crowd. And he never seemed to get drunk, at least not in the usual way. Like Dan Danielson, who would stand for an hour leaning on the kitchen wall, then sit for an hour with his back to the wall and his legs in wrinkled black gabardine sticking straight out in front of him, then for an hour lie flat on the kitchen floor with just his head almost upright against the wall. Then an hour later he would be lying flat on his back on the kitchen floor, his drink disappearing in a puddle under him. Eventually, after walking on his body for an hour, some of the stronger women in the crowd would pull Danielson's body to the basement door, always leading off the kitchen in Vancouver houses, open the door, and slide Danielson's body down the stairs, where it was usually found by strangers the next afternoon, ritualistically decorated from head to toe with bottlecaps.

But M had an odd metabolism. He said it was because he had been born in the North West Territories, on the roof of the world, as he liked to put it. He had ice in his veins. A beer upended into his mouth was doomed to meet the Terror of the Snows. At three in the morning M could be heard arguing the vacuity of the British Command at the Battle of the Somme, or speculating on the fate of European literature had Kafka decided on a chocolate eclair instead of a beetle for Gregor. G would never admit it until 30-odd (very odd) years later, but he was envious of M's quick three a.m. wit, and would hasten to overlook his shortcomings as a supporting male in most recent productions of the Players' Club.

So he was honoured to be employed as worthy opponent in M's verbal tennis game. When D heaved Carey into the middle of things, he was glad that M was not yet ready to wind down, who wouldn't be?

"Plant psychology has no place for impatiens," M smirked.

A beamed her appreciation.

"A sage in Abbotsford is soon acclimated," replied G, his heart sinking.

A looked at him with sympathy.

"Look on the face of international vegetarianism and weep," thundered M.

G turned his back, his shoulders stooped, and began to shuffle away. But D had him by the shoulder, or rather by the shoulder of his old air force trench coat, an item of raiment that G wore to all house parties, rain or shine or bleak of creepy night.

"Mein Herr," D said; then continued, true as ever to his own perception of what was relevant, "we have here some potential doubters, more than a half-dozen mass-debaters, too many term-paper lotharios, one crypto-masochist, three women with clean underwear whose fathers rode penny-farthing bicycles, and a sophomore with a fish in his jacket pocket. It is early in the party, people are paying attention or capable of doing so. Dwight D. Eisenhower has been asleep for six hours. Listen to me, G, listen, M, it is time that we stepped up to the mark of social responsibility and revealed to these churls and damosels the apparitions we observed just last night. Was it just last night?"

M took this as a cue.

"Was it," he roared, "thou, Morandia, who discovered deep in the dark night of the hole that the heart of the Anglo Saxon meat-bearing anthropoid was identical in chromosomic composition to the side of the Oreo cookie which, when the sides are snapped apart, does not bear the round dab of white goop?"

Against all odds there was a crowd or rather a shuffling circle of young inebriates forming about this tableaux. One of the bunch spoke.

"This lightsome mid-Pacific cajolery is probably an accomplishment that a West Point Grey mother might be amused by during the evening tooth-brushing observations," said Liam Chutney, reputed future owner of a crumbling but still aspiring castle in the west of Free Ireland, "but my erstwhile handyman D has promised me that I will hear this night a tale that will fill the heart of even a landlady with dread."

"He saw the archangel Pineal arising from a burning ski lift," shouted Tommy P, who was nearly horizontal on the couch, Miss Anthrax lying upon him and licking the panes of his smoked glasses. It was an amazing party in that while there was a constant noise of broken dishes and falling bodies and shouted profundities, most one-liners were clear enough to be recorded by all the aspiring playwrights in the crowd.

D took the floor.

"We may," he said, "be living the last night of our young and often askew lives."

A huge cheer went up from the crowd, and at least four glasses were hurled into the big rock fireplace. G hoped that Fee's parents were gone to the Bay of Biscayne. But D in his elegant Oxonian way simply raised his voice.

"Only twenty-four hours ago, we three observed a huge flash of light behind the North Shore Mountains," he said, drawing out the hiss at the end of the last word.

The audience went into a supercilious silence. Sssssss. They waited for a sound. D went on:

"We waited for a commensurate sound," he said, "but found nothing but silence." He turned to M with a look comingled of sadness and love. It was the look D turned on all of his acquaintance, but there were some in the crowd who didn't yet know this. They were impressed.

M opened his mouth to proceed, but G beat him to it.

"The flash of light, "he said, "was only as frightening as the sensation of one's pulse disappearing for five minutes. The more frightening event, the more puzzling, the one that might get us out of the endless deferral of this story, the one that might begin the machinations of a novel, were this fiction rather than unproductive early life, was the ludic writing on the wall of the Sick's Brewery."

"That is called advertising," said a wag in the crowd.

"No, listen to them," put in A.

She stepped in front of G, treading on one of his feet in the maneouver. Her hair was perfect, Avonic. He reached for her tail but she stepped further, into the middle of the throng. Tommy P rolled onto the floor, where Miss Anthrax seized his legs.

"Listen to them," said A, and began an explanation of that necessity. "When William Butler Yeats attested that beings beyond our normal ken had brought the sources of his poems to him, no one credited the miracle, but later he nodded his white head over the medal from the Nobel Prize committee. That night the dark air of Stockholm was permeated with the sweet promise of a Nordic Winter. Diplomats in Broughams, their serge collars turned up wore white silk scarves around their pink necks. Offshore the harbour seals contemplated a new patch of oil slithering in darksome evening shades across the moonlight above them. The world knew parity and justice, for on a mountain slope in Patagonia at just that moment lovers disrobed and celebrated the first strong rays of spring. Demosthenes had a word for this kind of Masoretic balance. In a speech to the collected citizens of Athens in the last year of his sclerotic decline he spoke of the rashness of youth who never give heed to the night. Look, he urged, with the eyes the gods have given you on the nether side of your heads. Had there been a sudden flash of light from behind the peaks of Olympus, Demosthenes would have known it was time to hark, time to seek portents, time to become a reader of what the gods may have writ. Had words of curious intent appeared across the facade of the Architecture on the Hill he would have read them; he may not have guessed their message but he would have known something of their import. He was not a wastrel with a glass of his mother's hidden sherry in his hand."

And as she said this Fee McMannic took a quick glug and hurled what looked like a cut glass goblet into the fireplace.

"Exactly – "

But M spake only that one word, though for a few moments he made gestures with his hands. He busied himself for the next few moments, with his front teeth and the naked shoulder and neck of an actress.

"We pretend so often," said A, "to direct our thoughts and even our lives and sometimes the way we walk into the Koffee Kabin, by the words we read in the books that come to hand when one is an Arts student, Albert Camus – "

Three people blushed, something not often seen among the swacked.

" – Malcolm Lowry, Emmanuel Kant, Ezra Pound, Guillaume Apollinaire-"

She turned to peer at her date.

" – or at least the young Cold War veteran, G. Mickey Spillane," she added.

He gave her a mock smackeroo with his loose fist, on the shoulder. God, thought G, what a knockout. God, he thought, I have to have a piss, but she wouldn't take my departure at this point with aplomb.

"We pretend to direct our lives by the words we read in these people's books, words that are most of their time squashed against each other in closed volumes. But how many of us attend to the words scribed for us on the walls before our eyes. We are estranged from that with which we are most familiar, as Demosthenes said on the steps of the Capital."

"Wait a minute," said G.

"On the steps of the Capital," said A, "on whose facade might have been found the words that proclaimed democracy for the citizens of Athens. But just who were these citizens? Of all of you here, perhaps the only two that might have been permitted that rank would have been Liam and D."

"Wait a minute," said G.

"Wait a minute," said M.

"Liam and D, and I am not so certain about D," said A. "As for the women, as for the slaves, they would have been dumped from the couch," she said.

Now A was standing on a copy of *Smoking Carrion*, which was lying closed on a square table made of thick glass and wrought iron.

Fee spoke for the first time, from the side of his mouth, with his lips almost clenched, with, miraculously perhaps, another goblet of sherry or was it tawny port in his left hand. He used his right hand for a significant gesture.

"My oldest friend, the boy who fed me the perfect passes so that I could sink the opposition's hearts with spectacular jump shots at the dying of the clock, this fellow M told me that someone is flashing the unknown aretes behind Lynn Canyon and scrawling graffiti on brewery walls," said Fee. "I suspect a Zionist plot."

Most of them drank as if there was no tomorrow. Fee drank as if there was no tonight. Everyone understood that.

He had a lot of good friends, and G, for instance, had leaned toward him early. As G went everywhere in his Bulgarian-length air force rain coat, Fee was never seen without his Bennie, an expensive but very bedraggled doghound's tooth overcoat. It was said that he often, for penance and the endurance of his heart, did forty lengths of the Aquatic Centre pool in his overcoat. He was an actor in the Players' Club, where he once acted Polonius in the self-same garment. He was M's equal as an actor, carrying his personality onto the stage with him, making Shakespeare into Durrenmatt, making Durrenmatt into John Foster Dulles, burning the hearts of black-stockinged nymphets in the Green Room, winning the heart of A when he compared her with the doe-eyed mistress of a Karamazov. "A Zionist plot," he snarled, and everyone knew that he was playing a terrific part. It was said that he had made love to every young woman, gentile or other, who had seen destiny in her nakedness inside his hounddog's tooth coat. There was not a young man or younger woman who did not admire his forlorn Rimbaudian doom. They all expected him to die in a useless accident, a large piece of furniture falling from the roof of a passing truck, a stack of Coke bottles collapsing on him where he toiled weekends.

G, thinking back on this tangle of besotted thespians and quite ordinary flesh from the vantage of his late years, wanted to go back and throw his arms around three people in succession: Fee, A, and the young G.

"The flash in the sky!" shouted M at last. "The runic inscriptions on the yellow wall!" He had found the word at last. "These are only the beginning!"

M spoke in exclamation marks for the rest of his presentation. He joined A on the glass table, but he was standing on an open-faced copy of *Guns & Ammo*.

"This morning!" he said, his voice quieter but urgent, as ears, pretty and malformed, were aimed his way. "I woke up! Well, it was this afternoon! Eventually I worked up the courage! I looked into the mirror! I looked into the parts of the mirror that are not covered with toothpaste and some stranger's lipstick message!"

"More words," said A.

"What did they say?" asked Tommy P, who was now standing close to the table. Miss Anthrax was rubbing the side of her head against the inside of one of his charcoal-garbed legs.

"That's not the point!" said M.

"Oh, is there supposed to be a point?" asked the almost comatose but still standing Danielson. "Is that allowed?"

In the den, all this time, a brainless young girl who looked exactly like Susan Strasberg was gazing intently out the window. She was looking for a sign. She had a bamboo leaf in her hair.

"I say, old sport," said Liam Chutney. "If yon Demosthenes promises a point, the least we auditors can do is extend him our faith. I, for one, expect a point, though previous experience urges that I do not rely on its profundity. M has been, in my experience, an agreeable colonial, a bumptious but relatively honest and often fervent subscriber to the armory of received wisdom, that wisdom coming for the most part from the civilizing islands that gave me my birth."

No one upbraided Chutney for the mixed metaphor, because they were always indulgent of his rhetoric and accent. There was a widespread sentiment that he was over here on the Pacific Coast of this colony because of a Fenian tragedy in his family.

"I have not finished with my exclamation points!" said M. "As I was saying before I was so egregiously interrupted! I looked without optimism into the bathroom mirror! And what did I see there! Look! Look at what has happened to my hair!"

CHAPTER SEVEN

In late February of 1961, two green cars, one a 1953 Dodge sedan and the other a 1956 Oldsmobile 98, green and white with portholes, crossed the border into the United States of America on, as they say, one another's heels. Sealed inside was the student cast of *Our Town Cops Pleas*, a radio play recently adapted and rehearsed for readers' theatre performance in Seattle at the University of Washington.

The author of the radio drama was a poet whose career had been marked by frequent and strange experiments. He had written in imitation of verse models in Ancient Finnish, True Norse, and Faroese, and he had some success as a painter and concrete poet and chain-saw sculptor. He often sang, or barked like a seal at public readings. He looked as much like a seal or a walrus as a skinny, gangling man can. He was, and is, an esteemed and estimable poet, and he was a great friend to young writers, though he hated teaching them creative writing. No one understood or accepted that.

Our Town Cops Pleas was a verse play, its basic line modelled on the Far Norse "stutterstolt," the notoriously difficult accentual verse form. His fifth book of poetry, it had been given a single performance by the Canadian Broadcasting Corporation, and Prester John was pleased that it would be performed again this weekend and that he would see it. John sat on the passenger side of the front seat of the second of the two green cars. His wife Pegeen, blinking earnestly, drove along the bumpy American highway, ignoring the Burma Shave signs.

Stuffed in tbe back seat between a student actress and plum-voiced Arthur Maguay, was G, trying hard not to throw up. His gorge had literally and strongly risen three times in Peggy John's blinking, jerky progress along the road. As a distraction from the nausea, his penis had also risen during the ride, hardening as it did so. This phenomenon was caused by a warm firm pressure from the hip, thigh, arm and scent (of cinnamon, gone just a little pleasantly rank) of the student actress, Dorcas. Dorcas Davenport, once referred to mysteriously but euphoniously as "Dorinda Brutska" by the satirical D in the arts page of the campus paper, *The Bad Seed*. G's nausea was caused by drinking too much Cherry Heering after a lot too much beer the night before. In the morning, just before climbing into the John's car outside his Kitsilano basement apartment, he had precipitously and without any intention or malice, vomited on his landlord's cat, Samba, hitting it with the heavy stream of creamed diced vegetables as it crouched, tragically watching in the wrong direction, on the cement walk that led to the basement door.

As G rode southward into the freedom and opportunity represented by a weekend visit to the United States, his gorge rose again and again, and he understood what the phrase meant, and he shuddered and gasped. The other passengers sat silent as shellfish, except for Maguay, who looked like a shellfish, an ancient, inedible one. Maguay recited limericks designed to amuse the presumed academic and puerile mind of Professor John. But John, a practitioner of some elaborate forms of humourous verse, including visual or concrete poetry, in fact hated limericks. So there they were, a carfull of silent sufferers, toiling in ignorance or desperation, travelling in the eye of anihilation.

G had visited Seattle just twice in the past, sleeping in cars or on a sofa? couch? Chesterfield? in a fraternity house at the University. These had been musical mystery tours featuring basement clubs in the University district. The cast of *Our Town Cops Pleas* was booked into two downtown hotels, about five blocks apart on First Avenue. The students were happy about this, for they observed it to be a seedy area, which meant maybe jazz, or drug dealers, or prostitutes, (or at least nymphomaniacs), or maybe just a good brisk knifing in the alley. D and G had naturally and quickly selected one another as roommates; their occasional rivalries and uncertainties were nothing in the face of the possibility of getting stuck bunking with any of the other strange types from the Player's Club.

Then it was off to the Rathskellar and the sombre glory of bock beer. Somewhere back in Vancouver was M, sadly no part of this expeditionary force, for as a freshman twice-flunked, he had been denied active student status and couldn't take part in this official exchange of culture between the universities. M had urged G not to miss the Rathskellar and the bock beer, saying "It'll gird your loins, G! Two tankards of that stuff and you'll become a stranger to decency, a foreigner to all human custom and observance." M then smiled widely. "Exactly what you want to be." G didn't know about that, but he did find the bock beer, two big dark mugs of it, marvelous.

Next came the The Italian City, a restaurant on Third Avenue where G and D joined a big table of their noisy compatriots. Ken Ellsworth, court clerk in the play, was loudest. "Broadbent will tell us about that! D is a man of literature, and he can tell us whether John is any good! Hey?" Ellsworth's eyes glistened, his muzzle was slick with foam, his hair was slicked back. His very long left arm had tendrilled around both Dorcas Davenport and Frederica Henry, the two female members of the company, who had been assigned a hotel room together and arrived at the restaurant in tandem. Ellsworth's snake arm hugged them together, made them inextricably a brace of woman.

G seized a salt-shaker and, concentrating on the little particle flow of white flecks, threw salt in four vigorous arcs at Ellsworth's front. Shuh, shuh, shuh, shuh. "Shrivel, snail-slime" he hissed, then, cackling with pleasure at his masterful enunciation, he collapsed onto the banquet to his right. There was consternation and various lungings across the table, but Arthur Maguay and Willy Jeep kept Ellsworth muffled, stuffed down in his place. Waiters appeared, bread and ravioli, more beer. Butterpats were thrown, and one landed in G's coffee, but since G didn't want the coffee anyway, he laughed with the others.

In the end the restaurant, a bar where jazz was reputed to be playing, the streets and the American night all dissolved and G found himself sitting stunned upright in the twin bed with D sitting likewise in the other bed, both fully clothed and babbling vacantly. D held forth on the colonial mentality of Canadians, the archness and preciosity of Prester John as a playwright, and something marvelous he'd seen done by Laurence Olivier in London, some scene in which "Larry was playing Eddypuss, you see," though despite the modern name the play apparently had been a classical Greek tragedy. G, lost in the whirl of D's words, kicked off his shoes, grabbed the coverlet around himself and settled for oblivion. For some time D remained sitting against the end of the bed, flourishing the stubby American beer bottles and talking to them, finding, as the Canadians did not, friendliness and reassurance in their resemblance to the little brown friends of home.

Hurled early into awakeness the next morning by a telephone call bidding them get up, get going, get out to the University of Washington by noon, D and G drifted downhill to the Pike St. market for breakfast. There in the cool shadows they had eggs and things, and also hash-brown potatoes and good coffee (appreciated by hazy G) and the cheerful service not to be found in Canada. D, tireless on three hours sleep and as always full of cheerful chatter, turned out to know a tune on the booth's jukebox list *The Frozen Logger* entire and by heart, and sang along with verse after verse to G:

> It froze clear down to China
> It froze to the stars above
> At a thousand degrees below zero
> It froze my logger love.

Our Town Cops Pleas was performed in a lecture hall before a small audience of drama club *habitués* and literary types. The actors carried texts, but most of them had, in their couple of rehearsals, memorized some lines, and G, lurking at a partly opened door of the shallow-staged lecture room, awaiting his cue to enter, alternately looked at and muttered to himself his final and most impressive lines "Eala beorht bune! Eala byrnwiga! Eala theodnes thrym! Hu seo thrag gewat, genap under nihthelm, swa heo no waere!"

On the far side of the stage G could see clearly Dorcas Davenport in the role of the prompter. This character was written for comic relief, and Dorcas had been put in a tight skirt, see-through blouse and permed hairdo to convey quickly that she was a vacuous functionary with little awareness of the profound issues the play raised. Unsubtle, punderous with implication, John had named the prompter "Miss Take."

From his spy's vantage in the doorway, G found himself looking at Dorcas with a removed but more intense interest than he had hitherto taken in her. In some way his despair over matters, and over the unlikelihood of other matters, with A, and also his confusion and despair at the cloud of knowing and the storm of understanding emanating from D, contributed to his condition. He noted, not for the first time, Dorcas's finely curved lip. He noticed that the legs of Dorcas were good ones, and realized that she had been cast in her small part chiefly for this. He clamped his teeth together and felt an iron band holding his head and his gaze inexorably at the knees of the student, actress, and prompter, at the tanned legs and knees and the bit of slip revealed as the skirt had ridden up. He felt, just for a moment before more frantic feelings, stage fright and nausea again took over, a merciful, tremulous softness and a slight, sweet ache. Miss Take had something for him. A golden explosion.

Prester John watched the plodding little performance from eight rows up in the half-filled lecture theatre. Unlike G, he was not in any way disturbed by what he saw, only warmed. In his mind's eye he saw not David Broadbent, sassy in red suspenders and Cockney accent, as Artless Dogger, nor dog-faced Nicky Dixon as the blustering politician Grubby Checkers, nor pop-eyed Barton Martlett as the wild-eyed, white-haired (courtesy Leichner #11 Grease Stick for Stage Characters) incarnation of Seymour Tissue, debauched poet, nor high-hatted, haughty Wesley Trotsky as Twirla Trunchen, the police chief in drag... Carried off by his own words, John saw people, the historical figures themselves, moving on the rudimentary stage before him. His world seemed the world.

While these worlds shifted and spun in their adventures south of the border, M, back in Vancouver, took advantage of the respite from dissipation enforced by the Sunday blue laws to visit his aged parents in Kerrisdale and cadge a dinner. In an after-dinner address notably brief and pungent, he informed the parents that their world was coming to an end, thank you, that there was certainly apocalypse now to be had for the asking, and that he, for one of a large squad of natural philosophers, was indeed asking. Thank you. Seat resumed, to silence.

"Oh, M!" said his mother, "Is that what they teach you at varsity?" M's mother's own university days had attached to her this never-never-land slang, still good, she supposed, a hundred years later.

M's meals were not pretty things. The evening following the Sunday roast at mama's, he cooked and forked into himself his standard rice glop, boiled rice topped with canned soup. The evening after that, he hunched in the ridged red velveteen seats of the Varsity theatre, eating two moist beef pies, one Melton Mowbray pork pie, a big kosher dill pickle, a small block of cheddar cheese, four deep-fried "drumsticks" of ground chicken, sweating and odourous, finishing the meal with a box of Glossettes raisins and a dixie of Pepsi-Cola. M was in one of his elements, lunch. This one was the registered trademark movie lunch. The chicken drumsticks were the trademark, the linch-pins of this affair, and M was known to alter his plan to see a 3 PM showing of a Grace Kelly movie (*Green Fire*, with Stewart Granger) because the Europa delicatessen didn't have the drumsticks out of the oven yet. He loitered in shops that sold ivy league clothing and New

Directions paperback books until the perfume of the fresh-baked drumsticks seeped out to tell him that Heaven had once again come to Granville Street, then, arms loaded, strode into the movie.

The ugly spectacle of these movie lunches had achieved some notorious notice. A young woman not herself entirely a stranger to debauchery in its standard forms had fallen in with M in The Georgia pub and had consequently had a movie date with him. "It was horrible," she reported to friends. "He said we had to have a 'snack,' and he brought all this stuff. I've never seen anything like that; I was appalled."

This Tuesday night M was wolfing his celebrated mess and watching the film version of Jules Verne's *Journey to the Center of the Earth*. It starred James Mason, mellow of voice and menacing, and Arlene Dahl, a Titian-haired beauty of impressive cleavage but even more remarkable dullness. Not necessarily a bad actress, just someone whose roles and personality melded in an unassailable nullness. Also cast in this desecration of Verne was the pop singer Pat Boone. This was one of Boone's few non-singing movie parts, and of course he was scarcely less loathesome as a straight actor than as a singer. Though he had not yet become a declared Christer, his callow cornfed face already shone with sweetly simple bullish goodness. Those who, like M, aspired to madness and badness found that this sort of face made them puke. "Pat Boone's pukey pusillanimous pupface makes me puke," confided M, at seven hundred decibels once over coffee at the arty-farty table.

Herbert Lom was the villain, and crude animation created a suitably gnathous saurian for menace and roaring and a climactic fight after the explorers crossed "the central sea" that Verne posited in the innards of the earth, but it was all like Arlene Dahl's bosom, pretty pastel stuff. Snarling audibly and hideously, like Verne's Ape Gigans, M lunged out of the theatre and thrust himself toward the Roundtowner Motel. Near the centre of the city, this was four nights a week the workplace of D, now returned from Seattle's astonishing theatrical triumph to resume his employment as desk clerk from eight PM until dawn, unless he slid out early, in the small hours for some fun in what was left of the night. In such AWOL behaviour he was encouraged by M, who was thrilled at D's job at the night attendant at The Roundtowner, and pleased too that D could be fetched out of there at two, three, or four o'clock in the morning, when M would make his way along sleeping suburban roads, over bridges and through downtown lanes to reach his friend. For all his brassy yammer, M was an aimless, lonely lout, hungry for the company of people like D and G who had lives more directed than his.

"Look I can't lock up just yet," said D. "There's something happening in one of the rooms. I've called the police." These statements instantly vested tremendous authority in D. Some big, ugly, real thing was happening, and D was coping with it, doing the job he was paid for, putting his thin shoulder to the wheel.

The police, two of them, only blue jowls and small eyes visible, arrived, and D showed them to Room 38, unlocked the door, stepped aside. A man perhaps a few years older than D or M lay on the floor, shoulders tucked awkwardly against the bed, the salmon-pink nubbled bedspread pulled out of place, the bed otherwise undisturbed. The man's mouth was half open, his thin striped tie slung across the chest of his tan suit in a messy way. The man too had been slung or cast, looked like that, at the foot of the bed.

To M, looking covertly over the shoulders of D and a policeman, the man looked surely and exactly to be Pat Boone.

CHAPTER EIGHT

He was definitely dead. And good riddance to him, thought A, who surely and finally put an end to the Pat Boones of her life when, one night, she accepted an invitation from one of them to an Evening with Mort Sahl at The Cave Supper Club – not a supper club at all, really, since almost no one ate there, but a place you could go to drink and be entertained by a variety of persons who ranged all the way from Mitzi Gaynor to Lennie Bruce. For some reason, the Pat Boone look-a-like had developed a crush on A who *did* want to see Mort Sahl and was willing to endure Pat's company in order to do so. What she was not willing to endure was the highschool gropings in the car following the performance. Pat seemed to regard A's enthusiastic response to them as the price she had to pay for the price he'd paid for their entry to the club downtown. The Cave was built to look like an actual grotto, its *papier maché* interior suggesting that all hope be abandoned upon one's entry. The denizens of the club frequently included Vancouver's shabby imitation of the elite of Tinseltown: Jed Goldenblum, resident intellectual for *The Vancouver Bun* and his actress-wife Blanche. In the 50's, dermabrasion and facelifts had not become commonplace, and A was alarmed out of her ambition to be an actress and torch singer. A made do with occasional performances (on table tops at parties when she was drunk) of *Love For Sale, The Man I Love, Ten Cents A Dance, Lover Man* and *Round Midnight,* sung in the style of Carmen McCrae, Peggy Lee, June Christie and Doris Day (from *The Ruth Etting Story*). She had, she felt, graduated from the Pat Boone class.

However, the Pat in the car beside her was not convinced. He persisted beyond the brief kissing session A felt was sufficient recompense for the evening's entertainment. Her need to extricate herself from his dogged grappling was made even more imperative by the two drinks she had consumed on an empty stomach which were now causing her considerable intestinal distress. When her polite efforts failed to persuade her persistent companion of her need to leave, A, in disgust, abandoned all pretense at civility, threw etiquette and caution to the winds and farted. It took only a few seconds of awful stillness for Pat to realize that A's protestations had been genuine. He leapt out of the driver's seat and opened the door for her departure, making no effort to delay her with a request for a final kiss. As she climbed the stairs to her bedroom, A witnessed his futile efforts to fumigate his car of her sulphuric contribution to the evening. He was swinging the door on the passenger side back and forth as rapidly as he could. When she reached her bedroom, A glanced out of the window in time to see Pat pulling out the lighter he had lit her cigarettes with all evening. The explosion that ensued lit up the sky for miles, and A watched a face-blackened cartoon character climb into his car and drive off while bedroom lights went on up and down the street and the silhouettes of people wakened from their sleep by the blast appeared in the windows of the silent houses.

Evidently Pat saw the writing on the wall; he must have understood that the end of his fantasy relationship with A was at hand, for he retired to D's hotel to rent a companion for the rest of the evening, a service discreetly provided by D, not indeed his only connection to the demi-monde of the sororities. So it was with some dismay that D realized no discretion was possible in this instance. The police, when they arrived, were puzzled by Pat's blackened appearance and concluded that some sort of kinky sex game had backfired. Which wasn't far from the truth, had it been known. A, reading the paper next morning, and relieved to be rid of Pat, was not so unkind as to have wished death on him, and thought that his punishment had far exceeded his crime. The events of the evening had wound themselves beyond her ability to control them, however, as such things often do. Keeping her head down, peering through the dark glasses she adopted for a few days as a disguise in case anyone should suspect a connexion between Pat's death and her date with him. A did not know at the time what fate had in store for her when she left behind her forever the Pat Boone world and moved out of the frying pan into the meatgrinder.

Years later A would laugh in astonishment when D's chapter five and M's letter arrived in the mail on the same day. Both included references to the Ancient Mariner. Both saw A's chapter as analogous to that old codger's glittering-eyed, skinny-handed, obsessive grip. When she opened M's letter, there he was, the central figure of a cartoon aptly titled *Crossed Paths: Icarus Meets The Ancient Mariner.* A dead albatross lay on the deck, arrow stuck in its chest, legs stuck up in the air. Definitely dead. The mad-eyed old man, cross-bow pulled taut, was taking aim at a young and already arrow-filled Icarus surprised in mid-flight. A couldn't believe that such a thing had happened by chance, despite her half-suspended disbelief in Jung's ideas about synchronicity, so she called M up to find out whether he and D had been talking to each other, but M said no, they hadn't. He seemed a little subdued, uncertain about whether A understood his careful cautionary note? A did. She wasn't surprised that D and M had come to the same conclusion, just surprised that they had both used the same metaphor and that their letters had arrived on the same day. She had been well-trained by G to recognize her limitations. She just didn't want to pay too much attention to them when the alternative was silence. She preferred, somehow, to continue rushing around like a fart in a collander until she found her own way of protecting herself. Or not. On the other hand, she didn't want to be seen as the killer bitch mother shooting down the ecstacies of the little joy-boys whose stories they were writing. Was she that? She might have known better. She did, but was not protecting herself with her disbelief.

When she read G's chapter the next day, she laughed and laughed and then she cried and cried. This porridge is too hot for me, she said to herself, remembering the silver dish she'd had as a child that pictured Goldilocks and the 3 bears on the bottom when you'd eaten all the porridge. She still had it, and though its bottom was tarnished now, you could still see the group gathered around the breakfast table. Though she'd said in letters to D and M the previous day that she thought the albatross was a little redundant, after reading G's chapter, she didn't think so anymore. A is G's albatross. And it is A, now, who is the arrow-filled figure – spiked on their wit. There is no room for me in this writing, she said. This bed is too hard. This chair is too big. What happens to Goldilocks? Do they take her in? A wanted to be taken in. And she was – repeatedly. But would they take her in? They were scary, but familiar, and There is no room for me in this writing, she said.

G had written a protective persona for her – the jolly joking cloak he wore which garnered him affection and afforded him protection now covered her. What could she be but a ponderous kill-joy if she protested? Or the thing on which they worked their wit? An occasion for a joke (which she, like the rest of them, didn't know how to take). G turned her memory of *The Books of Knowledge* into a joke: Oh yes, A had read *The Odyssey* by the time she was five, you know. This strange double compulsion to protect and attack at the same time is something she doesn't understand in men. Perhaps they are protecting the scars of their own babyhood for which they blame the mothers they are attacking. Maybe it is their recognition of their own cowardice and vulnerability that lies back of the insult they hurl at each other: Motherfucker. I'm outnumbered, A thinks. Sclerotic means scarred. And we all have many scars. G would like A to develop more protective scar tissue for her many wounds.

Her friend taught school in Buffalo Creek in the interior of British Columbia where she had a student named Mary Many Wounds. Her friend was herself wounded there, multiply, when, after being raped by another student's father, she was told by the police she called that they would tell her dying father (who did not know) about her illegal abortion if she tried to press charges against her rapist. They promised she would never get another teaching job in Canada or the U.S. She moved to England after she married, had her first child, became an alcoholic, moved to Singapore, gave birth to a second child, moved to Texas, went back to school, became a political scientist, lost one husband, moved to Florida with another, where she managed a health club, left the second husband, lost her job, joined A.A., helped to establish a women's centre, is now teaching black children in the Everglades, and has sworn off drink and men.

Back then, when A knew them all, her friend was losing her baby in the apartment where A lived. G and his friend were waiting for A to get ready to go to the party across the street. G's friend was the one A called Trombone, and he had just come back from 2 years in Japan, sent there by his millionaire father's effort to rid his son of his suicidal Japanese girlfriend who had, amazingly, lived through World War II in Manchuria, picking lice from the seams of Japanese soldiers' uniforms, washing uniforms in boiling water, the unheated warehouses in which the children worked so cold that their hands and feet, wrapped in rags, were bleeding. She had narrowly escaped being in Hiroshima with an aunt when the American bombs fell. One of her friends had been raped by either Russian or Chinese soldiers when both were moving into Manchuria as the war was drawing to a close. The friend had committed suicide, and Fumiko was dressed like a boy and hidden in an attic after her father had convinced a Chinese neighbour to offer his daughter's would-be rapists money to let her go. The transaction ended her father's friendship with the Chinese, and the fishboat on which her father had arranged her passage to Hiroshima was late arriving. She told A these stories years later, in Mexico.

Trombone married her in a disgusting ceremony at his father's house. The bride, dressed in a traditional wedding costume sent from Japan by her father, handed around the sushi while Trombone's father expatiated on the price and symbolic meaning of the embroidered gown, mispronouncing all the Japanese words. G and A were present at the ceremony. G got drunk, flirted outrageously with a young wedding guest, and turned pale green. A knew that he was going to be sick. He threw up on his shoes in the garden soon afterwards.

When Trombone was living with G on the third floor of an old house overlooking False Creek, they took turns having their girlfriends stay. It was a lovely old house that swayed every time the wind blew, and its lights went out. Running, wrapped in a sheet, to the bathroom across the hall where the stairs to the floor above came through was an adventure in not being caught. A often opened the fridge to find neat packages of sushi leftovers. Trombone spent most of his married life trying to keep his wife alive. She jumped off bridges into water, out of hospital windows into the street, bit her tongue half off, stabbed herself in the stomach, swallowed lye, liquor and pills, vomited them up and survived. She was finally successful in shaking off her painful mortal coil after the divorce had gone through. From time to time she called A, complaining madly that Trombone was stealing her alimony money. Mary Many Wounds. Her daughter became a cop. Trombone is going blind and prays for the convent-schooled soul of his wife in Catholic churches all over the world.

But at that time, while A's friend was losing her baby in the bathroom, delirious with fever because back then, abortionists did their cutting and scraping and sent their clients home to lose the foetus and *then* call the hospital – Trombone and G were waiting in the living room of the apartment for A to finish getting ready to go to the reception being held at G's former girlfriend's place across the street. They were laughing and joking and looking out of the same window A had been looking out of a few months earlier, waving goodbye to G, who was standing in the street, skinny and beautiful in his old blue airforce shirt and jeans, waving goodbye to her, waiting for his friend Tenny to pick him up. A's heart bloomed with love and then with horror. G stepped out into the path of Tenny's car as it drew up to the curb, bounced four feet into the air, got up, waved again and disappeared into the little Austin which disappeared into the line of traffic moving down Broadway. A stood at the window, shaken with what she did not then know was her future.

But at this time, A's friend called from the bathroom, and when A went in, her friend held in her hand a little beginning-to-be-shape, primordial E.T., and asked – strained eyes, flushed face – Is this it? A said she thought so and called the-woman-who-cannot-be-named because she cannot-be-implicated. She was A's landlady, and her sister was a nurse who worked for and was having an affair with a big name, married lawyer. It was a romantic story. The lawyer's wife was an invalid and the landlady and her sister spent long weekends on the lawyer's boat with his daughter and her new husband. The landlady told A about the time the daughter, water-skiing behind the boat, lost the top of the bikini she had bought on her honeymoon in Fiji and had to ski barebreasted behind the boat until they got close enough to shore for her to discreetly descend into the waters, to wait for a towel to cover her nakedness. The landlady also told A that her sister slept in her brassiere to prevent her breasts from falling. Now she told A to get the two men out of there – go to the party across the street – not to come back until much later. Conspiracy of women. How could A make sense of these relationships of men and women? She had no one to tell her how, and she felt bludgeoned by experience she could admit only as fragments, images of horror she steeled herself against, learning a new world her mother knew nothing about, or did not speak about. So she became her friend's mother, not knowing, then, how power worked, how her friend would hate her for it.

Out of her depth in this new female world, A obediently went to the party with G and Trombone and tried to get drunk, but she could not, though she was sure one of her major attractions for G was that she was such a cheap date. It took only two drinks to get her drunk, and she was willing after one, but that was for love, not drink. This was September, three and a half months before G and A got married. Everyone else was getting very drunk. The civilized proceedings earlier at G's former girlfriend's elegant father's house in West Point Grey had been too much for the arty farty crowd, so now they were really tying one on. A always suspected that G's former girlfriend had married her painter husband shortly before G and A's own marriage to get even with G for not coming back to her when she decided she wanted him back after all. This happened soon after A and G fell in love.

She tried other things. Like inviting A over to her apartment, built onto her father's house because her stepmother who was a famous composer hated her. She had arranged a ceremonial meeting to give A her photographs of G which were photos of G and herself. She cut them in half before handing A the half of the picture in which G appeared. A silently cursed her mother for not properly preparing her to deal with this side of things. She understood that G's former girlfriend was exercising the only power she had left, which was to claim G by giving him to her, but she remained silent, complicit. She even understood why. The girl's father was the most beautiful man A had ever seen. No wonder his daughter could not live with any of her other 8 stepfathers. No wonder she tried to make her father jealous of all her boyfriends. No wonder she told her father (who paid for it) and G that the child she was aborting was G's. Neither her father nor G believed it, but G pretended he did. He even bought the girl a ring. She laughed when she gave it back and called G a fool. Her wedding present to G and A was a white woven bedspread, which, A later found out, was the one she'd slept beneath with G. Her other present, a broken black leather chaise longue, was the one G had slept on when he stayed over. She gave G a drawing of Paganini that hung in his study for many years until someone stole it. A was finding out about variations on the Oedipal problem she hadn't conceived of before.

The former girlfriend invited A to the opera. Her family was musical and European. One of her grandmother's husbands had been Dorfendorf, a German composer who joined the Nazi party, having produced one son with the grandmother; the other was Bruno Hauptbuscher, friend of Albert Einstein, Jewish violinist, and father of the beautiful man who had produced G's girlfriend. The two sons fought on opposite sides in the second European war, sons of the House of Atreus. The first time A saw the girlfriend, she was at a meeting at one of the writing instructors' houses. She'd removed Dorfendorf's fur cape with a flourish and thrown it on the floor before settling herself on it. A was impressed, as G had meant her to be, when he told her these things.

The opera A went to with the former girlfriend, her grandmother, and the grandmother's husband, gay and twenty years his wife's junior, was *Faust*. There had been a little pre-theatre supper at the house – broiled grapefruit and cold chicken. A had worn her little black Ann Klein dress, the only really good one she had. The former girlfriend offered A her mother's pearls to "brighten it up," cautioning her to be careful of them since they were worth $10,000.00. In her confusion and dismay at all this Jamesian anxiety and complexity, A spooned salt from her salt cellar onto the broiled grapefruit, disgracing herself completely. The former girlfriend smiled triumphantly. A's sense of shame was only partly assuaged when the German grandmother emerged from the bathroom after dinner trailing a couple of yards of shit-stained toilet paper beneath her white crepe dress. Bejewelled and ready, she turned away to allow her husband to drape her fur over her shoulders, which he did, and as she moved to the door, deftly stepped on the toilet paper's tail end. It came away fairly easily; he had disposed of it and was at the door in time to hold it open for her. His wife was entirely unaware of the tiny drama that had taken place behind her back. A left the house filled with a churning mixture of admiration (for the husband), shame (for herself), hatred (for the former girlfriend who was so intent on making her feel like a hick) and a wild urge to shriek with laughter.

When they got to the theatre, the two younger women had to sit in orchestra seats while their hosts ascended the stairs to the loges, the grandmother bowing, nodding and waving all the while to the buzzing seats below. When A looked a question at her companion, she was told that the grandmother had been a very beautiful and famous actress in Germany. A understood that the grandmother was lost in another time and place. No one knew her here. A began to wonder why *she* was here, but the opera was *Faust* and Mephistopheles was most satisfying in his swirling cape with its red satin lining. Margereta wailing and dying in her prison cell was a perfectly beautiful victim, her sad plaint and yellow braids all that A could have wished for at the time. Later when she saw Bonynge's *Don Giovanni* with her own mother, she realized that the *Faust* production hadn't been all that good. But she'd become a grown woman by that time.

At the time of the wedding party for the former girlfriend, the world was hyper-real, the way it is when someone dies, and A didn't know why she was there either. People were crawling out of second story windows, and as far as A knew, there was no balcony. The rooms were blue with smoke, and a lustful pair were fucking among the coats piled on the bed. This offended the bride who was vainly trying to get her new husband to haul them out: What are you? A man or a mouse, she uninventively demanded. He was a painter who had done a portrait of G, one of G's poems embedded in its thick oils. He looked miserable, but refused to uncouple the two lovers, so the former girlfriend had to do the job herself. G and A and Trombone heard her yelling at the hapless pair as they descended the stairs and walked past the used furniture store that occupied the lower storey of the building. People were still making a human chain from the window above to the street below; in the middle, his belly exposed in the stretch, was the beautiful dark-haired painter who looked like a soccer player. The newly married couple were divorced in less than a year, and the painter husband came to live a block down the street from the apartment where G and A and Trombone lived. He ran every morning on the beach and collected driftwood to heat his studio.

There are 8 million stories in The Naked City and this is only Vancouver. But stretch it is the texture A wants. Not the stories so much. The baffled thickness of creatures blundering about in words and paint not yet realized, their obstinate questions, their laughter. Idiot joy, trailing toilet paper and cloudy glory. The darkening edge they tumble toward, rose-lipped girls and light-foot lads. Out of romance and into the 20th century, fallings from us, vanishings. Though she writes from the other end of this *fin de siécle* world, even A's laughter endures and erupts, from time to time, like the lightning bolt that hit the pavement outside the Yew Street (1719) apartment, burning it black, summer, 1963. Writing diabolic in concrete, close to the wall where their bedroom was. Put the lights out. And someone threw ink through the window onto G's books.

CHAPTER NINE

D had his head in his hands. What had he set in motion? He was mired in consequences beyond his calculation when so light-heartedly he had invented a couple of gestures then flung them to the wind.

This is called Having a Life.

"The toebone connecta to a footbone..." These were the words of the Lord. And the fear of the Almighty took D and shook him, there in his lair, in his rathole where Heaven's Hound had run him down. His, the Cosmic Hangover; his, the fault, Mea culpa, mea culpa culpa culpa, mea culpa culpa, he was crooning, head now a little to one side, listening-like, to the tune of *Que Sera, Sera*. Doris Day had long been his idol. He prayed to her now.

"O Dododay, hear me now and at the hour of my setting-forth, and at the hour of my kneeling-down, and at the hour when I envy my lover's car, for it supporteth her buttocks and knoweth the grip of her small hand upon its gearshift. It hath purpose, in following her; it hath ends and goals. But upon the likes of me, O Dodo, the bald blank world breaks into a million smithereens of erstwhile intention. Dodo, oh show me the way."

D prayed this prayer or one much like it several times each day. He liked Doris Day's earlier movies best, and held to this prejudice throughout the days of his long, long life thereafter. She had a certain vulnerability back then, and it made her indignation more credible. And her indignation and her anger, what else had she to offer? Her radiant smile was a dima dozen phenomenon. No, Doris Day spoke to his outrage. And spoke in a low, husky voice that transported him beyond sex to a realm of bliss such as he had only actually known in his mother's arms, infant-wise. There, on the edge of her infanticidal tendencies. "There is where we truly live,"

D thought, anguished. But the Good Lord in his infinite wisdom had taken Doris Day and scattered her qualities throughout a score, nay a hundredfold, of women. D was aware that the real Doris Day lived in Beverly Hills with her husband, Marty Melcher, and that she wouldn't hear a word against the nogoodnik and therefore would never give D a tumble, would forever remain beyond his possessing, forever condemning him to the Egyptian labor of reassembling her from the Daylike portions and qualities of other women.

An angry voice from the street broke in upon his self-indulgence, causing him to suffer even greater pangs of self-recrimination. When so many are substantially troubled, who wants to hear such private crap? If D had had a gun, he would have shot the lout then and there. Doris Day had felt to be but a skipping heartbeat away. He liked the movie with Danny Thomas best. But the innocuous Gordon McRae had proved a pretty decent foil, also. "We were sailing along, on Moonlight Bay; you could hear the darkies singing,… " For "darkies" substitute "voices". Transcendence there is, but never untrammeled; the past comes at us pitted with dents like a dead moon subject to meteorites.

They had hauled Franklin Garshaw off to the city morgue. His resemblance to Pat Boone, commented upon by A and by M, had become a passing one.

Franklin had been not shot but gang-raped, and penetrated finally by a mightier tool than this planet of the apes had intended to be used in such fashion. Pat Boone crooned on unscathed.

D feared that he would lose his job for not having noticed anything untoward during his shift. Surely there had been screams? Doubtless, but D had as per usual been catching forty winks on the daybed in the office of the Roundtowner Motel and so had nothing of value to tell the authorities. But it wasn't going to look good on his resumé. We aren't paid to sleep, in this vale of tears.

We are bent upon a quest, and if D's was to assemble the

scattered portions of an ideal bandsinger turned movie star, he could count himself lucky; so many drift without purpose in this Sargasso Sea of the second half of the twentieth century, fanning their flickering Existence with the palmetto leaf of Being. Of course, he counted himself no such thing.

"My God what have I done!" he wailed now, causing M, who was fiddling with the knobs of the office radio, attempting to bring in some late Schubert, and succeeding, to roar back at him "For Krrzzsake Broadbent! Decease and cyst! Isn't it enough that Pat Boone isn't dead?!? Must I also put up with your mewling and puking sensibilities?!? Good God man, get a grip on yourself! – No, not there!@! – Remember, Food teaches us that God is good." And he produced the remains of a Cornish pasty from under his black fake velvet Brooks Brothers-type jacket.

M had been noticeably on edge ever since the Great Flash incident on the bridge. Something weird had happened to his hair, as G had remarked. The chicken drumsticks had been late twice in a row, spoiling M's chances to review a couple of winningly artsy-fartsy flicks for CBC. He had been bumped from his role in Prester John's play, and much to his seething displeasure had been replaced by none other than G himself, who had used the opportunity – as M had feared would happen – to cop a feel of Dorcus Davenport, hot from Prester John's imagination. And to top it all off, he had believed he had seen the still-warm corpse of Pat Boone, his *bête blanche* (a rebel's hot lunch), only to find it was a case of mistaken identity.

"A Mace of Striking Misanthropy!" M's wrath, like his memory for words, knew no bounds.

But so what, thought D, so what? He had other fish to fry. Since we left him at that party, D had aged ten years, twenty. His brown hair was streaked with blond. He had wrinkles beneath his tan. Having been thrown out, eventually, as was the custom when D attended such parties, D had set out on foot, an ancient mariner looking for a wedding guest. Turned out no one at the party had given credence, despite muffled and muttered affirmations from M and G, to D's account of the Big White Flash that had blossomed for a breathless moment from behind the ducal skyline of the North Shore Mountains, then faded in a trice, like a cast of the dice, leaving our three anti-heroes waiting in the dark, the new dark, the darkness post-Flash, for a sound, the merest of muffled booms, anything but the *ingesting* that same dark had gradually delivered and kept on delivering. No one had wanted to decipher hieroglyphs, not while Seagrams continued to distill, and hormones to ring.

To whom should he unfold his tale? He was crossing a golf course, arriving at a street. There was a window. And at it, or in it, or protruding from it, two faces, faint and rosy, flowers reflecting the madrugada of northern midsummer. One of these opened and spoke. "Time for a sex scene in this fucken novel." D couldn't care less how he made it up the stairs. Her rough bud slithered along his tongue. Their breasts hung like pears, pairs of pears. Parts of them sprouted, like mustard and cress. The witching odor of Coal Harbour at low tide dragged him lower, deeper. Anyone has seen, and even eaten, a persimmon. The velvet loges of their theatres accommodated the silken buttocks of his glans. Somewhere, in a still room like a nun's cell, a Q-tip is being inserted into the corolla of a floral arrangement. Now a rough cut of a grave at dusk, with rain overflowing the runnels of the departed marblist. D was engrossed in his comparison and contrast assignment. The sticky seam gaped at his effrontery. Securely mounted, and one hand jollying up his mount's companion, D spoke: "Just two nights ago, or was it three, three nights ago, I stood on the Burrard Street Bridge in company with G and M – you know them?... " They shut his gob with the Greek salad of their attributes, the Renaissance Faire of their simian resourcefulness. Bats shrilled their radar in remotest caverns of the ganglia. Stop-motion photography was being invented on sepia postcards for the first time in this Kalpa, the thirty-seventh time in the history of the planet. Somewhere deep inside the British museum, a book slapped shut as Ezra

Pound scrawled "H.D., Imagiste" across the bottom of a sheet bearing the poem every one wakes up from a dream nearly able to recall in its unimaginable toto. Large raptors were dragging his naked body across dense tufts of lavender, marjoram, oregano, fennel. A statue of David, only with its knees bent, was ported by lustily chanting laborers in a prone position across a courtyard cobbled with raw filet mignon. Surrealism shorted out like a two-bit length of wire. The OED fell from the top shelf and burst into words like thigh, dimple, jamjar, derringer, aureole, follicle. Charles Chaplin ingenuously removed the piece of wood that was keeping the half-built ship on shore. Down the slip it slid, beneath the calm mirror, and its sinking would have been the end of the matter, save that vasty gouts of water welled up through its unreadied ribs. Emblematic beasts went nose-to-tail down a long corridor of some filthy European palace. Anomalously, that farting Royal Berkshire was trotting through the Louvre sporting Fee McMannic's raincoat. A welcome mat had been spread over his face, a magic carpet substantial angels were using for a surfboard. So far, so good. But later, he found palliatives and medicines in the bathroom cabinet that implied that his two companions of the night had diseases of a sexually transmissible sort. Also, the prescription labels were from a local prison. D fled, undeterred by their friendly shouts of See ya later and Come back for some more.

D knew the works of Malcolm Lowry, and the phrase "This unprophylactic rejection" entered his memory field as he jogged along Arbutus. Although it was still early, he could see Montgomery Incline fighting with his wife in the kitchen. A plate of ham and eggs went to the ceiling and most of its contents remained behind, dripping gradually onto the rapt combatant couple. D crept into a dumpster and went blank.

D sat on a log on First Beach, head in hands, recalling all this, aye, and more. Though not much more. What has been indited above very nearly covers the case. Something of M's beaded string of words – *fungible, autosynthesis, beeswax, corrida, sturm-und-drang* – now caught in his attention-net. He and M had wandered this way, once D had been released after intensive questioning by a Rottweiler and an Old English Bulldog, to watch yet another dawn come up on the greatest little city that literature ever had at that moment for inspiration.

"…fungible. So Fee said that he wandered off and two girls invited him up and yanked his pants off and had their way with him then and there and then he found out that they had escaped from Oakalla and were taking part in a gonorrhea experiment. He's quite upset."

What was this? Though he knew it was rude to do so, D interrupted, and adding to his list of social gaffes, demanded of M that he repeat himself. M, mouth in an oval O between its decorative frieze of black beard and mustache, eyebrows slightly raised as if in polite rebuke, obliged. "…fungible. So Fee said that he wandered off and two girls invited him up and yanked his pants off and had their way with him then and there and then he found out that they had escaped from Oakalla and were taking part in a gonorrhea experiment. He's quite upset."

"M, this is un*canny*. What you're telling me happened to Fee happened to me. How can such things be?"

"Broadbent, it's a sign of incipient schizophrenia to rime like that. I recently read some pretty jazzy poems by some American called Sylvia Plath who on the evidence of her chiming rimes is clean round the bend dementia-praecox-wise. Now I grant you that the events of this night – and the night before this – and the night before that – ahem, tell me, Broadbent, have you ever considered a visit to the campus shrink? Dog-faced Nick Dixon, with whom you acted in Seattle, swears by him. Reportedly he cured Nick of a very severe case of hydrophobia."

"Yes, he didn't exude his usual odor of lanolin and wormwood when I was crushed in Prester's back seat next to him. But tell me more about Fee, about his encounter with two bad girls next to the golf course."

"How do you know they live next to the golf course?"

"I could describe their apartment intimately. I could describe their parts intimately."

"Well that deplorable litany you'd better save for Fee. If we hop a bus right now we can probably catch him before he leaves for the VD clinic. I believe a bus headed in his direction departs this stop yonder in another five minutes. Just time for me to purchase a salami and two pounds of apfelstrudel at this delicatessen. Are you sure you won't join me?"

But D never ate before the pubs opened; scarcely ate before they closed. He shuffled amiably along with M on his errand. His mind was working overtime. "M, was I thrown out of Fee's party?"

"You were indeed. Rather splendidly, by Billy O'Shea. "

"And what happened then?"

"That I can tell you, because I was thrown out immediately afterwards. We went to the White Spot."

"It was still open!?"

"Alas, no. We damaged some of its windows, and then we walked to Trafalgar Beach. You said you wanted to see the herons."

"And we never crossed a golf course?"

"Not once. After a while, you found a public telephone and called your spouse to come and fetch us. Naturally, she did. I approve these unions of the bohemian with the middle-class. Their mutual need is so clearcut."

D wanted to protest that Beth was not so middle-class that she had refused his dare a week before to take her clothes off and walk home naked from a previous party, but his eye was on even bigger game.

"Then I don't have gonorrhea!"

"That's not for the likes of me to say. Perhaps you could go to the clinic with Fee. He might be glad of the company."

"But M, how can such things be? I recall it so clearly – what actually happened to Fee!" He made the leap. "It's that white flash. I've been radiated with some power to switch identities."

"And I haven't?"

"Because your name doesn't rime with Fee's. D rimes with Fee. The flash makes use of the power of rime, don't you see?"

"No, I don't. D rimes with G, too. Had any of *his* experiences lately?? Just more of your nauseating *understanding*, Broadbent, always anticipating others with your nigh-psychic sympathetic powers – it's revolting."

Just then, the bus rolled up. D dropped his fare-money, and stooped to retrieve it. M was already boarding. As D straightened up, he felt something hard and metallic nudging his back.

"Don't give us a hard time. Just get in the car."

M, looking around, glimpsed D being shoved into a black Daimler that had several black-coated figures already in it. He hopped back to the sidewalk as the car sped off. M made a note of the license plate. Anachronistically, it read NO ONE U NO.

The Daimler was taking him through Stanley Park. The man with a scar on his face was doing the talking.

"So shut up about this big white flash, see? Just shut up about it, okay? You didn't see it: it didn't happen. There was no big white flash. Got it?"

D shifted uneasily. He was squeezed between two other men whose muscles felt like triple-layer stove-piping. His interrogator was seated in the passenger side, twisting around to face him. This position was easier than it would be today, for he was not obliged to wear a seat belt.

"Got it?"

"Do you mean to tell me," D began carefully, "That the big white flash – the flash that uses the power of rime – Ugh" – here he stopped speaking, for an elbow had been jabbed into his stomach.

"I don't mean to tell you anything, asshole. The one question is for you, and it's this: do you think you can forget what we want you to forget? Cause if you can't, you're gonna end up down there." He indicated the tide race in First Narrows. "Sooner or later."

"Why not kill me now and save us both some trouble?" D found he had asked.

"Cause you been spillin' your guts already, and if you wash up it might raise some questions. But if you don't clam up, we're just gonna have to take that chance."

"No chance if he's garbage," put in the man on D's right.

"Right, drowning's too good for him," the interrogator agreed. "Let him be landfill, him and his fucken rime."

"I think I can remember," D said. "Ouch! I mean, forget. I meant to say, remember to forg – "

The elbow again. D couldn't believe how real this felt, how unreal. Now the car, having reached the North Shore end of Lions Gate Bridge, was turning to head west. D could see his friends Ham and Leona Bremser's shack, with Ham and Leona in front of it, yab-yumming. D could tell from Ham's beard that a stiff breeze had sprung up over the Gulf.

"Lookit there, willya? Dee-sgusting!"

"Dirty beatniks."

"Oughta ship em to Cuba."

"Jeez, is he really doin' that or do my eyes deceive me?"

The company of the Daimler had not been this animated until now. Thinking to take advantage of the more relaxed mood, D asked where he was being taken.

"Where would you like to go, your royal highness? Just name it, and Louie'll take you there. Right, Louie?"

"Whatever," grunted the driver, shifting his dead cigar.

"I'd like to be taken to Southwest Marine Drive," said D, adding "If Louie knows where that is?"

"Is that back? We don't do back. Try again."

"Well, okay, how about right here?"

"Too short," the man on his right said.

"We were thinking of somewhere like Squamish," said the man in the passenger seat. "To give you time to think. To remember, uh, to forget."

They drove on in silence for a spell. Finally D summoned up some courage and spoke: "Does any of you gentlemen know anything about, well, hieroglyphs?"

It was a bright morning, altogether too bright, thought G Delsing, his eyes screwed up against it. He would sooner still be asleep, nestled in his single bed with A. But he had to get to the stacks and get on with his thesis. And the next issue of *Hits* was overdue. He had to get to the mimeo machine in the English Department when no one was looking and run off a couple hundred copies free gratis.

He had padded outside barefoot to get the paper before his landlady could get it. Standing there in his very striped pjs, the sleeves cut off at the biceps, the thin arms of a poet sticking out, he resembled nothing more than a deckchair in a stiff breeze. *The Vancouver Province* lay rolled up on the sidewalk, when it should have lain on the front walk at the bottom of the landlady's wooden stairs.

"Bad shot," said G to himself, to himself and the grass of the lawn, and the shrubs of various shapes, sizes and hues, and to the birds and the sky and the trees of the street, and the big car just turning the corner, and he padded out to the curb and bent down. He felt something hard poking into his back.

"Don't give us a hard time. Just get in the car."

CHAPTER TEN

It is difficult to feel natural in striped pyjamas that should have been changed two weeks ago, but who has other pyjamas, inside a big black foreign car with several gunsels also in black, in fact to be sitting between two large and probably Slavic gunsels if that isn't a racist observation, in the back seat, and because this was back then, with one's bare feet up on the bump in the middle of the floor that he never had understood but it was something to do with the driveshaft or transmission or something, *n'est-ce pa*? But he had never been able to sit in the middle of the back seat, and especially next to serge overcoats, and especially next to black serge anything. He always got nauseated in the back seat in the middle, especially if there was *fabric* anywhere near his skin or eyes.

"I may vomit," he said, reciting the best line he had ever heard M pronounce on a stage.

"Like shaddup and listen to the radio," said the gunsel in the death seat up front. Solicitously, perhaps, said gunsel turned up the sound.

"*Aprilllll love, is for the very yu-hung*" opined the vapid voice that emanated from the tinny dashboard of the Daimler.

CFUZ was playing a whole hour of Pat Boone songs, and the radio was not tuned quite right. Boone's voice, which usually sounded as if it came from a throat that had been simonized and freed of all nodes, now had a kind of dryer-lint margin to it.

"I wonder, could you get something on CBC?" asked G.

"Shaddup, like," expounded a Slav.

"They play the Archers around this time of the morning," G persisted.

A hard object introduced itself between the two halves of

his jammies. G was happy if that is not an inappropriate word in such a circumstance, that it felt cold. He was quick enough to fear that these guys could have been the agents of Franklin Garshaw's misfortune in the Roundtowner. He looked around for clues, hotel matches, a towel with a name on it.

No luck.

G hated being in the middle of the back seat of a crowded Limey car while it was going over the Lion's Gate Bridge. He hated going over the Lion's Gate Bridge, because it was so high and so old and so narrow, and they didn't have anything like it back in Lawrence, BC in the middle of the gentle Okanagan Valley, where he wished he was right now, a sentiment he did not remember having during peach-picking season. Peach-picking always made him feel nauseated. He had often upchucked in orchards.

He had often upchucked while listening to Pat Boone, but this had usually happened just outside the kitchen of someone's apartment. Once he upchucked a mixture of Old Niagara Port and onion pizza on Fee McMannic's raincoat.

They had reached the other end of the Lion's Gate Bridge, and the Slav at the wheel stomped the gas pedal and got through the toll gate free. Then they proceeded west, along Marine Drive. G was awake enough now to be frightened, he told himself. He looked past the swart faces on either side of him to the ambient bourgeois life on either side of the verdant road. He did not know anyone in this part of the world, so his minimal activity was done without hope, without irony, without breakfast, but with an annoying stomach flavour in the back of his throat.

On a cedar shingle roof, among stray pine cones and what looked like a dozen issues of the old yellowed and baton-shaped *Vancouver Province*, he espied a man and a woman performing illustration 47.a of *The Illustrated Kama Sutra*. She was holding his ankle high. He was wearing a mortar-board on his head.

"It's enough to make you puke," said the gunsel in the death seat.

"Speaking of puking..."

"Shaddup," suggested the gunsel in the left rear seat.

"*Writing love letters in the sand,*" added Pat Boone.

"I wonder whether he ever thought of writing love letters on the side of the brewery," mused G.

All the gunsels turned their silent meaningful faces to him. As these included the driver of a large foreign car with the steering wheel on the wrong side, on a road that turned every time it had just turned, G decided to shaddup.

Why aren't these gunsels wearing fedoras, he wondered. A clue to remember when he spoke to the authorities without irony later on. If he ever got to talk to the authorities.

At this moment A was probably talking to the authorities on the telephone, telling them that he had disappeared in his pyjamas, again.

No such luck. Because with the irony shared between author and reader we are privy to the information that at this moment A was indeed on the telephone, her other hand idly looking for a less-full ashtray, but she was chatting with Rhonda Toogood, a sensible friend recently arrived from Toronto, telling her about something that had happened in the woods near a clearing on a Gulf island just after the War. If G had known about this he would have been relieved that at least a call to Rhonda was not long distance.

G watched the granite cliffs going by, the far shiny ocean on the other side. They had not turned down the hill to Horseshoe Bay. They were headed to the far north! Think think think think, he urged himself. Puke puke puke puke, his essential self replied. Think, he insisted, all this in his very loud head. Get all the details right for later. How come these guys were not wearing hats? What did they pitch playing cards into during their long periods of enforced idleness? Who killed Cock Robin? Shut the fuck up! You always throw that question in at inappropriate moments. What is the meaning of life? Shaddup.

The last time he had been in the back seat of a car was on the way to Seattle, and he had felt somewhat nauseated, that is for certain, but at least although he had not been sitting next to a window in the profmobile, he had reached across the promising heat of the personage to his right to crank it open a slit and allow the clam-scented air to bathe his face. And he had been sitting nigh not a gunsel but a damsel, sweetish Dorcas Davenport, a damson if there ever was one in the Green Room at the University on the Hill. Now this very Davenport was M's obsession. "What orbs, what fixtures, what recipience, what cosigns!" M had often exclaimed, his hand in his chin whiskers. "I would give my collection of Red Ryder comics and all my Mario Lanza '45s for a half hour of her chunnility," he appended.

"Really, chunnility, this is a word?" sneered Tommy P, a barbecued chicken leg in his gloved hand.

"She is chunnilitous!" averred M. His hand strayed from his beard and tentatively approached the dome of his head, then retreated chinward.

This all happened last Autumn, on a bench at a bus stop on Denman and Burrard. Crisp maple leaves gathered around the feet of these worthies. Tommy P's famous white teeth flashed among the flesh.

Anyway, in the flashback before that flashback, G was sitting beside Dorcas in the back of the green Oldsmobile. He did not know his lines, or rather M's lines in *Our Town Cops Pleas*, but on previous occasions he had somehow, miraculously, known the lines at the very last second, onstage, under lights, makeup drying on his face. He would give himself to the gods yet again. Besides, he was teleporting the spirit of M. He would open his mouth and M's stentorous voice would emerge, ending as M always did each thespian phrase, with a short whine meant to sound like something from Stratford on Avon. Besides, G had more immediate matters at hand.

His left hand, to be exact, though in the best of circumstances he liked to employ the dexter. Dorcas offered not a complaint. In fact at one point she placed her right leg, which had been atop the left, beside it, and fortuitously, beside G's left. These legs were attired, as was the custom of campus starlets of the time, in black stockings that did not shine and could not stretch. Said stockings were obfuscated at one end in desert boots such as Pat Boone fans were wont to wear save when they could get hold of white bucks, and at the other end by a mid-length tweed or plaid skirt, often featuring pleats. "Campus," this outfit bespoke. "The Arts." Yes, and "*Kurosawa.*"

Sometimes these black stockings had wrinkles at and around the knees. Sometimes, if one were lucky, round holes, through which mucilage-hued skin made itself known.

His gorge rose from time to time. Especially while plummy Arthur recited such renowned poems as *There was an old Codger from Wales*, and *There was a Young Darling from Dallas*. Sometimes when the maniaquess at the wheel wrenched the sedan back onto a southbound lane of Highway 99, Arthur Maguay's corduroy-clad leg would crush his own, alas. But nature and science have a way of evening things out. His gorge, he decided, if he were given time, would be expended to his starboard side, perhaps just as a final quintuplet was being launched.

These black stockings, then. Sometimes, sad to say, they were a kind of trouser outfit, called 'tights' even if they were not. They had been conjured by a disappointed lifelong scholar of the Belarus Kabbahla. They were always too snug or overly loose at the waist. They allowed no air to pass outward or inward. They looked sad on clotheslines. Their only felicitous use was as bonds with which to secure wrists to bedposts. They were flags flown by sere nihilists. They had to be purchased from ashamed stores in the less-sunny streets of downtown Vancouver. They were worn by ballet dancers more interested in pain than Venus. Tommy P had a pair dragging from the back bumper of his roadster for a winter.

Fortunately, fatefully, Dorcas was not wearing such an outfit. Her blackness stopped halfway up her loafy thighs, where oldfashioned garters such as your grandmother might have worn in West Summerland secured the stockings against unrolling and sagging. The injury done to her presumably whitish skin was imaginable but not, finally, of the first importance to G. G was a whiz now, taking advantage of every lurch of the sedan, his gorge suggesting itself while his sweating fingers insinuated, and that was the story. Later in Seattle Dorcas did not even look at him when she passed the salt.

But now in the purring Daimler that was approaching the obvious economic structure of Britannia Beach, oblivious as its driver to the political nuance of that community's title, G's woebeworn pyjamas had given way to his aroused yard, and two gunsels recoiled as best they could against the upholstered walls of the touring car. G's memory-filled roscoe stood as a young man's roscoe might stand, swaying slightly at its proud one-eighth of a meter.

"Get rid of that thing or we will get rid of it for you," remonstrated the more protected gunsel in the death seat, where just a few moments before G had been imagining poet and playwright Prester John.

"Stick 'em up!" intoned G.

He had not wanted to say any such thing. There was something that came over him at such moments, a weakness for jests on the precipice, a stupidity unknown among his confrères.

The Daimler crunched gravel, and came to rest in a small quarry beside Highway 101. Three of the four gunsels in black took the pyjama boy outside the vehicle and hit him several times with stones they especially fancied. "Are you sorry? Say you're sorry," one of them requested.

But G was still, despite the pain and the sudden loss of his eyeglasses, in the grip of his unrecommended impulse. "Each petrific blow is like a sudden flash of light," he managed to say. They hit him twelve more times, taking turns. Then they hurled his limp body into the car, this time permitting him only the floor with the bump in the middle of it. He did not feel like upchucking. Nothing was about to rise. Until Paul Anka sang something about his fetching high school teacher. The hour had passed.

G was lying on the floor, without spectacles, so he did not

see the man hitchhiking southward on the highway. The driver was sitting on the right hand side of the car instead of the left, so he did not really notice this semi-spectral figure. The two gunsels in the back seat were stomping G with their Bulgarian-looking shoes. The gunsel in the death seat may have noted the hitchhiker but he made no mention of him.

We are interested in this figure because he was D, clad in wrinkled gabardine slacks that were probably not his, and a sweatshirt upon which one might in decent light make out the words SQUAMISH SON ET LUMIERE. Now we know that D had always detested the North American habit of wearing clothing with words on it, no matter the language. Even when he purchased shirts with the label from Davenport's Discount Clothier hidden inside the collar, he scissored the offending words away. So what are we to make of this morbid figure beside the road in broad daylight, oversized huaraches flapping on his narrow feet?

Back in Kitsilano A was conversing with Rhonda Toogood. She was telling Rhonda about the adventure she had had with a fraternity boy who had made the mistake of feeding her creamed onions.

M at that very moment was consuming creamed onions, along with baked ham and green beans and mashed potatoes at the groaning board of a large family in Kerrisdale. Each member of the family was wondering which other member of the family had invited this handsome young man with the luxuriant beard and the practiced way with a fork and knife. Some of them were wondering what might have happened to his hair.

Arthur Maguay was in bed with Dorcas Davenport in West Point Grey. Well, not a bed, precisely. Rather a pair of air mattresses on Maguay's floor. The air mattresses slipped and skidded, turned over and flipped endways, as they might have been intended to do at the beach. "Here's a good one," said Arthur. "A lazy old Scot in Beirut… " Dorcas was already starting to giggle.

Angus Carey was impressing the living shit out of a

sophomore. "Listen," he said, standing with thumbs under imaginary vest. "If there was a man sitting in the forest trying to make the sound of one hand clapping, and the tree he was sitting under fell on him, and there was no one else in the forest within ear-shot, would there be, after this failed Bhuddist was no more among the living, any sound?" The sophomore had not heard anything after the word "clapping," and was still wondering about that. "Forget the tree," said Angus. "Suppose he managed to make the sound of one hand clapping in that forest. Would there be any sound? The sophomore did not know. "Suppose," said Angus, "that you are driving a big black car through the darkness at the speed of light, and you turned on the knob that is suppose to ignite the headlights. Would the headlights light up the way ahead?"

"Well, I suppose so," said the sophomore, "if they were working."

Angus Carey smiled his I-have-you-in-my-trap smile. He continued the questions. "If there was suddenly a giantific flash of light over the North Shore mountains, and no one happened to be looking in that direction at the time, would there be any flash of light, in fact?"

CHAPTER ELEVEN

Broadbent in a Daimler... An Offer too Good to Refuse... M Chows Down... G Continues to Vanish... A Tidies House ... A Shaggy Dog Gets Told

"...hieroglyphs?"

D's question hung on the breeze. The breeze caressed the exterior of the Daimler with a fine, warm stroke... its susurration, as so much else, was lost on the ears of the assembled company. Nor did they hear the song-thrush warbling amid the conifers. The wash of the waves upon the beach at Lions Bay was likewise out of their auditory field. But not their entire perceptual field. The dark blue, slight rollers formed a pretty sight indeed on the left side of their route as they rolled smoothly along in the direction of Squamish. D shuddered. Squamish! What rough beast might *that* be? He had never set foot in Squamish. But earlier in life, he had set foot in Bralorne, and Cache Creek, and North Battleford, and old Battleford, the old town across the narrow bridge, on the south bank of the North Saskatchewan River, and White Bear, Sask., on the north bank of the South Saskatchewan River, where in the White Bear Hotel one squatted to take a dump and heard the turds plummet a full three stories from the second floor into the basement... What a day *that* had been! Hornet had stolen an apple pie from a farmhouse that stood too close to the highway for the safety of its inhabitants. He had shoved it up under his shirt and of course it had leaked sticky stuff all over the front of his pants. What mirthful remarks *that* had occasioned among his companions, drunk as they were and fit to be horsewhipped, young scalawags and rascals all, scum of the earth and proud of it... No, D didn't want to go back to the boonies. Life for him had begun in a city, and a big one at that; and if he had declared London off limits for his own convoluted "reasons" (dark and deep, dark and deep, run the thick waters where Psyche must weep), then Vancouver would have to do. Personally speaking, as he had confided in Liam Chutney only the other night, he wouldn't mind never setting foot outside of Vancouver again. Oh, he might like to see San Francisco… And Seattle had been okay, come to think of it, one of those places one's artistic gifts had privileged one to visit, like… like… well, like Bralorne, as D had *not* gone on to say at that time, preferring to leave his thought uncompleted, leastwise out loud. It hadn't mattered. Liam had been too engaged with his posture to pay more than an eighth of his genius-class attention to D's inebriate ramblings.

"…Seattle. San Francisco…" It was pleasant, D found, to have his own private thoughts echoed in his ears in this way. Probably a phenomenon caused by the stress he must be under, kidnapped by crooks and I don't know what-all. He decided to try some more. He thought about the boonies, the years he had lavished upon them, gratifying his own need to go as far as the system of transportation reaches, staggering through the blizzard to Edna's shack with a mickey of Seagrams under his dumb Brit dufflecoat flapping open because his fingers were too cold to stick the pieces of wood into the rope loops that fastened it… He recalled strolling through Bralorne with Jimmy Parks, primo comedian of the UBC Players' Club, and how Jimmy had indicated a rope looped like a noose on the side of a barn, and had fingered at his own neck nervously as he expressed a fervent hope that the locals would find this evening's performance of "Charley's Aunt" entertaining…

D began unconsciously to finger his own collar. "Seattle… San Francisco." Funny, *that* should have been "Battleford… Bralorne." But no, there it was again, "Seattle… San Francisco." Was someone in the car actually saying those names? They *weren't* emerging full-blown from his own psychic depths? Someone in the car *was* saying those names. D was disappointed. But manfully he struggled to recoup the context.

He was prevented from remembering what else might have been said to him by his captors because one of them now demanded of him, "Take it or leave it, jerk. You deef or sumthin?"

"I beg your pardon," D said to his interrogator, the beefy man with a wart on his cheek. "Were you replying to my question concerning hieroglyphs?"

D regarded the wart more closely. It was a dilly! It had five distinct lumps, and was brick-red: from a flea's point of view, crouched there amid the stubble, it must have looked like one of those rock formations you see in westerns. The kind of bastion with a mesa up top that has been, god knows how, brought thence, wild stallions ranging its gullies, and bad hombres stalking them. And the heroine in the picture somehow, dimpling demurely in her dirndl... Beef-o was by now unmistakably snarling in his ear (er, ears): "You're a goddam idjit if you don't take it!"

"Take what?" D was ingenuous.

"Fuck you," said Beef-o, who thought D was being disingenuous. (This was always happening to D. People thought him aloof and ironic and condescending while he was actually susceptible, gullible and lost. Well, as Blake said, or leastways wrote, "Go love without the help of anything on earth.")
"It's no use trying to up the ante. That's our final offer and that's flat."

"Right," inserted another. "That's flat our final offer."

"Yeah," put in a third. "Work for the CIA in Seattle or San Francisco and retire a millionaire in thirty years."

"Or," resumed Beef-o, "disappear somewheres out there." He indicated with a vague flourish a million square miles of British Columbian wilderness. "Out there in Brutish Columbia."

The Hobbesean echo startled D. His interrogators had hidden depths?

"Haw haw haw," put in the driver ("They called him Al"). "Nasty, brutish, and endless."

"Really, 'Al'" sneered another, putting quotes around that

name with his voice. "Thanks loads for regaling us with the sum total of your recollections from Philosophy 100. Steve – uh, 'Al', spent a semester at Berkeley," he confided to D. "Next he'll tell us about how trapped he felt in the Berkeley human loch. It's his favorite pun."

"It's his *only* pun," said Beef-o.

"It may be my only intellectual pun," said Steve-Al. "But I know other *puns*." He turned to look at D, causing the Daimler to cross the midline of the coast highway and sending a doctor in his Volvo careening into Howe Sound. Or so D perceived. "Knight, back when chivalry was in flower, goes forth on quest. Big storm comes on. Here's a castle. 'Let me in for the night.' Done. But the storm doesn't lift, and the knight gets antsy. He's had dinner, chicken giblets and boar's brains, he's – "

"He's had the baron's daughter – " (thus Beef-o)

" – He's had the baron's daughter, okay, so now he goes to the baron and he says, 'Baron, I must resume my quest for the Holy Grill.'"

"Grail."

"Gray-all, Shmay-all, so he says to his host, 'Hey, I gotta get on with it, my homeland is laid waste by a plague and a murrain lieth upon my cattle, so storm or no storm, thanks for the meal, the dry suit of armor, now I gotta get going. So just give me a fresh horse like nobles have to for one another and I'll be on my way.' And his host tells him, 'Horse? I haven't any horses.'

"'Dont have any horses? What the fuck kind of noble host are you?' says the knight."

"Wait a minute, wait a minute, which knight? Is this the first knight or the second knight?" Beef-o's impatience was palpable.

"It must be the foist knight, because I'm feelin' noivus," Al-Steve put in.

"I know what you mean," D intruded pleasantly, "I've been a Person of the Theatre myself – Ooff!"

Beef-o removed his elbow. "Pray continue," he said to his

colleague sarcastically.

"Your colleague's name is Sarcastically?" D queried in mock surprise. "Ooff."

"Hey, I like the way dis guy never quits," said someone. "He's our kinda material."

"Yeah, well, I'm tellin' a joke," said the one who was. "So the second knight, the baron, says to the first knight, the knight who's just said 'What the fuck kind of noble host are you' – "

" – For Krrzzssake, look out where you're going!" Beef-o quoted Robert Creeley without knowing it, possibly, thought D. He quoted from *I Know A Man* [*For Love*, Scribners, 1962, but available earlier in which one of the poet's six or seven previous slim volumes D couldn't just at this moment recall: possibly in *A Form of Women*? If you know, please write us]. [I would tell you, but I'm proof-reading this in Denmark. G]. He quoted it (not Robert Creeley, but Beef-o) at Al-Steve, their driver, who had been headed more-or-less straight at a Greyhound, which swung wide as it rounded one of the many curves on the Squamish Highway. Al-Steve yanked on the wheel and the Daimler, white walls squealing, scraped a fiftieth of a metre of paint off the mighty silver bullet.

"Hey, kid," someone said to D, "You'll be able to get back to town easy. Just ride the Dawg."

"That was likely the last one today. If he don't give us the answer we want, he'll have the spend the night there – in Squamish."

D's mind reacted feverishly. What should he do? *What* should he do?? He knew the punchline of the joke – should he say so or keep quiet???

Also, he needed to go to the bathroom. Should he mention this?

Also, it had been a while since the topic "Hieroglyphs" had been broached. Would it be rude to re-introduce it?

Also, what should he do about their offer? It was the kind one could hardly refuse. It was thirty years in the States, or a night in Squamish… A shot rang in and D realized he had left it too late. Procrastination had always been his strong point, only to be countered by blind impulse; but now it was too late for blind impulse. He had been shot.

Once M had watched the Daimler with D in it turn a corner and vanish from his sight, he realized he needed to do some fast thinking. He sat down on a wooden bench, produced his yard of apfelstrudel, and absent-mindedly tried to light it up. Who had kidnapped D? Where were they taking him? And was there anything on TV that night that he might want to see badly enough to go visit his parents?

Then he remembered Serena Rapt.

Serena was a prodigy who was flunking tenth grade. So the Rapts had looked around for a tutor. Cosmic justice had brought M within their purview. M was bidden to their mansion in Shaughnessy for a bout of mutual inspection. SR turned out to be model-tall, with hot blue eyes and white lipstick.

"It must take forever, sliding one's hand slowly up her leg, even to reach her *knee*," M said to D.

D knew deferral was important to M, who had eight times attempted Russian 100.

"Felicitations," he replied.

Now M recalled he was invited to dine chez Rapt this very day. Their *cuisine* was rumored to be *haut*. Putting aside all thoughts of D, he hurried home to shower and trim his beard. He would wear the stovepipe pants purchased at Frederick and Nelson's together with a black turtleneck. Serena had let her fingers linger in his when they had shaken hands. A scent of fresh apples had wafted from her neck. And her hair – her hair had smelled of grilled sea bass *au gratin*. M was going to enjoy brushing up her Latin.

A turned over in the narrow cot and went on waiting for G to come back. It often took him up to five minutes to find the newspaper in the heavily wooded yard (Beautiful British

Columbia, fertile as all get-out and tended by Brits, Dutch, Germans), especially on a Sunday after a heavily woolly Saturday night. But today, he was being even longer than usual. And with G, usual was already impressively long. Smiling to herself like a model who had one hand on a unicorn, A stretched languorously, not easily spelled before breakfast. This was A the young beauty, Northern European Ice-Goddess, eyes green as the ten thousand and one lakes of Finland, graceful in gait as a white swan that swims upon one; meanwhile A the one who watches, who is ageless and misses not a figure etched or engraved in an eternal and continuous ground which is a field of force, this A with a slight smile of pity observed this self who knew too little and envied her also. Also only slightly: for narrative is a passion that allows little scope for other feelings. Should she leap out of bed and go look see if G had dropped dead of the fear of death? Or should she go back to sleep?

She took the leap. But she didn't go outside. She began to tidy the room. If only you could tidy up people the way you could tidy up a room! But people were too narrow or too big. And some wore giant warts shaped like mesas with stampeding mustangs... hmm, where had *that* figure come from? Rooms stayed discrete, this side earthquake, hurricane or war, whereas people overlapped, identity shadowing identity, thoughts streaming through the universe looking for a warm receiver, a plugged-in bunch of tubes and valves and copper wire... For herself, she liked to keep her gear in order. But she could know beyond that habit, however laudable. This Great White Flash which G and his friends had witnessed... this flash without sound or wave... told a truth of some kind, whatever its empirical existence. Had she paid sufficient attention when G had told her of it? Was this G's only pair of shorts? Suddenly tender towards the big lug, she moved towards the door, and the sunlit garden beyond. She wanted to find her man, and hold him close... She gazed up and down the blank street. Premonitions of trouble, grave trouble, stirred in her soul.

It was not until he was almost upon her that she noticed the short slight man with a countenance of Oriental cast. He smiled and bowed and handed her a slip of paper about the size and shape of a fortune cookie fortune.

A read it aloud. "Remember, the Chinese sign for trouble is the same as the sign for opportunity." The last word was misspelled.

Right. Since G was out of sight, and there was nothing to be done about it, she would not become depressed or anxious; she would practice Negative Capability. She would use this opportunity to phone her old friend Rhonda Toogood. She hadn't yet told Rhonda about George Oliver Delsing (GOD to his friends). G-Absent would become G-Present as she discussed him with her old helpmeet Rhonda. She returned to the basement suite and reached for the phone.

Arthur Maguey and Dorcas Davenport: ah, let us envy them their lot.

Once they had stopped writhing on his cot, Art said with a grin, as he wiped off his chin, "Let's do it again!"

"I've been shot!"

This cry was cried in five different accents, timbres, pitches.

Beef-o clutched at his gut. Another thug grabbed at his own shoulder. A third clapped a hand to his head, as if to snuff a pesky skeeter. Al-Steve had to settle for a wrist, since he was using one hand to wrestle the car out of the skid brought about by the blowout.

D was thoroughly convinced that the bullet had entered his ribcage. He could sense its presence, just above his liver. Then he remembered the gallon of Regal Sherry he had downed at the Roundtowner last night.

They piled out once the driver had steered the vehicle into a pullout zone, and watched him jack it up.

"'I sit by the side of the road, watching the driver change

the wheel,'" D said. "'There is nowhere I need to be. Why do I watch him with such impatience?'"

"He knows Brecht," chortled Beef-o. "Well enough to misquote him. Say, kid," he went on, "You could be a double agent. Talk Brecht to the commie rats and sell the goods back to us. Whaddya say? We'll pay your tuition and board and room… Berkeley: all those chicks! All that dope! And the Summer of Love is coming!!"

"Summer of Love?" D said. "What might that be?"

"Just a little something we're cookin' up by way of a distraction. It's gonna involve an awful lot of humping."

D thought hard, if not long. Sometimes a chep had to do the decent thing.

"OK," said D, "Where do I sign?"

" – But I have a big dog,' Al-Steve was saying, sitting on the ground and apparently talking to a spare tire. "'Great! Lend me a big dog then!' 'Oh, I'm sorry, I couldn't, I couldn't send a knight out on a dog like this,' said the Baron, indicating a stupid looking mutt that had wandered into the banquetting hall."

"So seems to me the life of a man," Beef-o opined into the dull silence (save for Nature's sweeter sounds) that now ensued: "He trots in at one door covered in muck, dries off as he shuffles past the fire, sneaks a bone fallen from the great table, then vanishes into the night out the far door, pursued by execrations."

He turned to D. "Therefore it seems to me to be right and fitting that we should believe in something – something that will deliver three square a day and a roof overhead and kindling in the hearth. But you don't actually sign anything. We don't need you to. And as for us, well, you'll just have to trust us, won't you? "

CHAPTER TWELVE

Visible as a few black grains in grey air, it came, at first, along the North Shore, a floating poisonous wheeze over the sulphur piles on the North Shore docks, and dawdling gently over creosoted fragments, soiled gull feathers, and lost cedar floats moved on up the slope of the city to spread depression and pleurisy.

It stopped lightly and quickly at the home of Mrs. Sarah Teasdale on Pioneer Street. It sneered at her snug home and frowned at her comforts. It gave her a hard look, a bad look, for her nephew, the last living relation of this decent old woman, widowed sixteen years. On lower Lonsdale on December 15th, Nephew Tommy, in a paroxysm of pre-Christmas tension but with no real motive but beastly boyness, had hit a little girl, a schoolmate, the eleven-year old sister of Lorraine Tartan, in the face with an ice-hard snowball. That this was the fault of Mrs. Teasdale, Sarah Teasdale felt suddenly and utterly certain when our spirit moved, in stealth and force, upon her.

Now the cold dark thing moved on westward. It harrowed souls bent to honest if selfish work in the shops of Park Royal and in the kitchen of the *Tricolor* restaurant, where Victor Selva planned for his wife's brother an unpleasant accident with a motorized meat slicer. It spiralled out over the Gulf of Georgia.

It moved gradually over the southern neighbourhoods of the city, alighting in moneyed Shaughnessy, where it found M lying on Serena Rapt, coiting vigourously. It brought him, as he laboured, a narrow, sharp and shadowed sense of unease and vacancy, flatness, materiality and dread. It suggested to him that he might as well turn himself in at the Campbell soup plant on the south edge of the city near New Westminster. "Chop me, brothers," he should say to them.

"Cut my gristle and bone for your giant soups! Render my bull's neck, my faun's ankles for your broths and gravies." But then, thought M, why the despair? I am after all a materialist. What I am doing here right this minute is simple enough, nothing but the old bump and squish. I don't need to be bothered by these dark hints, premonitions, emanations, night sweats. I think that I won't be bothered by them. Beneath him, pillowy, Serena billowed.

The cold northern spirit, nothing daunted by this juvenile bravado, hunted on its way. It found M again and threw at him its prowling malfeasant stinging aroma, its rank evacuating influence as this transportable polymorph perversely sat on a grey marine-painted bench in Vancouver's Coal Harbour. He'd been turned down flat in his bid for a tryout for the UBC rowing team (Junior Eights) despite or because of some vehement lobbying by Serena Rapt's big brother. Perhaps Roger Rapt II only wanted to drown the couthless M.

Now M watched a woman on the next bench in a dumpy bitter-grey tweed overcoat clutch a half-full Safeway bag and sit and stare without any hope at the frilly chop of water. M, softened by his own disappointments and by the dark northern spirit, could feel all that oppressed her, all the dismay that seeped into her in the office above the Krak-A-Joke shop on Granville St., the atrocities hurled into her by her man in the house on Hudson St., the pain from the daughter and the niece. M was ready to wrap great rubber pig-shaped bags of sand marked All Your Trials Dear around his ankles, and topple into the dark grey water for her.

But he was needed, is needed elsewhere. He must join his friends in the big dark car in which they have been abducted. He must, in truth, be the one abducted. He must take his turn. So we again transport him, astrally if you like.

The next thing M knew it was none other than himself in the back of the kidnap car, a Mercedes as it turned out. The wheel, or more correctly tyre, had been changed, and the menace-laden thing continued along the Squamish highway, though now the car headed toward Vancouver, for the addle-pated Al had put its nose the wrong way emerging from the pullout, and now steered back in the direction whence they'd come, not apparently noticing or caring. The interrogation and menace of Phase D of the ride continued though, and M was faced with hard, hard questions.

"What did you do to McMannic's girlfriend?"

"Why won't your father speak to you?"

"What's that peculiar smell?" (This from Roethke, of all people.)

"Where did you put the money?"

"How many a you seen that flash?"

"What made you think you could get away with that?"

"How many times you done that?"

"Done what?"

"What he done."

Every answer M made, and he tried, with dutiful and would-be engaging little smiles, to make several answers, was rebuffed. "Hawmphh!" said his interlocutors. "Cheep" (trying to be a good "canary") and "murmur" (trying, since nothing he said seemed to be right, not to be offensively definite) said M. For a time M supposed he had them going in his direction as he talked about patterns of violence in Kyd's *Spanish Tragedy* compared with those to be found in Shakespearean revenge tragedy, specifically of course *Hamlet*, though not entirely excluding Cyril Tourneur or Thomas Middleton, and paying full tribute to John Webster's two dark masterworks, *The Duchess of Malfi*, and, preeminent for M, *The White Devil*.

"Actually you folks remind me a good deal of Francisco and Antonio, two of the heavies whom Bosola brings in to do some cutting and strangling in *The Duchess*. I expect you know your way around that sort of work, eh? Could see your way clear to take on a bit of it?"

Now there was swearing, and five hands reached for the chattering, demented student. M sucked in his boyish rosy cheeks and sucked his spine as far as he could into the nasty imitation leather (even then, even Mercedes) seatcovers. The voices and faces wavered and wowed and became a quick babble of anger and jerking red masks. The car too wavered and wowed. M found hands hustling him forward on the seat and sliding him through the suddenly open door and through the sudden wind and into the gravel, skinning on his shoulder, chest, face. He felt his nose tear open and knew that he was in some way free now, but what impossible cost? And most dark of all, he knew that allies, friends, were nothing, nothing, and that the strong forces in the world had no regard for him. Wanted him out of the way. Out of the way of what?

He lay for quite a long time in the gravel, and he waited for something to come and redirect him, down a little deeper perhaps, into a shallow grave. Or off on a stretcher or a bier or a plank. Flights of saranwrapped angels sing thee. Off to the reformatory, the infirmary, the crematorium. Maybe something would raise him right up.

In an hour, perhaps two, something did raise him to his feet and start him walking slowly and uncertainly along the shoulder of the road. In what direction he was going was not clear for a time, was not a matter of interest to him as he bobbed along, dreaming elsewhere, elsewhere, and looking zebra-striped with raspberry marmalade over the right side of his neck and face and head.

Lorraine Tartan walked down the lane behind West 37th Avenue, a few blocks from Angus Cary's house. Thither was she bound. No young person was ever really welcome in the Cary home, for they were seen there as agents of corruption and springtime, influences which the Carys wished to deny to their son, and to the younger brothers, Sean and Patrick. Besides boasting the spiritually upward-mobile Carys, the district was the home of the semi-fictional Alma Dukes. This vicious and legendary neighbourhood gang was composed of such neighbourhood hoods as Patrick Cary, and it excelled in beating up primary-school kids, girls preferably, from St. Mary's School, and stealing the candy they purchased at Earl's corner store. Patrick Cary had done a couple of worse things than that, too, but he had never told anyone except his older brother Angus about these things. Once, suddenly and considerably drunk on two bottles of Lucky Lager beer in the Henderson's garage, he had blurted some threatening information to Lorraine, hoping to impress this splendid older woman. She sneered and turned away from Patrick. After all, what good was a fifteen-year-old would-be hoodlum to an attractive eighteen-year-old widow with an I.Q. of 168 on the Richter scale? Brazen, brainy, budding, bee-hived philosopher that she was, she had sights half set on Angus, who had wit as well as delinquency to offer. Angus could be winkled from the Cary house by an apparition at a basement window, and Lorraine knew this. Thither she walked. A car radio nearby gave forth The Kingston Trio singing "South Coast" and the lyrics offended Lorraine. "My heart died that night with my adoring slave," she thought.

Ahead of her in the lane a clapboard garage was spilling grey things, a human cargo, incongruously dressed up. In movies Lorraine had seen guys who looked something like this – sallow shirts, ties, suity suits, the big overcoats, hats, oh, the hats! But in the movies they looked spiffy, impressive.

They stopped in front of her, stopping her. "Are you Lorraine T?" said the nearest one.

"Yes."

"Have you seen M, G, or D around here today?"

She was confounded. What did he mean? "What do you mean?"

"You seen any of these guys around this neighbourhood today?"

He looked nasty, and so did his companions. They looked full of anger and official or very unofficial aids to angry action. The grey and navy topcoats draped down over who knows what. But they carried themselves in a way that said that they were either not out to or not able to pull just any old bystanders or bystalkers into their cars or their cells or their lineups or offices or whatever they had behind them somewhere in the city. She felt bold.

"Why would they be around here?"

"They'd be around here," the sneer readily responded, "because they're not going to be around the University, that's just for students, as I think you know. They're not going to be downtown because they haven't got any business and they haven't got any jobs and they haven't got any suits. So they can't go downtown. And they're not going to be anywhere in this city that there's work to do, because they haven't got any work to do and they wouldn't know how to do it if they did have it. They can't do it, they can't learn it, they can't take it." Here the eyes of the sneer grew large, and he advanced his face at Lorraine. "Too friggin' soft! And that's about the end of it on those guys. Isn't it, Miss Tartan?"

"I haven't seen them."

She walked past the suited man, past the group of them, and the wind, a hinting bit of the dark and cold thing that had earlier come into the city, grated its way down the lane. It didn't trouble Lorraine, who sensed it as only a very small disturbance in the ether. She was not bothered by it; she had her brains to keep her warm.

And other things. Yesterday, standing dark-eyed and flat-eyed in front of Brock Hall, Tommy P had offered to sell her the huge raccoon coat he was wearing. The great pelted thing was draggling on the ground behind Tommy P's dirty heels, and who knows where he had found or stolen the thing. "My special offer this month! My College Special. Next month maybe I'll have the Duesenberg Phaeton for ya! The pennants, Smith and Swarthmore and Fordham! Where Marshall McLuhan's on the faculty, Lorraine! I can give you all this stuff and make you a coed to wow the other coeds, kid! Teach you the varsity drag! Not to mention the Frug! I can make you *authentic*, Lorraine! Of course you might have to dismantle that beehive, get a short bob, a becoming Betty Coed cut."

If I wasn't an atheist he'd be Satan, thought Lorraine.

"Get behind me," she said.

CHAPTER THIRTEEN

The problem is that A is sitting here trying to be everything at once: person and storyteller and character and reader. She doesn't like the character they've drawn for her and doesn't seem to know how to invent one. That's anybody's problem of course, not particular to her. She isn't the Snow Queen, the Compulsive Lecturer, or Goldilocks, or the Killer of Little Joy Boys, but how can she wade her way through this morass of male bonhomie to anything that seems remotely authentic? Authenticity isn't even something that matters to them. It matters to her. That's the problem. What's upsetting is that she's beginning not to like them much – all that bafflegab about their little oolicans, measured in fractions of yards, comparisoning off each other's personae. All that triumphetting, disappearing into their own stories – the ones they make up and the ones that have been made up for them.

"IAMB!" says Angela-Misplaced-Belonging to David-At-Sebastopol and George-Oliver-Delsing and Mike-Omigod-Greatheart. AMB, DAS, GOB, MOG? Only Connect! Flotsam and Jetsam of Medieval morality play rites, Samuel Beckett or Kafka, the difference being in the amount of flailing about we do. Dregs and debris, brief lives, evidence of our beginnings or watt? Sheep in a blanket-toss and blank misgivings. What AMB is suffering now.

She supposes DAS is right about narrative. He is also right about AMB talking GOD into presence – or trying to. She is never successful. He is wrong about her not becoming anxious and depressed though. GOD was beginning to disappear into his own stories a lot. He was somebody else for everybody. What there was of him for her was only her own fiction. His words went into his writing or into others. She never knew when he would next write himself out of her life and into someone else's bed. She knew when he was disappearing. He was an endless supply of black holes into which he could disappear and become someone else's story. He claimed to have no control over it, though AMB didn't believe that was true of any one of them. So she talked to other people on the telephone, in coffee shops, at kitchen tables, later in various therapists' offices when she felt she herself was disappearing into her nightmares. They got transported in their stories. She just got misplaced. Or displaced. They seemed able to replace themselves with their writing. AMB could never do that, though she was transported by talking.

More and more, they seem like alien creatures to her. She doesn't think they inhabit the same world at all. Sometimes they pretend to when they want to seduce you, but it is all an invention. *Isolato* GOD used to call himself. He took pride in that, to AMB's surprise.

When he didn't come back after going out to get the newspaper, A became depressed and anxious. She called all their friends and acquaintances, but everyone claimed not to have seen him. A's powers of invention were sorely tried as she conversed with Rhonda Toogood. Sometimes she and Rhonda would sit around drinking iced tea and lemonade laced with white rum all afternoon when G was gone. Rhonda was a good friend. She sat and listened while A went through the ritual invention of G. First of all, she had to piece together the bits and scraps he'd given her all those nights they were necking in the car, and out of the few encounters she'd had with his family, out of what his friends and enemies said about him, out of their gestures – reachings and leanings across pub tables – while he leaned back in his chair, laughing, inventing himself – a distance, slippery as an oolican, impossible to catch. There were other fish.

But what if he had been caught, she thought. What if he was in trouble? She tried to console herself by thinking about the time he'd gone out to pick up a cheque and had come back in the evening with purple-stainéd mouth, stained with Al Purdy's home-made blackberry wine. They'd been drinking it all day. G and A were very poor at the time. He was reading scripts for the CBC, and A was waitressing at the Vancouver Yacht Club for a dollar an hour and no tips. You left me all day with no food, she said. No cigarettes, she said. You dont care about me, she said. You didn't even think about me. You didn't even care enough to come home and give me some money, she said. He threw his money at her. Fuck off, she said. He did.

That next day, he still wasn't home and A was going a little crazy, calling all the people she thought were their friends. Nobody had seen him. Carol told her he'd hitchhiked to San Francisco. The woman poet from New York chastized her for her lack of cool. Oh God, A thought, all the ways men have conned women into thinking there's something wrong with them: You're not cool, hip, existentialist enough. He'd once said, I want a woman who will suffer indignities. He thought it was self-mockery when it was the simple truth. Tenny finally told her he was at Carol and Ebbe's place after all, stoned on peyote. Tenny drove her down there in curlers and housecoat and she'd fallen on G's chest weeping with relief while he, up close, smiled and smiled and said over and over again, Don't hassle, baby. Don't hassle.

Even at the time, the lingo of hippydom had seemed inadequate to A. Little shocks sounded inside, warnings of what was here and to come Death knell. And Gaston Helios, across the room, chanting: The horse with horns, the horny horse. Everything dissolved. There was no more anchor in her world. He came back home. They were careless people. Though they pretended to care. Those hippies headed for the sixties. Victims, they pretended to be. Some of them went mad and shot themselves. Or were beaten up and jumped off bridges. Or became acid-heads. Or nearly died on macrobiotic diets. Dropping wives and children along the way, they said, these boys, Don't hassle, don't hassle. The naive and sentimental and irresponsible lovers of the sixties that drove their women mad on acid or rotted their innards out with unattended venereal disease, or got busted, leaving babies, wives and girlfriends to manage as well as they could on welfare or the kindness of strangers. These flower children stood on the steps of the White House and bravely stuffed roses into the barrels of guns with bayonets fixed to them, or held love-ins, smoking dope in the parks and eating brown rice and lentils out of disgustingly dirty dishes. Much of it was fashion, idealized. A despised their sentimentality. That cheap romance. Beautiful. Don't hassle. Ballin' my old man. My old lady. All ya need is love. Sloppy language. Sloppy morality. Sloppy art. The self-indulgence of spoiled children. They probably stopped the Viet Nam war, those children of the sixties, but what a price they paid. The good of the intellect, gone.

A, remember where we are in this dangerous story, where and when, they told her.

That's where *you* are, she told them. I have my own story to live, and you don't know the *meaning* of dangerous.

A is impatient with lost generations, though she read *The Sun Also Rises* and was enchanted by it when she was 18, like everybody else. She is too judgmental. She knows it. This rollicking of people who don't believe in characters is fun for them, but they seem to A not to believe in character either. At least not in their writing. A feels compromised. She doesn't like the way they talk about their women. About women. This bed is too narrow. She wanted to tell her story. G said he'd never thought of it as telling his story. It's just a lark, he said. It doesn't have to be Strindberg, a confession to your psychiatrist. It doesn't have to be serious. G accuses A of being Miss Julie a lot. But what if it is serious for A? What if it's not a lark anymore?

> You can't holler down my rainbarrel;
> You can't climb my cellar door.
> I don't wanna play in your yard;
> You don't love me anymore.

> You can't dum-de-dum-de-dum-dum;
> You can't climb my apple tree.
> I don't wanna play in your yard
> If you won't be good to me.

Why do you have to control everybody else's writing? G asks. Why don't you just control your own? A wonders why G thinks it's a matter of control. Is it? she wonders. It doesn't feel like that. It's meshwork, and it feels like a trap to A. Is narrative a trap? Like women? Like the unfolding earth, folding them in? Is that what they think? So they have to explode it, tangle everyone up in the holes. But they're the ones who keep insisting on plot. I mean what is this business about all of them being kidnapped anyway? Who do they think they are? Princes stolen from the cradle? Reared by gypsies or women unworthy of the task? A wonders whether she'd better just write herself discreetly out of the story into the direction of a black hole, come out on the other side of all this implosion-explosion-grail stuff. She doesn't want to be trapped inside this silly plot. She can see which way the cookie crumbles. She can read the writing on the wall.

> Beware the frabjous jub-jub bird.
> Beware the Jabbercock, my girl.

She doesn't care about the rising and falling of their divining rods. What do they think is in there anyway? Misguided Don Giovannis looking for love in all the wrong places. Giacommettis poking their women full of holes. Reviling them when they discover their mistakes about this one, they go after the next one and the next one. Boats against the current, part and parcel of America's dream of Hollywood starlets with silicone tits worshipping at their sceptres, rods, staffs. No comfort here. No rest for these wicked women, inadequate to the dreams of their heroes – which persist through the mockery, the self-reflexive exposure of their own bathos, their laughter. Where's Barbie? they cry. Where's Mummy? Where's baby? A feels uncharitable. She doesn't care about their Woody Allenish preoccupation with sex and death.

Does A really want to play in their yard? Maybe the best we can do is tell the other half of each others' stories. Out of the ashes of each other we rise, knives and forks poised over the corpse of love. A broken lance, an empty cup. How early in the morning we enter the Maramar caves now. Too young. Too hard to write about then with what we know now. Impossible task to unravel the past, be now what once we were, or even to remember. Flotsam and jetsam. Winsome and wontsome. And underneath the arches this enormous rage. Snap goes the endentata-ed trap.

I yam what I yam. What I yam? AMB cries. Watter we? Water all these liddel wee wees? Liddel Joyce-boys in Blunderland? Wattemeye? Explosions in the Iyambics of their Iamb? The lady vanishing? Banished in The Big Byambybang.

CHAPTER FOURTEEN

D was now walking along the starboard side of the Upper Levels highway, one huarache gone, his bare yellow lizardish right foot learning to go beyond the pain of the pebbles. He had just achieved the top of a rise, and the whole of the city was spread out before him, grey and low in the mist. He counted himself luckier than most men because most men were dead. And also because about a mile earlier he had found an Eat More bar, still in its wrapper, lying among the sun-bleached cigarette packages along the verge. On a muddy spring day not long before, G had taught him the felicities of what G called the ideal varsity lunch – an Eat More bar and a bottle of Creme Soda. D kept one eye on the misty city, one eye on the road traffic, and one eye on the verge. If someone had ejected a bottle of creme soda – or even Hires Root Beer – it would not be too warm to drink in this weather.

He did not know it, but a mile behind him, right where there had been an Eat More bar still in its package, trod M, trying to eat up the miles with the illusion that he exhibited a military bearing, and reciting to himself all that he could remember of the poems in the thick pinkish Oscar Williams anthology.

"onetwothreefoursix indians, just like that," he intoned.

Neither D nor M knew that far behind them G was still a captive of the thugs in the Bulgarian gloves. He and the thugs were sitting in the Oolichan Hotel beer parlour at Squamish, watching an early-season game between San Francisco and the Cubs. G had been trying to build a reputation as an expert in baseball, hoping that it might distinguish him as a poet, but here he sat, unable to put a name to any of the players on the blurry screen up high above the bar where the radio used to be.

Neither could G invent a method of extricating himself,

and if it came to that, his fellow knights, from all these overcoated people and their expensive cars. He decided to give himself up to fate.

"What the hell can we do," he said, surprised that he had said it out loud.

"Never give up," said one of the large fellows, with a Hapsburgian accent. "Willy Mays is up third in the eighth."

Back in West Point Grey a beautiful young woman with a long white neck that ordinary underclasswomen would maim for was standing in the front yard of a stucco bungalow, with a damp newspaper in her hand. She looked up and down the avenue, cast her eyes to the roof of the house and the nearby trees just in case, and with her other hand did up the top button of her white blouse.

This modesty was inspired by the banal stare of a swart man whose face was framed in the rear window of an ugly and oversized automobile with *déclassé* white-wall tires. It was snugged to the curb across the avenue, and there were already new patches of white pigeon shit on the roof.

A held the newspaper so that she could scan the headlines on the first page. Brewery Receives New Paint Job, said one. It was a slow news day.

Now a burly man in an overcoat and homburg and gloves got out of the driver's seat of the big car. He walked slowly toward A, who was buttoning the sleeve of her blouse.

"Okay, Goldilocks, get in the car," he growled.

"Do you perhaps mean 'get *into* the car'?" she inquired, allowing no condescension in her voice.

"Get *into* the god damned car," said the bozo. He had not had the manners to remove his hat when he made his invitation.

A did not obviously grip *The Vancouver Bun* any tighter. But she shifted her feet slightly, so that they were positioned according to the second illustration in the textbook she carried to her weekly night class at the Point Grey Community Centre.

"I don't think so," she said then. "It's a rather ugly car, and not very clean."

The plug-ugly in the coat stopped in his tracks. His forehead furrowed like a septic pool on a windy day.

"That's a Rolls *Royce*!"

"Since when did they start making Rolls Royces in Bulgaria?"

"Get in the car, Cinderella."

He was walking again.

She saw the other doors opening in the Rolls, but her attention was mainly for Igor under the hat.

"You can forget it about the car," she said, sweetly. "I do not go for rides with strange men, and I certainly do not go for rides with even lower species."

Igor had apparently not run into this problem in his earlier grabs. He approached more quickly. He reached out his gloved hand. The hand was about the size of Scrooge's turkey. He was making what his bosses would later inform him was a mistake.

A executed the procedure on page twenty-four without a hitch, and the behemoth was soon lying at the base of a thick poplar, the top of his homburg at an acute angle against the bark of said deciduous tree.

Three other overcoats came as hurriedly as their rectangular shapes would permit out of the car. One slammed a door and a pigeon that was just about to land on the roof veered away.

The first one to reach the lawn in front of G's landlady's bungalow was induced to keep going, without reducing speed, until his homburg came to an abrupt stop against the third step of the concrete porch. A threw the unread newspaper into the face of one of the remaining goons, to delay him for half a second while she used page twenty-six on the other. As she did so she plucked at his overcoat pocket.

Thus when the other man got *The Bun* out of his face he was looking at a handgun that, while it had first been fired seventeen years ago in World War II, was still impressive enough in the length of its barrel and the excellent European styling overall, that he lifted, unbidden, his gloved hands into the air.

"Drag them," said A.

"Duh?"

"Those sleeping simians. One by one, grasp them by some item of their clothing and drag them to your hideous automobile. Put them inside. Then drive away. Tell your masters, wherever they are, Washington, Plovdiv, the UBC Players' Club, tell them that you found that your assignment needs more planning."

"Huh?"

"Take slobbos. Put in car. Vroom vroom."

"Can I have Alexi's pistol?"

"Drag. Or I will make boom boom."

The man in the overcoat started dragging his co-workers toward the expensive British car. He tried to repair the three homburgs, but then settled for throwing them into the car after the sleeping men.

"You!" intoned A.

"Yes, ma'am?"

"If you people have G and D and M, I would appreciate it if you were to let them go."

"Uh, you want them, lady?"

"I didn't say that. Listen carefully. Let alphabet men go. Do not return here."

She watched the English steel proceed up the avenue, belching smoke from its tail. She hoped that if she and G ever got married and she learned to drive, that she would not end up with an English car.

She buttoned up her other sleeve and went back into the basement room. She took the gun apart so that G would not hurt himself with it. Then she made some instant coffee. It took a long time to make. She let the kettle try its best while she thought about what she should do. She should do her hair. The hell with it.

To divert her mind, she opened the English 435 essay that

G had at last finished. Taking up a ballpoint pen with the name of a Canadian bank on it, she set about correcting G's more egregious errors.

"No, no," she said to the empty little room with the odor of basketball shoes. "Kafka was the fiction writer. Rilke was the poet."

When she had met G two years ago he was a c+ student. She had managed to get him up to b and occasionally b+. Once he had got an A in a creative writing course, after she took all the hokey similies out of his long poem about cigarettes and beer.

The water boiled, and she poured some into the IGA crystals in the coffee mug that had been used by hundreds of mouths at the UBC cafeteria.

She reached under the cot and pulled out the novel that G had been writing since the day after his seventeenth birthday. She was on page 111, and she would do her usual twenty pages, sipping the hot liquid that tasted like horse skin. At first she had simply smoothed G's spelling and punctuation. Lately she had taken to removing and replacing the most jejune clichés. It was a novel about a young man smoking cigarettes and drinking beer and trying to describe women's paps.

Today she could do no more than eight pages. This may have been partly due to the rudeness of the four animals in the big car. But some of it had to be because of her life of romance. For a moment she thought of messing the room up, bringing in all the detritus she had carried out to the garbage bin.

Cary Deneau appeared before her eyes.

Not the whole, corporeal Cary. Just the certain fresh beauty of his scarred face and the deft angularity of his body in repose. She remembered that when he put the fingertips that usually touched saxophone keys to certain areas of her skin she felt like the growly low parts of "'Round Midnight." Cary Deneau had made her a melody when she was eighteen years old. He had ears that stuck out at the sides of his head, and they moved when he was playing anything above high C. She liked to grab his ears in her hands. She would never do page twenty-four to Cary Deneau.

But now she did not know whose club Cary was playing in, and she was a poet's girl. She prayed that he would be reluctant to publish.

M stood on the side of the Upper Levels Highway and tried with all his might to extricate an insect that had been carried in the wash of a passing Rolls Royce and plunged into M's ear. A passing motorist mistook his gestures for antic hitch-hiking, and yanked the family Turbocharger to a stop a hundred feet in front of the gnat-maddened man.

But habits and expectations die hard. M hobbled to the car and climbed into the back seat, to find himself sitting next to a little old lady who reminded him of President Dwight D. Eisenhower, and a pre-teen boy with mercurochrome on his fingers. A woman and a man were in the front seat.

"We just been overnight in Squamish," volunteered the man as he looked hopefully for an opportunity to pull back onto the road. "Took in the *Son et Lumiere*. Liked the *Lumiere* part the best."

"A wise choice," said M, trying to tone down his gestures aimed at insect-extraction.

"How far ya going?"

"Oh, Vancouver will be fine, anywhere in Vancouver. The Georgia Hotel, if it's not out of your way."

The preteener stared and stared.

"What happened to your hair?" he asked.

Just then two things occurred. The insect, which M had mistakenly thought dead and even eviscerated, crawled like a Seabee out of his earhole. And he saw D limping along the verge, his head down, his beard like that of a saviour carrying a cross through a heartless mob.

"Stop, please," begged M. "That is my friend D. He's a sad case. We all try to look after him. He won't do you any harm. He once published a villanelle. Please."

The dad pulled over, and they waited for D to hobble to the car. M had to lean out and pull him into the Turbocharger.

"How far ya going?" asked the driver.

"Seattle," said D. There was a chocolate stain on his teeshirt. "San Francisco."

CHAPTER FIFTEEN

After much rain, it was a sunny morning, Monday, in early October, 1961, and John Holsun's breakfast was ready for him the instant he brought his last and best foot down off the last linoleum-clad step. The stairs were those of his fine south Cambie Street house, and the breakfast, Kellogg's All-Wheat cereal, Jersey Farms homogenized milk, Rogers sugar, and Nabob coffee, was prepared and served to him by his wife, Marlene Nisbett Holsun. Marlene Nisbett Holsun, born a Nisbett, wooed in a Pontiac, married to a painter, went by that three-sided monicker only on the most formal occasions, such as her memorial service in the Broadway Funeral Chapel, on Monday, October 12, 1998.

That same October morning Brian Stewart came downstairs in his parents' house in the 7000 block of Larch Street and tucked into two Fraser Farms eggs expertly and lightly fried in Parkay oleomargarine, and two slices of McGavin's (brown) bread, toasted and spread with honey or raspberry jam, this latter adulterated with "added pectin," both from Woodward's Food Floor. These items prepared and served by Dorothy (Dot) Stewart. Her family of origin and expiry date not known or not important at this time.

In mid-egg Brian tapped his knife against the edge of his plate, and again, and again, a sharp chink chink chink. "Brian, stop that," said his mum. But the young fellow was in a brown study, or let's say a muddle. Peculiar dreams had assailed him as he lay in his bed under a map of the world with Tanganyika and Bechuanaland depicted in strawberry red to show British responsibility. He'd had, in these dreams, intimacies with the Stewart family dog, a Lab named George, and Brian could neither countenance such images, events, and feelings, nor connect them usefully with any part of his real life or his restless libido. He had had some difficulties with his girl friend

Marjorie, difficulties that were driving him crazy. A guy is a guy, as Doris Day crooned. He headed off to work.

Getting off the Number Ten bus near Apex Painting, Brian fell in, just outside the office, with co-worker Dave Powell. Powell had narrow hunched shoulders, several prominent yellow hounddog teeth, and yellow freckles and freckle-coloured hair. He attended the University of Oregon, where he managed athletics teams. He had worked as a copy boy in the sports department of the Vancouver *Bun*, and he knew well the downtown East End and the waterfront, including the street that bore his own name. He knew Hastings and Water Streets. He knew all about Carrall Street, whose name alone, turning in the mouth, made a bitter taste. History, orient winds, the seaport, rusting iron plates, shadows, opium!, stabbings in the alley, a drawn-out sigh as a body slides down a wall, glistening blood, horror and boys' delights. Grown-up delights, the delighted imagining of the boys in-between. Powell knew all about Frince's rooms and what men went up there with what kind of creature, and what they did, illustrated with startling gestures, fingers and tongue.

Hunched and hustling he guided Brian into the lunch-room, where the young men sat at varnished plywood tables and rooted in their black lunchboxes for cookies or cake that mum must have put in there somewhere, gobbling some down and yarping up gossip and hearsay.

"So we're up the side of the Coca Cola building and Holsun says it's supposed to be at the seventh floor, but he says I can't see any letters, do you see it Brian? And I'm looking up maybe eight, nine feet over my head, we're at the fifth floor, and I can see just these big shapes, not letters but these wiggily shapes."

"*The Bun* said they were letters, they were hieroglyphics."

"They weren't letters, they were just wavy dark shapes. But in the middle of the bunch of them there was, it looked like, letters tee, eeh, and something not so clear, and an ell, or two ells. It was maybe just more wavy lines. And there was another word beside it."

Danny Charles, silent to this point, absorbed in the blinding clarity of a darkly secret vision, said, "You're full of shit, Brian."

"I'm not, I saw a real word, at least two words, up there."

"So how come Holsun didn't see anything."

"I'm… "

"Holsun said there wasn't nothing up there but some smudges, like the bricks were dirty or something."

A giggle from Dave Powell.

"Jesus Christ, I know what I saw, I saw some words, some letters… "

"You're so full of shit, Stewart."

Silence fell on Brian Stewart; silence fell from him.

Jack the crew chief leaned in the door. "Who's going to Malkin Brothers?"

"Me and Tim," said Danny Charles, getting up and following Jack out into the hall. The lunchroom group dwindled out after them, leaving just Brian Stewart there.

After a minute a navy blue uniform appeared in the doorway, a man in it with a lot of white skin around his ears and hairline. Another behind him.

"Brian Stewart?"

"Yeah?"

They walked in.

"We want to talk to you."

On the hospital's fourth floor, by the elevator, faltered a man who could equally have been patient or visiting relative, a man in that age and condition where there is no real difference between hospital visitor and visitee. He uttered a sighing snuffle from deep in his throat, like the Atom Man in the *Superman* serial on Junior Radio Theatre, or the Mummy in *Edge of Time*. He wore white leather shoes and a sweater the colour of arterial blood.

At the nursing station of Ward Four West a nurse recounted her Sunday endeavours.

"I had the table laid with peach place mats and a white cloth with dark green napkins and pink roses, and it looked really neat. I made this really nice rice... meringue with a tart, creamy sauce."

Nearby, under white hospital sheets, M lay aswoon. He dreamed of Davis, California, where he had never been. He knew, he saw its broad macadam streets, eucalyptus, palms, giant cactuses in the back yards, red tiles, the swimming pool. Davis, the calmness of the landscape by the Sacramento river, the broad valley, the drying, healing heat. Mexicans nearby? He could nearly taste the sombreros.

But voices pulled him away from his dream. Voices, and a Demerol-hazed glimpse of two forms near his doorway, one in deepest blue, another in deepest red. Voices pointed quietly at M.

"...don't want him yet."
"...should do that right away... "
"...want to send him home first."

The forms faded. M nodded again in slumber.

And twelve days later, he resurfaced at an infamous "pub" (for "publication") party, this one hosted by a brushcut law student named Gerry Lambskin, a winsome lad, half (in his won words) faggot, sometimes dated by A. With his face looking like an old leather waffle, M was in the kitchen, wearing his black corduroy suit. He was whirling and shrieking in front of a huge black iron dutch oven, two-thirds full of nude spaghetti. Four empty blue and yellow Catelli boxes were on the counter. M was saucing the spaghetti with tinned tomato sauce that thopped into the kettle like flung melted lead, and thorp after vigorous thorp of Paterson's Worcestershire Sauce. Again and again the young man pushed and thrashed into the mixture a wooden spoon laden with Rogers Golden Sugar. "Damned dirty heathens!" he cried to D, "They have no demerara!"

"I didn't know one put brown sugar in spaghetti," said D, whose ideas of food, being English, were quite limited.

"Who the hell knows what they put in spaghetti?" said M, "And who the hell cares what they put in spaghetti? This is what I put in spaghetti, and what I put in spaghetti – "

Here he flung a full handful of black peppercorns out of a Spice Islands jar into the kettle.

" – is what needs to go in spaghetti! Nuff said!"

M was, in truth, as drunk as a lobster, on gin and soda water.

"Now that is solipsism," said a blonde girl in poison-green taffeta from the kitchen doorway.

M half whirled, wooden spoon clutched knoutlike before him.

"Tartan, you sharpmouthed philosophical! Keep away from my mixings."

Growling, he spun away. He fixed his small red bear eyes on Kathy Richards, who'd unluckily stashed her mickey of rum in a kitchen cupboard and was now about to pour herself a refill. M harangued her about house-building. His brother Ron, an affluent operator in commercial circles, areas quite beyond the ken or interest of the bearded younger brother, was having a house built for him on a rocky and woodsy outcrop in West Vancouver. M, himself unable to saw a straight line or get a pup tent up (do you inflate the thing perhaps?), was entranced with the arts and complexities, the portentous mysteries of joinery, plumbing, electrification, the building trades. He compared these arts to the fine arts, and found all advantage, all merit, in the former.

"Next to a good carpenter, Praxiteles was a prat," he bellowed.

Kathy R clutched her rum and coke, ducked her head and shot for the hall.

Gerry Lambskin's parents, just arrived home by Mutual Taxi, gazed at one another with a wild surmise as they started up the walk toward the house. Out of the mock-Spanish frontery of their very own lil home in the west rolled and reeked a great effluvium of yeast-ridden youth, vomitings, noises, cries, rhythmic lurching, bell-like smashes of things, sudden, sharp grunts of pain, the popping of tears, wails, whales dancing in the dining room, eight thousand crows shitting and laughing in unison. Their house was in danger.

Hear the guests, locked into the drone of their own voices, let knock at door who may:

"So they have this neat floor, black and white squares …"

"…kick your frigging teeth in – "

"Anyway, Audrey is writing her novel in longhand, not using a typewriter."

"Marlene!"

"And they have these new french fries; they're crinkle-cut… just root beer, you can only get root beer."

"And what's going to happen when Russia gives atomic weapons to China? You know they're gonna do that."

"I figure the eyes at the window are The Asp, and Punjab is standing behind him in the dark, you can't see him."

"Marlene!"

"He tried to grab my leg and I kicked him, kicked his hand, and he's saying that I broke his thumb… but you know I was laughing, I couldn't stop laughing, can you imagine, I could have really hurt him and I couldn't stop laughing."

"I can't give you a ride home because she's sleeping in my car."

Against all this hubadeehub and Beelzebub came a stentorian knocking at the door. 'Twas not the Lambskins; indeed those bonny folk, about to plunge with courage into the house, were thrust back against the railing of their own front porch doorjamb by a lank and skinny arm as the door was opened by A, to whom a voice cried out, "Collecting for the heart fund!"

It was an old woman, scrawny but endowed with demon strength, with a leather case, a purple shawl, and mad, bulbous eyes.

"Well, I don't know… " A was in some confusion. "Mr. and Mrs. Lambskin aren't home right now" (The Lambskins in fact teetered and gibbered in the shadows just outside the doorway).

"Now look here, dear. Don't you claim that you don't know what the heart fund is all about," shouted the crone. "Here!"

She grabbed A's wrist, circling it with her bony grip. A was frightened, felt four years old, the witch had her. The old horror clamped A's hand against the witch chest, no breast at all. "Feel that!" she shrieked.

A felt the great, mad engine banging the cage, the little ivory bars, felt a black spirit swooping toward her.

Then came another sound, a wailing behind them in the night, and the Lambskins are once again pushed aside, and the old crone, in the midst of her diatribe, fade into the laurel hedge bordering the walkway. Four of Vancouver's Finest now barge through the door, march down the central hallway to the kitchen, and without pause seize the tilting, snorting M, the largest cop grasping a Goliath's handful of black corduroy jacket. With another large cop shoring him up under the shoulder, M went down the hall, his desert boots scarcely touching the floor.

And out into the night, the five of them, no words, no warrant, no by-your-leave. Jesus, thought G, thronging on the porch with several others, gaping at the dark car sliding away. They're going to get us.

CHAPTER SIXTEEN

G stood before D and exhorted his attention. Now, G had goo on his pants and fear in his heart. His pulse was racing like Fangio over a Keremeos backstreet. But D was in a reverie. He had a bag of ice on his head, but the bag was really a poorly-tied dish towel, and the ice was melting. D was wet, and clad in narry but a nightgown that had once belonged to Ms. Tartan. G had given up asking him where he got such things.

"Will you, for God's sake – ?" began G.

"No longer believe in God," said D, his voice obviously hurting the inside of his oddly-shaped cranium.

"Will you, for the Universal Life Force's sake, listen to me?"

Good, he had managed an entire sentence, though an interrogative one.

"That's an interesting religio-sexual phenomenon," said D, taking the slushy cloth from his head and tossing it into his sink, atop three TV-dinner boxes. Turkey? wondered G. Why three servings of turkey? The meat loaf would have been a nice respite. Comes with peach cobbler in the triangular indentation at 12 O'Clock.

"What?" he asked, beginning to surrender. D had an English accent that intensified from time to time. G, having been brought up in the dirt-road Interior of the Province, was conditioned to feel secure and uneducated in the presence of an English accent.

"Until this year, I always called upon the name of the deity while experiencing a climax of a sexual nature. It seemed natural to do so, especially while the partner of the occasion was calling my name out, louder and louder."

"Dorcas?"

"Dorkus? Just about kill us!"

G looked around the kitchen-sitting room-bedroom for

something to eat while being instructed. There was nothing but some dried sauce the colour of his desert boot. This sauce was on the wallpaper.

"So you see," said D, now combing his hair with water out of the saucepan beside the sink, "I find it ludicrous trying to exclaim Oh Universal Life Force while ejaculating."

"So, what do you exclaim?"

"Usually I call my own name louder and louder."

Now D began to remove Miss Tartan's peach-coloured nightgown while roving the living space looking for items of English male attire. G averted his gaze. He looked out the sooty window at the creepy plants in the Shaughnessy back yard while D was probably checking under the rollaway bed for underpants. G took this opportunity to describe their calamity.

"M is in the hands of the police. He is probably even now whimpering under a hail of billyclubs," he said. A smile tugged at the corners of his mouth, but he fought it.

"What has the miscreant done this time?" asked D. "You can look now."

D was attired in brown seersucker slacks that hung like soft air ducts around his legs. His grey shirt flecked with silver thread was done up at the neck button. He was holding in his hand a necktie that appeared to sport a design part Stewart plaid and part UBC cafeteria beef and barley soup.

"A metric ton of policemen grabbed him while he was throwing a handful of capers into the spaghetti sauce," said G. His voice rose as if he were connubing Dorcas, or as if he were enunciating one of his *faux* Corso poems in the quad.

"Are you certain that they were policemen?" asked D. The way he did so impressed G more than any English accent could do. D spoke the words in a kind of intradental hiss while his alarming beard neared G's ear and finally abutted it. It was like Chaimss Mayssson hissing into Randolph Scott.

"Well," and now G's hard-won urbanity fell from him like dust from a moth's wings. "They were wearing police uniforms. They had guns and moustaches. They were all wide in the hips."

"Eggsackly," intoned D. His tie was now perfectly knotted though not dead centre. He had a brown oxford on one foot and a strange sock on the other. Now he stood in apparent distraction while he should have been looking under something or perhaps outside for the other. It was not distraction, however, but reverie. Finally he spoke, the English accent nearly gone, replaced by a kind of unpracticed democracy.

"Tell me, fellow poet and true, when you were playing footsie with Amanda Tunefork under the long table in Creative Writhing 302, was that an idle moment, opportunity idly taken? Or did I miss something?"

"Amanda had eyes only for the bard. Amanda wanted Prester John himself," replied G, evasively.

"I am not reminiscing here about eyes, Delsing. You will remember that Miss Tunefork walked around squishing. She descended upon our leafy campus from the high mountain country, an innocent valkerie unaware of her beakish powers. One day she walked before me into the Gorp Building wearing, it appeared, nothing but high heels and a knitted dress of a dove-grey shade. When she mounted the heartbreakingly few steps into the Gorp, I nearly perished in the Herrickean sense. I broke into a sweat. I heard a ringing in my ears and said ringing was not a subtle electromagnetic buzz – I heard ringing such as a bat must hear in the belfry of St Crispin's Cathedral, Snarlton-upon-Twylle, Bucks. At eleven in the morn. I am asking you, man, did you ever swizzle that apéritif? Did you play handsies with the creature?"

G was trying to remember the words spoken by the four uniformed lardomorphs while they were bouncing M toward their van, but the image of Amanda Tunefork intruded upon his panopticon. He viewed all her parts. He viewed all her elements. He recalled the squeak of her skin. He began to mumble:

>   Her eyes, the sheets her fingers
>   work over like lapels.

> Morals, faded labels from foreign hotels
> we slept in, our luggage.
>
> How pretend nothing has happened
> when precisely that is your conviction.

D had somewhere located a leaking ballpoint and a college binder.

"Would you say that more clearly?" he urged. "I want to remember what you said here today."

G was always happy to comply on such occasions. He repeated the words, careful with the end-stops, breathing the way he imagined Gaston Helios, the doyen of the San Francisco Renaissance, to do. D scribbled in his binder.

"White globes with not a lick of perspiration between them," G murmured.

"Cad!"

"Two dorsal dimples you could lay twenty cents in."

"Dog in the manger!"

"Tongue like a frantic *escargot*."

"I wish to talk about M and these purported minions of the law," said D, now wearing his thick unpressed tweed jacket. It looked pretty good with the Stewart tie, though the soupstains were of another origin.

But now G was thinking of Tunefork. Sugar fell from the sky. Glistening worms emerged from between moist leaves on the forest floor. Blazing quaggas crossed the southern firmament. Oysters leapt into wheelbarrows. Peculiar inscriptions appeared on the yellow wall of the Sick Brewery.

"Lorraine Tartan!" shouted D, his beard touching G's nose.

He woke from his dream into the squalor of D's room. He thought he saw an inflatable doll protruding from beneath the rollaway, but D's foot moved quickly, and it was probably all imagined. Coming out of a vision can do odd things to the ocular organs.

Now D placed a tweed arm over his companion's shoulders.

"Let us go out and procure two Eat More bars and two Creme Sodas, and see whether we can make head or nail of this puzzle," he suggested, something like a cultured leer in his voice.

"That's tail," said G.

"I told you I no longer want to hear about that. Our friend M is, I fear, in dire straits. Maybe even Georgia Strait. If we stumble upon his body, I must tell you, M and I made a verbal agreement whereby I get all his Calypso forty-fives and the rest of his *New Yorker* subscription."

They did not trust the telephone. They went to the Public Safety Building and enquired about the possible presence there of their chum. After a long wait, during which time D smoked cigarettes and G eyed the female typist in the blue shirt with ironing creases, a doughnut-eater denied all knowledge of an arrest at the Lecovin residence.

Just as our duo was about to depart the building for a few quick ones at The Georgia, they heard loud voices behind a pebbled glass door. Then the door opened and two young men in paint-spattered coveralls emerged, talking loudly and angrily while a policeman with ironing creases and two stripes border-collied them before him. These civilians were Danny Charles and Brian Stewart.

"I'm tellin' ya, they were letters, real letters. There was lots of funny looking squiggles too, but there were these real letters!"

"We have your report, Mr. Stewart," said the border-collie.

"You're so full of pure moose shit, Brian," said Dave Powell.

"I seen a t for sure, and an e, that's no shit," shouted Stewart.

"We'll call you if we need any more information," said the border-collie.

And they were outside. Brian and Dave and G and D.

Brian and Dave looked at the two poet-students casually, and then looked again, recognizing them.

"Hey, we seen you on TV," said Brian.

"Yeah, with that broad and the other guy with the beard."

G and D looked modest. They were thinking of the afternoon darkness under the sidewalk at The Georgia Hotel.

"Boy, that broad really got you guys good," said Dave. "I couldn't understand a word she was saying, but she really had your number."

"Fuckin' eh," agreed Brian.

G and D mumbled their genial agreement. Now all they had to do was edge away, westward.

"That other guy," said Dave. "What happened to his hair?"

"We are kind of in a hurry," said G. "We are trying to locate our friend right this minute. There isn't a second to waste." And Kathy Richards was usually in the Women & Escorts by four o'clock.

But the two young men in coveralls didn't get to talk with television stars every day. They began to walk along with the poet-students.

"I thought I would die when you guys started shouting about the white flash and the wall writing and the kidnappers," said Brian, with a big smile. There was a Craven A in the middle of the smile. G gestured and the painter gave him a Craven A. G had been craving one all afternoon.

"'Cause I seen the writing, too," said Brian. "And now I remember the second word I could make out."

Now G and D were walking at regular speed, and the painters added up to a foursome. But G and D were word people. And G wanted another cigarette.

"What was that second word?" he asked, while they waited for a green light on Main and Georgia.

"Where ya going? The Georgia? I'll tell ya there if you buy me and Dave a barley sandwich."

CHAPTER SEVENTEEN

In which M's concussion becomes a vision of the past and future mixed.

So here he was, in the hoosegow. The linoleum, a deep colour of old dry McIntosh toffee, shrieked and whined under hectic traffic. Screeches and banging doors as Vancouver's worst of the evening were bundled away. Walls and cages behind walls reared before M as he was ushered from the van, up the stairs, through the grey corridors.

Being booked at the police station was just like the great comic book bust at Kerrisdale School, many years earlier. The frog-marching on that occasion (and it's only fair to report that M's mother swore to the end of her long, busy, and honorable life that M had never, ever, in *his* life actually been frog-marched. Might have done him some good, she chuckled, a bit of frog-marching. Dumb boy) the frog-marching was to the office of Mr. Amarillo, the principal, the white haired terrifying ramrod who lived with his strap under the stairs. M feared the strap, and he thought he was gonna get it for having a desk full of comic books, forbidden, forbidden. It had started with cranky old Miss Dreckshin finding mess, mess, mess, in M's exercise book, and on M's desk top. What kind of mess? Ink, snot, unfocused thought? Likely just grime and evasion, the staples of M's career as a student at every age. Sent for his inability or refusal to see where the apostrophe must go to Principal Amarillo's's office, he looked down the length of the hall and saw a file of classmates that went back to the stairs, and didn't seem to end even there. Each of his classmates carried an armful of comic books. This was contraband, forbidden stuff. M wept from fear. Mr. Amarillo had beaten many pupils; the screams were heard, the red hands and wet red faces were seen. It was all known. He would beat several more. He was a scoutmaster. And he beat M. Five on each hand.

Now M stood in fear and consternation in front of the authority charged with keeping order in the city. A slight commotion behind him, the clank of a heavy glass door and a scuffle of hush-puppied feet produced the long, squirming figure of G. Astonishing. Where had G come from, how, why?

G was hustled to the desk where rude hands took his nice watch and his belt. He produced, on command, what was in his pocket – some coins and a small black notebook. The officer behind the desk reached across and removed from G's nose the dark brown hornrimmed glasses.

"Hey, I need my glasses." said G, reaching slowly across the desk toward the items taken from him. "Gimme my glasses." He said this not loudly. Immediately one cop grabbed him and held his arms behind him, while the cop on the other side heaved a punch into the middle of his stomach. G went right down like something empty and was pulled down the hall backwards, one cop at each arm, pushed into an elevator, disappeared.

M stood goggling. God, they were so fast, just waiting for him to be just a bit out of line... they shouldn't get away with that... true, G had a big mouth, a big fat mouth, a mouth as big as all outdoors, an ego the size and shape of a barrage balloon. But whomped like that, the mealsack, heelwhack hall departure... it couldn't be allowed. It couldn't be stopped. It was history, and M just stood gaping until nudged and turned toward an open door. "In there, sonny."

"Officer Aliel, he's a honey of a guy," said the constable, pushing M up to the desk. Aliel looked as if rats had borrowed his juices for the evening. And replaced them with rat juice. With his consent.

"Who are your friends, Mister?" was all he said. And he looked at something happening over M's left shoulder.

Something small and metal whacked M just under the bone of the cheek and in an instant filled his mouth with blood. M's body jumped. M swooned.

The world went far and near, went wild and wacky. Sounds of thunder and sirens. Wooga wooga alarms as in *The Man From Uncle*. "They hit M," friends were shrieking as they ran down vast hallways like frenzied mechanical mice. "Tell Mr. Amarillo! Tell Reverend Harry Lumm! Call the police!"

M, aswoon, found himself lost in the ice caves with Mandrake and Lothar. No sign of Narda. Or standing with Rip Kirby, spreadlegged, arms in a warding-off gesture, as a black panther springs from the limb of a tree. Great Scott! Four-footed company! No sign of Honey Dorian. The Mangler going heh heh heh behind the heavy drapes of the study.

God! The wolf! The clarinet – poor little Sasha! Where are the woodcutters?

M spent the night in a blue funk on a metal bunk thinking of anagrams of the towns of Ontario. G, a puzzle freak and whiz kid, brainy though thick, had always in his room a forty-inch stack of magazines: *The Romanian Review, Baseball Illustrated, Sport, Ladies of Lapland, New Arts and Baseball of Japan, Women Comrades of Cuba*, the *Tamarack Review, Boink, a magazine of uncapitalized poetry*, etc. He also subscribed to the journal, *Etc.* M collected the overflow of these mags and read them for the personal advertisements in the back pages. The Ontario puzzle was scrambled names of towns in Ontario. Chimnord was Richmond. Sandud was Dundas, and Agraina was Niagara, but M was stumped by Stiltslevit. Test your own wits.

G spent his night in the hoosegow in a salle privée, a broom closet. Woken at six in the morning, he was told he could make a telephone call, and given one of the dimes taken from his pocket the night before. G's phone call was to D, and it found that young worthy in the middle of personal negotiations with Byrna Brytellson, student poet and raven-haired meaty. "Brytelly-haired Byrna Raven," D had described her in a *Bad Seed* review of her book *Kitsilano Felonies*. Published by Fiddlesticks Press and Subtitled *The Peckered Shade*, it was a sonnet sequence detailing the ins and outs of her two years' love affair with the head of the UBC English Department. The ins and outs were not literally described but rather rendered as a narrative of an incubus and its maiden victim, with Byrna and her Professor in the main roles. A key sonnet was a hymn to her innocence, stolen by the ghostly, ghastly lothario:

> And when to love our bodies down we laid
> I found full well you were a peckered shade.

D had a high and penile regard for Byrna, but roused by the call from G, he left her promptly, darting out the bathroom window as was his frequent custom. Dawn found him at the White Lunch on Broadway. Thence, after a quick fuelling, he spread the alarm throughout West Point Grey, rallying for help a small army of odds and sods. M and G are drowning under a hail of billyclubs in the hoosegow, he informed the Players' Club and *The Bad Seed*. Kerry Feltham, Dan Danielson and Rupert Brooke-Buchanan, pen-names all, responded for the newspaper, Wesley Trotsky, Fee McMannic and Arthur Maguay for the actors. Also Liam Chutney, Fred Clivus, Gloria Hilcoot, iron-jawed Trevor Howard imitator Roy Gooper, Pat Manzer, Deidre Fuller, and a mobile unit from CBC-TV. We're back in the days when the regional mandate meant something.

Flying down Blanca, Fourth and Cornwall streets that evening were McMannic's Hillman convertible, and antique Bentleys piloted by Liam Chutney or T. Gammelfelt. *Les belles dames de Shaughnessy* participated in their MG's. Tenny Rughead appeared in a three-wheeled Messerschmitt, so clapped out that he'd converted it to pedal propulsion. Ebbe Coutts came on a unicycle. They joined a growing crowd of curiosity-seekers and *poets manqués* converging on the Public Safety Building.

It was a wave of protest, fueled by popular rage and celebrity visits. Debbie Reynolds and Carleton Carpenter in summer dress, striped blazer, ice-cream pants, white shoes, ukulele, straw hats and picnic basket sang "and then he'd row row row," and suited the action to the word, grinning like hyenas. In the next boat, Gordon MacRae and Doris Day, likewise warbling their false little red cellophane hearts out. Stokely Carmichael spoke from the steps of the Vancouver Courthouse. Tom Hayden appeared. Linus Pauling waved a bottle of vitamin C. Benjamin Spock hoarsely exhorted a group of mothers standing in a circle around him, and Leonard Nimoy spoke on behalf of those with longer ears. The Beatles donated the proceeds of their concert at Empire Stadium, though the Rolling Stones refused to do so. Jean Chrétien said Grace in one of the official languages.

A short-wave radio hummed and whistled, and submarines were dispatched from a secret dock in a remote fjord in Norway. They slid in single file down the inlet toward the North Sea. Swimming with consummate ease and power just ahead of them was Submariner. Meanwhile half a world away, Stukas dove on a Jap warship. Stuka Stuka Stuka Stuka Stuka, they shrieked. Henry Fonda, James Cagney and Alec Guinness watched from the bridge of an Allied battlewagon. It was an international joint task force and one of the three was a Canadian. One hopes it was Henry Fonda.

A squad of Australian bathtubbers, delirious from thirsty weeks in the mid-Pacific, missed Nanaimo by miles, crossed the strait at full throttle and roared through the third floor of the jailhouse, shredding doorjambs with the custom propellers on their six-horse engines, doctored to the legal limit (and beyond it) for the Big Race. The Harvard University swim team, the Crimson Tide, led by its captain, the doomed breast-stroker Teddy Kennedy, surged through in the wake of the Australians. Crimson rubber caps, prominent ears. Attack helicopters from Cold Lake and Comox thrashed overhead.

Across the inlet Malcolm Lowry roared with joy and held up an empty glass. "I'll have another gimlet," he smiled at Marjorie. "Assuming you were able to buy gin in this God-choked presbytery of a city."

The atom-powered sub *Poseidon*, with the speed of fiction, passed Ferguson Point and slid into Coal Harbour near HMCS *Discovery*. The craven, complicitous Royal Canadian Navy yawned at its radarscopes. "At your service, Submariner," they muttered. The *Poseidon* surfaced beside the Rowing Club, and its first salvo hurled an 80MM. artillery shell from one deck gun, and, from the other, Prince Namor himself, sizzling through the aether, a human cannonball.

"Circus must be in town," observed Wystan Buckett from a vantage point on Pender Street, as he watched Namor hurtle through the roof of the Public Safety Building.

More shelling from offshore – poum, poum, poum. Smell of cordite drifting over Point Grey. The marines hit the beach at Spanish Banks. Richard Widmark with his helmet strap undone waved ashore his platoon. John Agar was there and, yes! a glimpse of Montgomery Clift, which meant that old blue eyes, playing Maggio in *From Here to Eternity*, was likely to be on hand. With Burt Lancaster, and you know he did that movie just for the fun of wearing the brushcut, lying on the beach somewhere, pseudocoupled to Deborah Kerr. In that black bathing suit, a *décolletage* twenty-five years ahead of its time… but no time for that now. Eddie Albert and Jack Palance led the attack and there was wiggly eyebrows, John Saxon, as the Strange One. Which meant that Robert Redford might be there, years before *Barefoot in the Park* with Henry Fonda's poopsy daughter. Redford then a stage actor, and Demi Moore just a piddly little gleam in someone's eye. John Wayne stood on a concrete picnic table, his eyes wide and bugged in that insane look, and yelled "Get your men up th' beach, Mr. Dunphy," sounding (as always) as if he had terrible sinus trouble. Just offshore, Humphrey Bogart, on the deck of his yacht the *Santana*, gazed ashore from under a baseball cap. He wore khaki. James Dean, wearing black, sent regrets.

Most marvelous of all was Ernest Hemingway, done up like Bogart in khakis and navy-blue baseball cap, debarking from the *Pilar* at Kitsilano beach, wearing a hundred pounds of expensive sidearms but taking no heed of the screech of artillery or the bang and rattle of small arms fire. Why should he? He still had two years to live. From an old-fashioned leather briefcase he pulled a battered, well-used, and much-oiled prose style. Our earnest aspirant G, said Arthur Maguey, speeding along Cornwall in the back seat of McMannic's Hillman convertible, thinks he's entitled to have that when the old man dies. M wanted that snazzy old briefcase, never mind the prose style.

Led by the Justice League of America, the Silver Surfer, or the Fantastic Four, (M and G later, comparing notes, couldn't agree which, and D remembered only the rabble he'd himself collected), the marines stormed across town to the jail and burst it apart, routing the police and grilling Officer Aliel and Hanging Judge Les Pewley on pointed sticks over a bonfire. As M and G scurried out of the building, a lunatic strode purposefully into it, a man with a cap pulled down over his eyes and a balloon floating over his shoulder, attached to his arm. "Here's the cop shop," he cried over and over. "Here's the cop shop."

"Hey!" cried G, looking back at the odd fellow. "That has to be a helium balloon, which would be an anachronism."

"Shut up and just keep walking; don't look back," advised his comrade.

D found his jailbird friends in the middle of Main Street. Dazed and giggling, they briefly hugged. A, watching from a little distance away on the sidewalk with her friend Feather, snorted and muttered something that gave Feather the giggles. Outside the Jade Garden restaurant, Peaches Dobell smoked from a long cigarette holder and smilingly, sneeringly observed to companions Mike Valpy and Murray Farr, "My heart leaps down when I behold these guys, a bunch of pansies that can only get out of a tight spot by calling in the Americans."

But there was one serious casualty in the affair. A man just a few years older than D or M lay on the sidewalk, shoulders tucked awkwardly against a hydrant. His mouth was half open, as if he might have been in the midst of singing "Friendly Persuasion," his thin gold-and-black-striped tie slung across the chest of his tan suit in a messy way. The young man too had been slung or cast, looked like that, against a fire hydrant. The face was peaceful, smooth and shining, as if he had Taken Christ. Far too seriously.

To A, now quietly and covertly peering over the shoulders of G and D, the man looked surely and exactly to be Pat Boone.

CHAPTER EIGHTEEN

Future continued: The Sixties

I thought he was dead already, A mused, delighted by M's prose, though not surprised by it. He was like that, always had been. Ready to erupt out of his own dark and understanding recesses into a gabble of enthusiastic anarchy. No wonder he gets arrested. In some ways he was worse than G, who at least proclaimed his challenges to authority in pointed aphorisms which baffled his audiences long enough for him to get away. M was always caught mid-sentence, still raving. G made himself feared, hated and adored by others, depending on how one read his histrionics. Anyone with any intelligence at all doubted all postures, every persona, A thought, as she certainly did, having been forewarned early by G's friend Carrots, who, grinning but serious, said, "Never trust a man who says he loves you for your mind; he only wants to fuck you in the ear." Long after Carrots was dead, A thought of him nearly every time she looked at the Simone Martini Annunciation that hung at the foot of the stairs in the house she shared with G.

Carrots was A's favorite of G's friends back then. He'd been a cook in the air force when G was serving out his self-imposed penance there for failing first year university and losing his girlfriend and his job within the space of a few months. Carrots, white-faced and skinny, had arrived in Vancouver after his stint in the air force was over, caught up in a fascination with G that looked like love to A. He was a coiled spring whose white intensity shone through his pale red hair and made his freckles luminous. He moved with precision so that every gesture was a ritual act, a thing of beauty, whether he was flipping pancakes or fried eggs, snapping a cap off a bottle of beer or unfurling, in one swift gesture, as if he were performing a magical trick, a bottle of West Coast Berry Cup, the cheap red wine he drank and offered to others. He was always engaged in a ballet he had choreographed himself. A was grateful to him for his reminder that not all persuasion was friendly. He seemed to be perpetually astonished by people and endlessly interested in them. He invented real people and told their stories for them and to them. That was another thing A loved about Carrots. All the persons in his life were mythic – Jack the Bear and Harry the Hummer and G and Ebbe, whose place Carrots lived in down at the waterfront. Like Troilus, he looked at the peopled earth from the seventh sphere and laughed, but without bitterness – with affection and wonder. A was never sure whether it was Carrots or G who had taught the other most about the fictional character of our lives.

Carrots lived on the edge of the water, on the edge of the *Hits* cabal, and drew wonderful cartoons about them, reinventing them as characters from a wild west show. A remembers one that lined up Ebbe and Furd and G on one side as the bad guys and Frunk on the other as a sheriff with a star on his shirt. Frunk was the straightest of the lot of them in those days, and the most unrelentingly intellectual. Somehow he had managed to grow up without the need or ability to temper his intelligence by brutalizing it. The North American practice of intellectual self-mutilation – blunting, disavowing, deprecating – was not part of Frunk's psychological armory. He paid for it in other ways – as in the cartoon by Carrots. "F-f-f-fuck off, you guys," he is saying, pistols in hand, pointed at the three lackadaisical unshaven rowdies he confronts. Ebbe is a mean twisted little critter – another version of Jesse James; Furd is big and wide with a squint and a sticking plaster; G stands tall and lanky, a cigarette dangling from his scornful grin. A laughed and laughed when she first saw it. Carrots had them down cold.

M was right, though. G's mouth would always get him into trouble. He could not forego a witty quip when one offered itself to him. Like the time at one of Ebbe's parties when he was yakking it up in competition with Ed Dorn and Robert Creeley, for whom he had so much respect he'd never visited him. Trying to impress them, he'd merely angered Creeley. A felt the threat in the air, but didn't know where it came from. Mostly, A was bored at Ebbe's parties. There was hardly any furniture, so everyone sat around at the edge of the big room overlooking the water and smoked dope in the candlelight. Ebbe never paid his electrical bills, so it was almost always candlelight at night. A remembered only one occasion when it wasn't, but in the middle of the party the lights had gone out suddenly, and no one knew whether it was the result of a thunderstorm or of Ebbe's failure to pay the electrical bill. A, in love, had thought of the possibility of a romantic interlude in the dark, but G had seized the opportunity to begin wisecracking like a yahoo. A was a student of literature, so she knew about foreshadowing, and, accurately sensing that this was a promise of things to come, decided that it might not, after all, be a smart idea to marry G, and suggested as much to him. She had not been prepared for G's reaction, which was to attempt to put his fist through a burlap-covered wall. He had been unaware that the burlap covered concrete. So had A. She relented when she wakened the next morning to see his broken hand lying on the pillow beside her head, swollen to the size of a football.

At this party of Ebbe's, spring, 1963, the candlelight looked romantic, but, as usual, everyone was sitting there stoned, waiting for something to happen. Usually, it didn't. They hadn't grasped the fact, A thought, that if you wanted something to happen, one alternative was to make it happen. They were a television audience without a television set. Or maybe something was happening for them. A didn't know since she didn't like marijuana. She turned away when Ham Berry asked her to smell a big bony chunk of stuff lying on the floor in front of the fireplace and giggled sillily when she wrinkled her nose in recognition and bewilderment. "It's Sperm Whale bone," he said – just a boy from St. George's

Academy playing a prank on a girl, two years before he shot himself in the head. They were so young.

But then Creeley roared with booze and amphetamine-fed rage and threw himself on G, hammering and pounding – a literary lion gone berserk, his wrath far in excess of anything G could have deserved, though, remembering her own earlier disenchantment, A understood Creeley's refusal of G's imitation comic-strip character. She saw G straighten with shock and deliberate for a brief moment about whether or not to deck his clay-footed would-be killer. After Ed Dorn and some others had peeled Creeley away from G, A took him outside and wrapped him in cooing condolence. This was no time for judgment.

The next day, the story was all over town that Creeley had tried to kill G. They'd found out when they went down to visit Carrots at Ebbe's place. A sat on the mattress staring idly at the evidence of a recent Pete Oxhead visit – a row of cigarette ends turned upside down and left to burn out – and wondered why there hadn't yet been a fire at the Pender Street house. Carrots popped up, grinning, from behind the kitchen counter, whipping a bottle of Berry Cup from its brown paper wrapping, and told G of the rumour. A heard G, feigning nonchalance, tell Carrots that Creeley was just drunk – he'd even tried to punch Dorn out earlier. The light fell away as G and Carrots talked, two shadows against the window. Behind them, the lights came out across the water from the downtown. The Shell sign floated above the barge anchored in the harbour just as it had for Malcolm Lowry. Five years later, G and A would go to a poetry reading in Detroit and Creeley would smirk with his gaze dropped in shame for the memory. Pawing at the floor with an apologetic foot, he would look up at A who would feel her face refuse the absolution he was asking for.

But here now, in the story, back on Main Street A has turned to Feather and said, "Sparrow Matbooze will have a field day with this one." Feather burst into tears, which A thought was a strange response until some time later when

Feather told her she didn't even know who Sparrow Matbooze was. Feather felt insecure, and like they say now, marginalized around all these literary folk, despite the fact that all the men wanted either to fuck her or protect her – probably both – though in the condition Feather was in, A couldn't see how they could do both. Feather McFiddle-Dee-Dee, A called her, and so did the rest of them. She would let some of them lie with her, but the abortion was still too recent and traumatic an event for her to take on anything serious. She was funny; she drank until she vomited her teeth down the toilet and, swaddled in heavy scarves, had to make her way down back alleys to the dentist to have them replaced, the plumber having failed in his efforts to retrieve them. Wrapped like an Arab in her bedspread burnoose, she drank with Carrots and Ebbe, who were frequent callers.

"Trust M to bring in the marines," A said, "and a host of Hollywood actors and comic strip characters besides."

But A had a sense of M's serious side, his solidity and his elegance, which she didn't want violated by his affiliation with G's hyperbolic presentation of multiple personae. M was Comforter, source of solace in a wacky world. She liked him just to be there, a big gentle person. If he went crazy, things would come undone. Once, still in the Future, she'd heard him crooning into his wife's black despair in the middle of a summer night on the edge of the water at Yellow Point and had felt justified in her sense of him as protector against the darkness, although she knew that was an estimation of him, a burden he'd probably just as soon not bear. You could tell that by the way he erupted when he unplugged the restraint and let all that exuberance run. You could tell that by the way he drove a car.

But it was certainly true that restraint went out the window that summer the American poets came to town. It was as if all that waiting around the edges of Ebbe's room had finally paid off. M, of course, had turned it into metaphor, but A doesn't believe metaphor is worth a damn unless it is grounded in the actual. "Unremittingly referential," G calls her when she attempts to sort out the names behind the names in the story they are writing now about the stories they were making up then.

"But I have to have it come out of my bottom nature," A wails, "and I can't unless it has some ground in theirs, in it ."

So she reads M's writing as metaphor grounded in the events of that summer. "How are we going to get out of this jam we're in?" she hears them ask, but she has to know what the jam is, first. Her friend Rob always said that A began her stories "Shortly before I was born… ", but it's probably worse than that. All around the edges, there are other stories going on, and like their friend, Greg, she wants to paint every leaf on the tree and knows she never can. They are both dead, these beloveds, but their words are part of A' s world forever. They become their words and sound in A's heart and mind, resonating there, making rings in the tree of time, tree of the world, torn out when time ends, according to the Norsemen who are A's ancestors, so how can she believe in anything uprooted? Anchored in words, she is anchored in the world, but it's a speaking world for her, first, not a writing world first, as it is for G. "We have come to bring you metaphors for your poetry." Old Georgie Yeats knew what to do to hang onto her man, but A can't do it. It's cheating, A thinks; uprooting is cheating. It's ungrateful. Perhaps because she's been uprooted so many times. By her mother, by G, moving from place to place. No refuge for him save in words written, a place on the page. For A, there's a place on the page when it's anchored to speech, to the real words that real people speak when they make up the world. Writing is the effluvia that remakes the world when it's read and anchored by its readers to the world again. No ideas but in things. Writing is deepest solace.

It was a summer of writing, that summer, or of waiting for there to be writing. Vancouver was invaded by the American poets, but it was a summer of other things as well. It was the summer A's life began again, moved in a new and bewildering direction. Cultural holocaust, another uprooting. Soft springtime rain, people tumbling about in the warm rainy nights. Two years later, Jack Spicer drunkenly stumbling through a bed of daffodils carefully laid out by Japanese gardeners – no tiptoer through the tulips, that one. Abominably dressed in a white sports jacket flecked in black, leftover stylelessness of the fifties, worn in honour of a dinner at the university faculty club whose flower beds he was destroying. Strange ugly Persephone, going to hell in his own way. This was only a prelude of things to come later that summer. Alien Ginseng in white robes, rushing about the Chalkfists' garden, looking for his hungry fix, a boy, any boy, a jar of KY jelly in his hand. "I have seen the best minds of my generation."

But they were having fun, these poets, being lionized and listened to by hundreds of us, all sitting at their very clay-ey feet, eyes open, ears cocked. Gaston Helios turning a UBC auditorium into an open field in which he was dancing, dancing, dancing to the sound of his own song. My mother was a falconress. Naomi with a long black shoe. The first time A heard "Kaddish" on tape, it shattered her. And Chelsea Octopod, giant man in workman's boots, Colossus of America, striding across three countries and up the aisle of a Vancouver classroom, towering above everything, fell in love with a teenager. All the young men were in love with Bobbie Creeley – beautiful, fierce, disdainful, Helen, high on her tower, impossible love of the prince of these islands. All the young poets fell in love with Robert Creeley, quoted him all over town. Oh it was high romance. We had never seen anything like them before. Mythical bestiary come to life in Vancouver, shining on their pedestals – words, words, words, all over everything – patches, illuminations, branded into consciousness.

Furd and Polly had a party. Their little three room apartment was jammed with the poets, thronged with adoring fans. Furd's home-made brew supplied most of the refreshment at that Dionysian frenzy – that summer equivalent of a rock concert in a very small space. The anonymity of astonishment enacted itself there. A, starting down the hall, saw

Octopod lift a long, gangly boy-girl Polly in his arms and carry her horizontally over the heads of the feeding frenzy – we all consume our gods – and launch her onto the pile of figures heaped on Furd and Polly's marriage bed. Confronted by this display of *droit de seigneur*, Furd said to the room at large, "My wife, my wife," a small protesting voice drowned in a sea of noise. Polly smiled her benign indulgent smile. She never lost her head, never would – looked on tempests and was not shaken. Built houses, raised her children, taught her classes, provided lasagna for the visiting poets, wrote her articles, swam in the lakes, travelled with Furd all over the world, kept a purse full of medications for whatever ailment she confronted. Polly and M were both like that – still points in a churning world. A could not sustain herself in the midst of it. What is this animal, she thought, all arms and legs, entangled limbs and steamy, laughing bug-eyed faces? The animal forced her down the hall, ejected her into the room where Hannah Chalkfist, from the bed said, "Poor girl, are we frightening you?" A disappeared. Outside in, inside out. G found her some time later, wandering on the street, feeling the air in front of her face, speaking in tongues. She had no idea of who she was or what had happened in that chasm of consciousness. The light foot hears you and the darkness comes. What did you do to us that summer? What did we let ourselves in for? It was an enchantment. The lovely enchantment of words. Did you save or damn us? You American poets, bent on your own salvation, damnation. Explosion of light – bodies and words.

Eventually, the police came and broke the party up. The neighbours were complaining, they said. "What neighbours?" asked Furd, who was worrying about his illegal home brew. They lived above a print shop, empty at this time of night. "Us," said the police, whose shop was around the corner. The hangover lasted for decades. Did we ever recover? No, thank God. Yes, thank God. That was the real writing on the wall. They marked us as their own. We had to write our way out of that rapture we'd been caught up in, not to be overcome by it. D moved to California and became friends with Helios, became a writer. Furd and Polly moved to Albuquerque to study with Creeley. M failed Russian 200 nine times, lost in another language until he finally found his own by becoming an actor, finds it now in crazy rhapsody, this writing. G, caught in the rapture, wrote himself into being. A lost her language, lost it again, years later in a Jack Spicer poem, opened her mouth in a seminar, lapsed into Babel-gabble and silence, wrote herself out of silence in G's office, listening in the middle of the night to the language whispering in the room all around her, talking amongst itself, was healed by another one who had been wounded by it – Robin, playing tape of man singing in ancient Greek: "Of arms and the man, I sing," he sang, playing tape of Dada babble gabble that, with extraordinary effort, resolves itself into a single word: "Ich." Isn't that where we all begin? That separation? The creaky sound of one's own voice, as Bobbie Creeley Louise Hawkins has it? Furd breathing his name with a sigh: "Wah, wah," trumpet wailing, baby bleating, crying in the dark following the blossoming of the light we are born into. Later, when Sheila Watson sang her inside out, A would begin to write for the first time. But this isn't A's story. It is their story – story of the little joy-boys still dancing, dancing, over the hills and far away into their battle, their rapture, with words.

CHAPTER NINETEEN

Ten days before we meet Brian Stewart, Dave Powell and Danny Charles [the painters from Chapter 15] for the first time, and exactly two weeks before the party at Gerry Lambskin's, A,G,D, and M gathered in the TV studios of CBC for a program CBC called "Youth," which our heroes, despite their willing participation, called "Youthless." It was very popular with all manner of persons in the Lower Mainland and Northwestern Washington, not for any intrinsic merit but because there was nothing else to watch on CBC on Saturday mornings, and because you never knew what the one called G would do next. The week before, he had unzipped, rezipped, reunzipped, rerezipped his fly quicker than a lizard snags a waterbug, and (no tape) people were still disputing among themselves whether it had happened or not. Word of mouth saw to it that the sets were tuned to this show in the Stewart and Powell households. What would those college cutups do this time!?

The producer had wanted to ban G from future shows but had caved in when A, D, and M objected and threatened to walk off: yes, thought Melchior Mobb-Barnsley bitterly, he could find another quartet of UBC twerps, just like that!, but one or more of them would likely prove even less ductile than the shitpiles he was currently using. And these four were undeniably photogenic, Melchior said to his fiancee, Fiona Futt-Tweenie. "For horror-films, darling," Fiona had replied, unkindly close up. She was jealous of A. "Well, at least, they can talk," he had growled, like the silly young middle-aged bear that he was, and so teddibly kewt, thought Miss Futt-Tweenie to her adorable self.

Her man Melchior was unjustifiably proud of his program, an earnest public-service CanContent feature in which university undergraduates held forth on various topics of current interest while the rest of the Provincials learnt how to chatter by studying their behavior. It was for this that D,A,G,M (Dam with the Silent Gee, as they were known, with deliberate irony) practised practically incessantly their party-going; at these events, one talked against rigorous obstacles – ukelele-playing, increasing intoxication (especially of oneself), intellectual brilliance (Angus Cary) or its simulation (Liam Chutney), but above all else, one's own ignorance. One learned adaptation. At first reluctant, D had eventually caught on, and began to say that he had read books that he hadn't. Even without Cliffnotes, after a number of these parties he knew what to say about them, these great masterpieces that he would one day get around to (if only these parties would stop!). From this, he in fact learned almost as much as he did when he did come, years later, under duress of graduate school, to actually read these repulsive tomes – *The Faerie Queene, All For Love, Moby Dick, The Collected Poems of Bliss Carman,* or the book Wystan Buckett (pron. Boostit) referred to as *Lord Weary's Asshole.*

Wystan Buckett was an exchange teacher from Brighton & Hove Redbrick College, whose parties some held superior even to Tarragon Chalkfist's. While weed was introduced to one at the latter's, fine wine flowed (like rye whiskey elsewhere in Vancouver) at the highly permissive entertainments of Wystan and Desirée Buckett. D preferred the Bucketts' because one was less likely to be lectured and hectored there, and because D didn't smoke dope. At Tarragon and Hannah Chalkfist's, the only place where one could get stoned on a regular basis, one might then smile at this paradox: Life was Real, Life Was Earnest there, whereas it was so only through the negation of such an attitude or policy, chez Buckett.

This worked better for D Broadbent. As it probably did, he mused, for Malcolm Mandrake, otherwise 'M'. He was distressed to know that George Delsing ('G') and Angelica Helsingfors ('A') were being drawn more and more into the Chalkfist ambience. They were going to get so American, hanging out with those two yanks, one of whom had actually gone to college with Gaston Helios, the Neo-Romantic poet and preacher, doyen of San Francisco in these late 50s and early 60s that supply the materials for this account of a couple of weeks in 1961. Buckett, of course, being British, could fake being serious as readily as he could fake being frivolous and trivial: "We're the West-Sussex Bucketts," he had said to the people sitting on his rug, and giving his name the West-Canada sound that synonymized with 'pail'. "The Worcestershire Bucketts pronounce it 'Boosh-it'." ("Marvelous," said Eduardo Viejo Pink-Meadow-Pink in a loud aside to D, "What I always say. Boosh it first and find out its name later, if any.") "Then again, the Northumberland Bucketts pronounce it 'Botch-it'."

"Wyst, what? 'Bat shit'?" D inserted.

"Ha ha, haven't heard *that* one before," replied Buckett, imperturbably beaming. "I've even heard there's a London branch – not too well-connected, y'know, come dahn a bit in the old standard of living, like, holed up somewhere like Stepney, and they pronounce it 'Bouquet'. As in (and he sang: it was horrible) 'A bouquet of roses/ for you and for me'. Ha ha 'bat shit' how about that. So" – and he put into words what D had already thought – "you louts and lubbers can call me anything you feel like from bat shit to bouquet to botch it to bucket as long as you don't kick it and as long as you don't call me before ten in the morning, and as long as you remember that high expectations breed misanthropy. Now who would like another glass of this splendid Kelowna Red? You, Eduardo?"

And Eduardo did have another glass, one in a long but not infinite series, for the sequence came to an end sordidly some twenty years later when his radio fell, or was dropped by himself (or another), into the bathtub of his California home where he had gone to sponge off the evidence of a three-week bender. Never again would D have to enter Eduardo's filthy house at three in the afternoon to find his friend sitting, surrounded by his circle of fifths, on a grungy green couch watching a TV screen gone equally green and grungy from overuse and neglect while a long-dead seagull simmered unwatched in a pot atop a stove inch-deep in grease. Never again would he have to kidnap and deliver him to Bel Azur Retreat (while Eduardo had some money left) or to the county treatment center (after the money had been pissed away: half a downtown block of Regina). And never again would he sit with his old friend and bathe in the glow of his permissive yet waspish personality. To this end came all Eduardo's charm, gifts and gaiety! (Was D today writing of it to deny that churchyardy *Aufgehoben*?) And at what ends would D and his bright young chums arrive, long years or short down the so-thought road? D-on-the-rug certainly didn't want to know: didn't even want to think about it, and so he dwelt in dread, and in denial of dread, and so there was that special reason for him, too, to have another hit from the wine jug. But this was before the White Flash, and the hieroglyphs, and the murder of a pop idol look-alike, and the being-kidnapped and forced into a contract with powers possibly diabolical. Before, that is, life got more interesting.

So that for now, seated on the rug at the Bucketts, getting drunk, negotiating with it so as not to show how drunk he was actually getting, listening to the insights and banalities of this dear chap from West Sussex, and being beside the rakish and consoling big-brother figure of Eduardo Pink-Meadow, D knew himself happy just as surely as A, had she been at this party, would have known he was not. And after all, D might have died that night – dropped dead on the spot or been killed by Eduardo's driving. It would falsify the record to show D at this time being aware of the falseness of his persona and the thinness of his means. At this time D was like a phrase on the board at the start of (which came along a few years later) a famous American TV show. It was all there, but only a couple of the letters had been named so far. And in this, he was not alone.

Meanwhile back at the Bucketts… what one got was the faking, which was first-rate and, as all such, an excellent challenge to oneself. Sincerity was found from within, not pounded into one from without. It was not determined in the town square. And it was seen to be an act – perhaps the finest of all acts.

Something of these musings came to D as he sat, a panelist, at the fake-wood desk (the plastic swirled to look like tree-grain) in the TV studio. The topic for today was Love: Different Things to Different Genders? It was striking in that it even referred to gender. Dictionaries had been widely thumbed.

D was going to talk about certain differences in terms of the Great Love-Pairs of the past. That is, he had been going to address this topic in this way. Until Angelica Helsingfors had said what she had just finished saying. Angelica had let loose broadside upon broadside at the good ship Male Bonhomie [v. Chapter 13], which was blocking entrance to the Harbour, she maintained, of Authenticity. Of course, she added, she realized that authenticity didn't matter to them. Show them a tale, even a little piece of one, and those escape artists would disappear down it like Alice down the rabbit hole. They were always turning into something or somebody else, were males, A informed the folk in TV land, as if death wouldn't find them anyway, anywhere, anytime: if not in Samara, then Vancouver would do. And at the end, then, what would any of them – these inauthentic males – have to show for it? Rags and patches, wandering minstrels. Always singing about their peckers. These last A referred to, D thought, as "Hooligans". (D hadn't heard of the slippery little fish that offered themselves to the hand in the luminescent surf of summer nights). "Hooligans" was about right, thought D, with a shock of surprise at the unusual application of the word.

There had been more. D sat there appalled, not so much at A's hostility as at her accuracy. Spot on, he thought, ruefully, grieving.

But not for long.

For this was *deja vu* all over again. D had confronted this during the Blitz. Authentically, he was about to be blown apart by high explosive. There was nothing he could do about it. So he began telling himself stories, stories he might hide in. He was only five, but he figured that out. He would be dead before he knew it. There was no afterlife, save for what people made up about you. Therefore, as far he was concerned, he would never die. The threat of death led to this conclusion.

Of course, says the grimly comic chap who looks a lot like you, or you, there's missing people. She left the room. She would be back.

And there are long nights… who could ever have imagined how very long some nights would be. Nights bereft of invention.

So he would defend the male illusionist, saying there are a hundred ways to feel up an elephant.

He would iterate that the basic difference between men and women concerned, indeed, the sex organ of the male, in its unpredictability. D was decades later to read a story by Winnifred Golden, about growing up in San Diego County, about these two girls, one of them the narrator, disguising themselves as boys and picking up a girl and both of them making out with her in between them in the front seat. "It was pretty squishy inside the stranger," Winnifred wrote, a sentence D would ever treasure.

But even if it isn't squishy, it can be greased to accommodate. Men, on the other hand, find their penises let them down. So no wonder all their braggadocio, their touching incredulity when they penetrate – the velvet dark. It's not like orgasms are everything. But they hadn't all heard that yet. Blame them? Blame the women for not telling them! Blame no-one. It's history. And it's specific, as in species. No wonder their bigger and bigger erections: The Empire State, the breast-phalloi of the Pyramids; or Sydney Harbour Bridge, the Albert Memorial (some guys hated their dicks), the Taj Mahal.

All of this D thought to say, none of it he said. Because, as he developed conclusions from his premises, a leap took place between his brain and his mouth, just as his turn came up. If there was no death, there was only truth. If there was death, there was only the story.

"Some nights ago a giant white flash lit up the northern sky. There was no blast nor sound. Coincidentally, hieroglyphs appeared on the wall of the Sick Brewery. Subsequently, attempts have been made to stifle any news of this. I myself was offered a choice between premature death and a cosy career in California. I accepted, but I shouldn't have. I reject these bribes, these threats. Stand forth and testify!"

But G was already speaking. "Hey, these fellas kidnapped me, eh? They said I could win the Governor-General's Medal for Poetry if I'd only keep quiet about what I saw. They told me I would be rolling in literary lolly, rewarded like no poet ever was before. But fuck them – Oh, that's 'But, fuck, them,' not 'Buttfuck them' – If I can't make it on my own, who wants it? Eh? I too saw the great white shock wave of which Broadbent has spoken to you recently. I – "

" – Aye, and I too!" put in M.
Abruptly the cameras pulled away . The producer came out of his booth.

> By yon bonnie banks and by yon bonnie braes
> Where the sun shines bright on Loch Lomond,
> Where me and my true love were ever wont to gae,
> On the bonnie, bonnie banks of Loch Lomond.

Donald the Editor wept – wept into a scrunched-up copy of *The Bad Seed*. Ugh, felt D, imagining the rough touch of the crinkly newspaper against human skin. Donald raised his head. His face was all smudgy with newsprint. It was hard not to laugh, and D opted for the easy way.

Donald regarded D with some dislike, wondering perhaps whether he ought to rebuke this tyro for his insolence. But he needed his support, not his enmity. He swallowed his pride (what a big gulp that must have been!) and smiled his charming smile.

Donald's ancestors had a proud history, including

support of Robert the Bruce in his independence battles with the Sassenach. Their ownership of Halvinch, an island on Loch Lomond was confirmed by charter of King Alexander II in the 13th century, and King David II officially recognized the family in the 14th century. Later, a clan member reached historical fame as a tutor both to the beautiful and tragic Mary Queen of Scots and to her son James (later to become James the Sixth of Scotland and First of England).

"If there's one person I know who's astute enough to get us out of this mess, it's Marianne McLuster. You can't call her – she doesn't have a phone – didn't pay the bill – she's always broke so she won't expect payment. Which is good because we can't pay anything. Take this hastily scribbled note to 1212 Haro in the West End. You have a car?"

"No."

"Is Eduardo Viejo Pink-Meadow-Pink on campus?"

"I believe he is."

"V. good. Commandeer his vehicle. I'll meet you later – say at eleven tonight. Good luck."

> O ye'll tak the high road and I'll tak the low road,
> And I'll be in Scotland afore ye,
> But me and my true love will never meet again,
> On the bonnie, bonnie banks of Loch Lomond.

But when D reached Eduardo Viejo Pink-Meadow-Pink's office, it was locked. The note on the door read "D-D-D-D-og down with the doggie flu. Must take him to the vet. Ta ta." D went to the Green Room intending to use the phone to call Montgomery Incline, CBC propsman, the only person he knew, apart from Meadow-Pink and Tommy P (currently on a bender) who had a car.

In the Green Room, however, he found Dorcas Davenport and Smetyana Gnarowski, huddled together under a mangy blanket on a leaky couch. They spoke to him and he went into a dream.

They asked him where he had been and with whom. He

replied, the $25 reply, mentioning Robert the Bruce and adding, "But Loch Lomond is loved not just for its history. As you drive from Glasgow ("frae glasgie," put in Smetyana) and the Lowlands ("Lalands"), in less than thirty miles the landscape is transformed by the grandeur of this loch and its dominating mountain, Ben Lomond.

"Real Highland splendour continues unbroken as you go up the loch and beyond into the wild and mountainous northwest. It is of this lovely loch that Scotsmen the world over sing this nostalgic song:

> 'Twas there that we parted in yon shady glen,
> On the steep, steep side of Ben Lomond,
> Where in deep purple hue the Hieland hills we view,
> And the moon comin out in the gloamin."

The twin ingenues of the UBC Players Club joined in with D on the next verse:

> The wee birdies sing and the wild flowers spring,
> And in sun shine the waters are sleepin,
> but the broken heart it kens nae second spring again,
> Tho the waefu' may cease frae the greetin."

At this point a heap of what D had taken to be old coats left over from a production of "Her Scienceman Lover" stirred, took form, spoke:

> Will you can all that crap
> Will you stow all the scots
> Will you drop dead and leave me in pea-eace
> For if ye will nae
> Like asses cease to bray
> You will all verra soon be de-cea-eased.

It was Arthur Maguey. If Oscar Wilde had been a British Columbian actor bearing a passing resemblance to Alistair

Sim and taking forever to fulfill his Arts degree requirements at the West Point Grey campus in the late 50s and early 60s of the 20th Century, he would have been Arthur Maguey. D was always pleased, in his puppydog way, to see Arthur, whose drolleries were quite to his taste. But this time, Arthur was preoccupied. The coats parted further and revealed the comely thighs of Philomena Ghastle, a stage-struck person of more than usual size and lack of talent. "G!" She cried, for it was beyond her abilities to tell D and G apart. She had always had trouble with the alphabet.

"G! How's *Hits*?" Wrong man, wrong mag.

"You mean, my dear," cooed Arthur, "'D! How's *Jackdaw*?'"

"Gee, Jack, how's *Dits*?" Was the best P.G. could manage. D's mind was working. Her parents, he recalled, had given her a convertible for getting straight Cs in her sophomore year.

"Philomena, how would you like to take me to the West End? We haven't finished reading the manuscripts yet." Philomena had submitted a suite of love-&-insomnia haiku dedicated to "One A.M."

They did not improve on the ancient form.

"You can let me off at the G," A.M. put in. "Together with these young beauties. I know you can't join us. Since your speech therapist sees you tonight."

He next indicated the frowsy duo blending in with the stuffing of the other couch. "*If* they have the price of a beer between them."

As these five crossed campus, they spotted the lean, Piers-Plowman form of Prester John sloping towards the library, with Amanda Tunefork in close attendance.

D went into another dream.

It was in one of Prester John's poetry writing workshops that D resolved never to present one of his own poems to the students for comment when he should have a poetry writing workshop of his own.

D was sitting there, one of the dozen around the long, seminar table, but, unlike them, playing footsies – legsies, actually, that had started out as footsies, but had quickly advanced – with Amanda, the most conventionally gorgeous of the females present. Unlike most of them, but not all of them, for G was also playing legsies with Amanda – D had sneaked a peek, after counting one too many limbs down there; sure enough, one of Delsing's desert boots was rubbing up the inside of Amanda's toreador-panted legs. (This must have been a little while before G met A.) Playing legsies with Amanda Tunefork made D nervous. It was a delicious distraction amid the boredom of listening to other people's stupid poems, but D was pretty sure that Prester John himself was getting into Amanda's toreadors and he didn't want to fall foul of this father figure upon whom his grade depended. It hadn't been D's idea. Amanda had initiated the action. But it felt good, and D was bored. He was also programmed to be chivalrous, to accede to a lady's request, however dumbly delivered. He didn't really know what to do with Amanda if she did want him to go further, as he was already involved with Beth, had a full course of studies, his nightclerk job at the Roundtowner, and an obligation to spend Hockey Night in Canada with Tommy P once a week. He had also promised himself, in his spare time, to complete the seduction of Tamara Nevers, the scandalous wife of Dean Rind, who had allowed him, the previous year when they had found themselves alone in Notting Hill together, to insert her tampax for her. It had been by hand that time, but she had declared to D that, should the situation ever arise again, she would permit him to push it in with the tip of his prick.

Last night, ah yesternight, betwixt left thigh and right
Began a poem of D's, the middle of which the reader shall be spared; it ended, of course,

I have been faithful to thee, Tamara, in my absence.
(At this time, all of D's poems ended with the "in-my-absence" phrase. When asked where he was, then, at such times, he would respond "Trapped in the poem and trying to get back to my desk.")

Those who knew of this attraction supposed D wanted

Tamara for the usual reasons men wanted her – her full red mouth, top lip flattened back as though she had spent her formative years staring up at a waterfall exploding upon her face; her big breasts, made, she maintained, only for grown men, never for a baby, to suck on; her long legs (of which more shortly), her risqué – if not actually foul-mouthed – small talk, her heavy head of hair, carrot-top from a bottle that had never been cheap. But to D, these were all incidentals; he wanted her because her maiden name, Nevers, was the same as the surname of the girl he had fondled in Gladstone Park one teenage night, the first girl he had ever fondled, Vera Nevers. Mick, Jim, and D had met Vera in the park: they went to different high schools, but had all been in elementary school together. Mick, it was soon obvious, had seen Vera since those days. He and she strolled ahead, hand in hand, lovers in an idyll of innocence, whispering sweet nothings. Then Mick rejoined his chums, with this proposal: they should each spend ten minutes in turn with Vera; Jim first, D next and Mick last.

It was dark by the time D's turn came around, darker under the chestnut tree that draped itself like a canopy above the bench where Vera Nevers sat. D had no idea what was expected of him. He kissed her and she kissed back. He put his hand on her breast outside her clothing and she began to talk of her plans after graduation. He put his hand on her breast inside her clothing and she told him she wanted to be an actress. Telling her he was going to be a journalist, he ran his other hand up her leg under her skirt. He had nearly reached her crotch when she slapped his hand away, meanwhile discussing the relative merits of RADA or LAMDA. She was already an accomplished thespian, D noted, for she hid her sexual excitement very well behind a calm and matter-of-fact exterior. But now it was Mick's turn, as Mick came to say, looming out of the September Cricklewood night. Vera greeted him a trifle too warmly, D felt. He had grown accustomed to her unruffled manner.

After they had walked her home, Mick said to D and Jim,

"What did you get?" Titty, they both told him. "Is that all?" Turned out Mick had gotten, whatever that might have meant, "Everything." He had been much longer than ten minutes, certainly. Poor, benighted girl! Felt up by three different pairs of male hands, warm young unaccustomed hands feeling all over her young body, her delicate and rewarding nervous system! Had she bought into the patriarchal system, or hadn't she? Unhappy wretch!

D had taken Vera out on his own a couple of times after that, but, whether in the bushes by the tennis courts near the pool in Gladstone Park, or in the bushes behind the Bull-&-Bush on Hampstead Heath, his progress had been arrested at the breast. That he had found thrill enough at fifteen. He never was to hear Van Morrison singing "Brown Eyed Girl" without remembering Vera, although he couldn't recall what colour her eyes were. What had become of her? He had not ever seen her name when watching British TV. Maybe she had changed it, although Vera Nevers sounded poetic enough to D's poetic ear.

Yes, Tamara Nevers-Rind was fun to be with, a challenge to try to fuck, an attraction-repulsion pain to be infatuated with, and perhaps her being a Nevers wasn't all that crucial. She was theatrical, and D was a sucker for theatrical people. She was one more claim, however, on D's time, and so he worried that Amanda Tunefork would prove, even if laid, an embarrassment. But legsies with A.T. sure made Garlin Scott Crankshaft's poetastings more palatable. Soon, it would be D's turn to read, and he could hardly wait. He had knocked off two new Audenesques only the night before. But he worried that he wouldn't be able to give an adequate reading while intwining his nether limbs with Amanda's. He would have to relinquish to G the sole rights for as long as he himself was reading. He resolved to read the sonnet, not the sestina.

But before D could read, Prester John interposed with a new poem of his own that he had decided to read to them, he said, because it shared something with Garlin's last poem.

What had Garlin's last poem concerned? Or his first, for

that matter? Anyway, John was reading by now, a sad twinkle in his bright birdlike brown eye. Some fish had swum up his private creek and his cat had stalked them. Then the fish had swum off and the cat had licked its paw. The poet had seen all this from the crotch of a hemlock. So what? Jejune D was embarrassed for the great man, so obviously pleased by this piece of crap. He understood that it meant something in Existentialism – "The cutthroat trout flick off to other banks" – but again, So what? D then and there resolved never to repeat this move himself. He often forgot this resolve, but he always regretted it.

If you wanted poetry, D thought, hazily, not making the connection yet to his own practice, you had to listen to Tamara when on a roll. He remembered her staggering back home from the Spanish restaurant near the Ladbroke Grove tube where they had dined on calamari and some powerful Roja, and Tamara talking about women's legs. She went into peals of laughter – our young D was a sucker for women whose laughter pealed. "Legs like Indian clubs – legs like milkbottles – legs like pipe cleaners – legs like carrots – legs like Waring blenders – legs like Stephen Spender's – legs like Claudette Colbert's – legs like concrete culverts...." There was the true genius of language, inspired invention tumbling out of Tamara Nevers's bright-red mouth, and D was the luckiest fellow in the world, to be strolling the Portobello Road with her arm-in-arm, headed for her flat and her tampax box.

After they had wrestled cosily, and with Tamara flat on her back on the floor, D placed his hand on her breast.

Next morning, over breakfast, D had, at her bidding, told Tamara about the play he was writing, which was based on his experiences in the Provincial Mental Hospital in Jackfish City, Sask.

"What was your scariest moment there?"

"It would have to be the time I was working nights on the violent ward. I was taking a leak and two maniacs grabbed me from behind."

"Then what?"

"I shouted and my ward-mate Phil Avecroi came running. When he saw what was happening, he blew his whistle. They let go of me. Then four guys from the day shift appeared and dragged them off and beat the shit out of them."

"That must have been a scary moment, alright," Tamara said, musing. "It must have been – it must have been like last night, when you put your hand on my breast." And she went into peal upon peal of laughter. D felt lost in her teeth, mouth and throat.

A year later, when she had returned to Vancouver (leaving D still languishing among the Young Angries in West Hampstead with his wife Georgia Littlewood), D penned her a card: I miss your laugh, your teeth, your hair,/ Your cruelty, your underwear./ Come back quick, for you I'm sick/ To push your napkin with my dick.

She replied, on a p-c of the Grand Canyon: There is a young fella called D/ Who fancies his chances with me/ If he tries one more time/ He could find it sublime/ Or told to fuck off, wait and see.

Through D's life, as through the lives of many of us, twisted this dark, glittering thread of unaccomplished deeds and vanished persons which even he would at some point cease to mourn. Ah, but how keenly real, how suddenly to memory substantial, the living flesh of undone business, washed clean of habitual, remembered replays of what didn't happen, washed with the vinegary rainlight of the dawn of that particular kind of loss – the loss of what (no doubt fortunately) one has never possessed!

It put D in mind of a late night in an after-hours jazz club at Main and Broadway where his party had drawn to it a couple of Yanks up from Seattle for the weekend. One of this pair, D had taken a shine to. He liked the way this man, Danny Schwartz, had weathered the usual Canadian flak about being a Yank, and he liked the sense of humor Danny had employed so adroitly to win these drunken bums over.

The talk had wandered into zen buddhism, currently a popular topic, and thence to a more general discussion of enlightenment. Danny Schwartz said:

"A man in a gray-flannel suit found life meaningless on Madison Avenue. He quit his job, kissed his wife and kids goodbye, and set off on a quest for the true meaning of life.

"For years he ranged across the face of the globe, swimming rivers, paddling across whole oceans, trekking through deserts in the blistering heat of the tropical sun."

"Cut to the chase," suggested Tommy P.

"He climbed a mighty mountain range because he had been told that a guru at the top knew the secret. He climbed and climbed, and he got to the top, and there sat the guru, cross-legged, his arms out sideways, index finger touching thumb in the approved manner. 'O Holy One,' our seeker exclaimed, 'I have swum rivers, crossed deserts, paddled – '"

" – the chase?" Tommy P nudged.

"'And now I come to you to ask you, 'What is the Secret of the Universe?' And the guru immediately says, 'It's the fountain.' And the seeker starts to scream, 'The fountain? I leave my job, my wife and my kids, I suffer all kinds of hardships – swim rivers, cross blistering deserts – '"

" – the chase, man, the chase," urged Tommy P.

"First eight times I heard this one, it wasn't the fountain, it was whole grain bread," said G.

"' – Climb this goddam mountain and all you can tell me when I ask you for the Secret of the Universe is "the fountain"?' So the guru looks at him for a moment and then he says, 'Oh, it isn't?'"

Danny and his buddy lived in a big house in Seattle and Danny insisted that D and Beth and their companions (Tommy P and Caroline Anthrax and G and Montgomery Incline; Ida Ride was supposed to have joined them, but had to stay home and wash her hair), should come and spend a weekend on the shores of Puget Sound.

"It's one long 32-hour party," Danny had told them. "We were all at college together. Like you guys," he added, to Tommy P's amusement. But D had lost the piece of paper that Danny had scrawled the address and phone number on. From time to time he recalled Danny and mourned this loss. He felt they were meant to be friends.

In 1971, D went to welcome the new hire of the department of English at Hydrangea State College. It turned out that Dr. Danrather Black was none other than Danny Schwartz.

"I got so sick of my family, and so into R and B," Danny, who now sported a Zapata mustache, shoulder-length hair and a hippie headband, told him, "That I changed my name. Hey, great to meet again, man! I hear the Secret of the Universe is somewhere around Hydrangea. Say, do I smell doobie?"

But that's a later tale, and Tamara Nevers, a faulty parallel. For in 1971, she had fallen from a rope bridge crossing some Andean gorge while working as a Carmelite nun with the poor and sick peasants of Peru. When he heard this news, D's first thought was "Now it's never." He was immediately flooded with a mingling of grief and abashment. Yes, D was abashed.

But that was ten years down the line.

"And to what do we owe the luminous pleasure of your dubious presence, D?" Maguey was purring, as Philomena Ghastle dragged the Buick from Dunbar onto Point Grey Road. "Why the West End, and not the G? Will you never weary of going too far? Mind you," he went on, warming to his sentences, "it becomes you, this way of toppling over without ever quite doing so. You're always adding one more brick to the stack. Why not insert having ten or fifteen beers with us in between one of your pressing concerns, and the next? Wouldn't that just complicate things," he smiled happily.

D, wanting to wipe that grin off Maguey's face, agreed to this suggestion. He figured Maguey wanted both girls for himself. So, D decided to drink with them simply to spike Maguey's plans. It was a petty gesture, one not worthy of a hero, and one – to mitigate the case against our D somewhat – of which D stayed unaware. Or does that make it worse?

The evening passed. It was all great good fun. The dark wood of the small Romanesque arches – three of them, whence beer and tomato juice were dispensed to the surly slingers, beneath the ornate clock (always ten minutes ahead), did not trouble D's vision that evening, for they were out of view from the Ladies and Escorts section.

Only when closing time was announced did D remember with a guilty start that he was on a mission. Saying goodnight to the others, he headed for Haro St. Late as it was, it was noisy in this part of town – a giggling trio of revellers brushed past.

"Aha!"

One of them was Montgomery Incline.

"Ink!" D yelled. "The very man I just remembered I'm – uh, I'm NOT – looking for. Good to see you."

The couple Ink was with were Ham and Leona Bremser.

"Hey, man," said Ham, "You bin a stranger too long. Come see us and we'll boogie on down some more."

"Don't make yourself a stranger," added Leona, who liked D's looks – legs, pants, a torso and a head. D knew how she felt. Sort of furry. Um, fuzzy, he corrected himself. Funny.

"Saw you two the other day," D blurted. "Fixing the roof."

"We were balling the jack," said Ham. "Fine day for a roof party." For an architect, he gave passable jazzman.

Leona, who resembled the Japanese version of Olive Oyl, was not exactly trapped in a preview of "The Shining." Ham was intense but laid back.

"We're going home to ball – want to watch?"

"Awfly decent of you – but cawn't, frightfly soddy," was D's offbalance reply. He reverted to this kind of English when taken aback. The last time he had watched them, it had been by accident, opening the wrong door on a drunken Sunday afternoon. What a lot of muscles and tissue had to be deployed to bring two small zones into concordance! They were certainly wrapped up in what they were about. D found himself less interested than he would have imagined. D wasn't ready to face his curiosity head-on. Besides, he recalled, "Besides, I'm on a quest. I've got to find Marianne McLuster, and I've lost her address."

"I can take you there," said Incline, the man who knows his way around and gets things done.

The Bremsers bent and screwed their ways into their own personal Hitler's Revenge and puttered off to West Van. Incline led D to a two-storey apartment building , the kind that has four or six apartments in it, and is sprayed with gray-pink stucco containing bits of colored glass.

"It's a bit late to be visiting isn't it D?" Incline wanted to know. "Unless, of course, that is, ah, well,"

"I've never laid eyes on her before," D cut in. "How late is it?"

"Oh not very, not from *my* point of view. But she's an A student. Probably studying in bed."

"We'll bring her some flowers," D told him, and began tearing up plants by their roots from the neat front yard of the wood frame house next door.

After Incline had brought him right to her door, D knelt as his partner knocked. Almost at once the door swung open and a woman more interesting than Tamara Nevers was standing there. Had D been a Sensation Type and not an Intuitive Type, he might have registered that Marianne McLuster (for it was she) was younger, more buxom, and with more and redder hair than Tamara, and with a laugh every bit as scintillating and infectious; but as it was, he would need months and years to articulate such information as he had already taken in at a glance.

"Well don't just kneel there without anyone under you," she said, "Come into my boudoir. Ink, who is this chap? He's lean but intense. Can I try him out and keep him if he passes muster?"

"Aha! This is the fellow I told you about, Marianne, the one who aided me in the art hoax – "

"I'm D," D interrupted, "and I'm in love with you. Have some flowers."

By now they were inside the apartment. For the abode of a person allegedly penniless, it was surprisingly well-appointed.

"Roots and all," said Marianne. "You don't mess around. I like that. I hope my neighbors appreciate it. I have a feeling I've seen these flowers before." She began to chop off the roots. Then she rinsed them and put them in a vase.

"I have a message for you. A problem to solve, actually." D threw himself onto the sofa. Ink hovered around Marianne.

"Uh, I warned my young friend it might be a tad too late to be knocking you up – " Ink enjoyed supplying the straight lines to such known quantities as D and Marianne.

"Never too late for that," she said pleasantly, meeting D's gaze and smiling the Smile of the Wicked Glint. "Let's drink some scotch. I studied enough tonight. I was about to go to bed and masturbate, but I can do that later. It'll be even more fun after flirting with you two charming chappies. Or maybe you could stay. Now, tell me, what's this mysterious message? You sure it was a message and not a massage? I think I'd rather have the massage, if it's all the same to you, which it probably is not. In fact I can tell you're dying to get your hands all over me. But let's settle the lesser matter first."

She plumped herself down next to D, letting her body rest pleasantly against his. Ink continued to pace, his face going through the exaggerated contortions of a melodrama villain, as his eyes rolled to heaven at the scandal of Marianne's speech and demeanour, and his mouth pursed into a tight anus of disapproval: and this was funny, because as they both knew, Ink was unshockable, and at least as bent as themselves. But he was ten years their senior, and this masquerade of the censuring elder was one way he had of entertaining the college kids of today.

"The message is from Donald McDonald."

"Oh that dear man. I deflowered him recently, and he was so very grateful."

"?"

"A friend of mine told me that Donald had been complaining that he was still a virgin at twenty-two, so I told him to send him on over. He took me out to dinner, and then I brought him back here for dessert. He too arrived bearing flowers. A little less earthy, though. And the message? Surely he doesn't want to be deflowered again! No, no, he wouldn't send you to tell me that. What's up?"

"*The Bad Seed* has already gone to press bearing the news of a giant white flash and some resultant or concommitant hieroglyphs on the wall of Sick's Brewery. Now various agencies are saying that no such events occurred, that it is alarmist and unCanadian to give credence to any such reports, and UBC Admin has sent us a red-alert memo that the paper's to say nothing about all of this. When tomorrow's issue appears, we'll all be canned."

"Who put this story in there?"

"I did," D allowed modestly.

"Aha! Once the hoaxster, always the hoaxster," cried Ink. "I've trained you well, my boy!"

"No hoax," D said. "I saw the flash, I saw the hieroglyphs. There's something big being covered-up here."

"It's just a female torso, sweetie," said Marianne. "44-28-38."

"And you mean to expose it!" added Ink.

"I don't want to get expelled from college. I worked for a living far too long," D answered, although it might be fun to suppose that line was Marianne's.

"And it's too late to stop the presses? What if you simply don't distribute it?"

"The advertisers will sue. And that'll be the least of our worries. Anyway, it's being distributed at this very moment. You see, I was supposed to get here about four o'clock this afternoon. But the only ride I could get off campus took me straight to The Georgia."

"He's not ALWAYS irresponsible," Ink interjected. "He's almost a Family Man."

"Almost?"

"Ah well uh, there is a wife or two at home. But I know you'll be charitable," said Incline, going to bat for his buddy D.

"Yes I feel quite charitable where this young man is concerned, and boy does he ever look concerned! – I look forward to meeting your wife," she added, looking directly into D's slightly evasive gaze. "What's she like?"

"Well she's a lot like you," D found he had said, tactlessly.

"An honest answer. Then no doubt I shall like her. Love her, even," smiled Marianne McLuster. "Red hair? A lawyer into bohemians? Smarter than you? Big boobs? Born and raised in Moose Jaw?"

"All of the above," replied D, awed by this psychic divination of geography and topography.

"Don't be awed by my psychic powers," she told him. "Do you know Tamara Nevers?"

D saw that Tamara Nevers, too, was a redhead built along the lines sketched in so recently. He saw also that Vancouver, if you had gone to high school there, was a small town.

"Don't you KNOW?"

"I do now," she said pleasantly. "Thought she might be your type."

D was still baffled by the discovery that he had a type. He had thought he was omnivorous.

"Oh, a lot of us are redheads this year," Marianne told him. "These hair colors come and go – as I'm sure you've observed. Next year, who knows? I rather fancy a blonde Joan-of-Arc hairdo myself."

"It would look ravishing," Incline said. When the propsman and hoaxster indulged in flattery of the female, his strange posture became even more pronounced. The torso bent one way, the neck and head another, while one arm was semi-extended, the hand with one finger up saying "Whisst!" The other arm, bent double, was up behind its shoulder-blade, a balancing act. His blue-black hair, slicked straight back, allowed several strands to fall across his forehead; his eyes glittered like pieces of anthracite. His nose was straight and his face halfway between humourous and handsome, the skin white like that of one long in city pent.

"I'll play Warwick to your Joan of Arc any night of the week," he added, with the usual over-emphasis that rendered all of his words camp, thus empty of primary meaning, so that signification ping-ponged behind the spoken lines. Incline's was a parodist's nature. One of his allusions here was to a recent production of *The Lark*, which had included both D and Incline in its star-studded cast of amateur thespians, although Incline had not played Warwick. That vital but woodenly-written role had fallen to the lot of M.

The play had been adjudicated by Someone from Back East, someone therefore Important, D realized, beyond any importance any mere Vancouverite could ever – in Vancouver eyes – attain to. After the play ended, this worthy gave his public summing up. D was pleased and surprised to learn that he, D, had given this savant "a moment in the theater." The best critique of his acting D had received up until then had been of his role as Colonel Sir Francis Chesney in *Charley's Aunt*, from Fee McMannic: "You looked like you were standing next to your character saying 'if I were going to act this role, here is how I'd do it.'" Spot on! D's subconscious yelled, as D tried to come up with something equally hurtful to say to Fee.

The difference this time, D reflected, as the adjudicator rambled on, was the leek. As La Hire, the rough soldier friend of Joan, D had to eat a leek on stage each night. It had grounded him.

The nightly leeks were supplied by Incline, who doubled as propsman. Ink liked to tell everyone that D took a leak on stage every evening. It was a pun that linked up with Ink's sponsorship of *Tobacco Road*, that play where a character does fake a leak on stage every evening. It was the outrage of two little old ladies over this act which Ink, the production's publicist, overhearing in the lobby, encouraged, advising them to carry their complaint to the police.

The police came to watch the play, and shortly thereafter closed the show. This led to a court case (at which Erskine Caldwell, the playwright, testified) and the subsequent reopening of the play, whose "redeeming social features" outweighed the indecencies of public urination or simulation thereof. The lines stretched round the block. It was Ink's first successful ruse, and he never missed an opportunity to recur to it, directly or otherwise.

Returned to the present, D listened with alarm as the adjudicator panned the production. One "moment in the theater" wasn't enough for him, it transpired.

The show stank. The hiss of air escaping a dozen punctured balloons was metaphysical. But someone would invigorate even this cast party. . . .

In *The Lark*, after Joan has been martyred, Warwick declares, "We made The Lark into a giant bird, who will soar the skies long after our names are lost and forgotten." At the party, Ink went around announcing, in his stagiest manner, "We made The Lark into a giant turkey thanks to which our names in this town will never, damnit, be forgotten!"

Marianne and Montgomery were trying to solve D's little problem.

"Say it's a hoax. You put out one hoax issue a term, right? Say that this one is it."

"That's right," said Ink, "Have a rubber stamp made and stamp every copy."

"There you go," said Marianne. "Well, the rubber-stamp shops don't open for another six hours. What shall we do till then?"

"But there are other stories in this issue," D wailed. "The story about the rapes in Nightingale Hall, for instance. The story about Otto Hunzinger's huge donation to the Art Gallery. The story about President McGonnigal getting a big award. The story about Prester John winning a Canada Council grant. The review I wrote praising the issue of *Jackdaw* I've just put out."

"Aha, it's a lesser-of-two-evils choice, Broadbent."

"You have only these alternatives," said Marianne.

"How am I going to stamp every issue before the students hit campus?"

"We'll help. Won't we, Ink? And Donald must help, too. I'm sure I can get him up."

"And I know a little old rubber-stamp maker who is in his shop by six every morning," added Ink.

"Four hours to party," calculated Marianne. So party they did.

They partied, teeny-boppers, by getting Uncle Ink to take more medicine and then tell them (for maybe the tenth time) about some of his principal japes, the ones before their time and the ones they had played bit parts in. Ink embellished. Each time, something new and untrue would have been added; the stories grew. It was a lot like Homer.

D liked particularly the one where Ink, forbidden by city officials to paste a poster announcing a play on the walls of a new civic building, had let it be known – widely – that he would go ahead anyway. On the night he had named, Vancouver's Finest gathered in force to preserve law'n'order. Punctual to his schedule, Ink had made the poster appear.

He was projecting it via magic lantern from a storefront opposite the public building. Police wanted to arrest, but several of Ink's old lawschool associates were on hand to opine that Ink was doing nothing illegal.

It took considerably longer in the telling as Ink told it. Many personalities had been involved at one or another stage of this scheme, and Ink had to evoke each and every one of them. But it wasn't exactly boring. No, mused D, thinking how to convey the experience to a future generation, it was rather like having Eugene O'Neill's father do the Count of Monte Cristo with the intermissions handled by Clarence Darrow doing *Sunshine Sketches of a Little Town.*

Nearing dawn, with Ink on bathroom break, Marianne asked D about the flash and the wall-writings. He told her all (Ink, returning, hushed up for a spell), and she accepted the truth of it – phenomenologically, anyway. D thought Ink wasn't so sure. He smelled hoax.

"It reminds me," he began, "Of the time when – "

Daylight arrived.

"The rubber-stamp, Ink!" his audience carolled.

D and M were in Nanaimo. D had been suspended from campus for two weeks for his part in the hoax-hoax issue; a light enough punishment. Donald McDonald had been threatened with expulsion. In order, he said, to save the hallowed name of Clan McDonald from further shame, Donald had gone on his knees from Brock Hall to the chapel, where he had repeated "Mea culpa" one hundred times. The entire route had been lined with Sciencemen in their red sweaters, granted special dispensation by Dean Brute to pelt the ex-editor of the hated Bad Seed ("tells the truth about Engineers") with the veggies left over from an agricultural experiment that went wrong some weeks before.

M, ever eager for excuses to goof off, had generously offered to accompany D. Besides, there was less likelihood, they hoped, of being kidnapped here. Foreigners seldom arrived at Nanaimo: they couldn't pronounce it, so how could they ask for directions to it?

D was sick and tired of campus and of the plot of the novel he was now trapped in and created by. His arm still ached from his part in stamping one thousand copies of a newspaper. (He and Ink had tired of this solution and had dumped the remaining nine thousand copies in the ocean off Wreck Beach; two days later, several soggy masses – happily unidentifiable – washed up on Gambier Island; the locals dried them out then built fires with them to heat their primitive huts. Ham Bremser, in on the caper (not the kind of secret Incline could keep), called to say a wad had ended up on the beach in front of his house. Leona was using some of it to clean her paintbrushes.

Beth had more-or-less tossed D out for being gone all night and not phoning her; she needed time to get over it, D figured. And Marianne had taken off with Donald once the deed had been done. She, too, would think differently soon. He relaxed, there by that still, northern sea, lapped in the syllables from the mighty mouth and mind of M.

"To a man of my intelligence, the proliferation of literary magazines is scandalous. If this seems a reactionary attitude, let me remind that nine times out of ten, to be reactionary is to be right. There is a horrible phenomenon whereby our bright, mindless progressing is making new problems for us faster than we can solve the old ones. This is so in literature as in politics, economics and science. And in literature it tends particularly to a geometrical rather than an arithmetical rate of increase, as each creative work automatically spawns a squadroon of critical material.

"Everyone is so busy vomiting creativity that we have more art than life. To combat this noisome imbalance I propose the banishment of any would-be writer to the frog mines for a term of not less than a dozen years. And if this experience only inflames him with an austere passion to transcribe into little tracts his found bonds with the workaday earth and his workaday fellows, why then chuck him back for as many more terms at hard labor as may be necessary to break and humble him." M barely paused, sure of D's attention, or indifferent to it.

"Writers, by and large, have the emotional tonus of a squid – all mushy and grasping, gutless and tenacious. The plain fact is that the army no longer absorbs enough of our youth. So they go to the universities, learn about sides to take on moral and political issues, and write. When they are too lazy and poor to go to the universities they compensate by becoming socialists, and writing.

"Despite the generic imbecility of fiction as a literary craft, I think the poets are the more personally disgusting group of artists. Present company possibly excepted – but only if you let me keep your Sigma Tau Xi badge and the pen from San Francisco with the woman who undresses every time it is turned upside-down.

"They are inevitably clever, in the unassuming rote way which is the product of tacking to the dogmatic sensibility of the trained and uneducated mind the most subtle and ghastly quirks and personal nuances of Neo-neurosis."

"Neo-neurosis?" Queried D mildly. He had scarcely heard a distinct word M said. The mellifluous, trenchant harangue appeared to excuse thought and put one on the shortcut to mindless pleasure. But D felt he ought to do something in return.

"Neo-neurosis, D: ivy-league haircuts – heavy blue-black hornrims – "

"Oh, like Jack – "

"Exactly – the man with all the pens in his breast pocket – your powers of observation are improving Broadbent – on with excoriation – homebrew (beer or saki) – "

"B-b-but Beth and I brew both – you came by two Sundays ago because your bootie is doing time – "

"Yes and when Serena spilled some on her velvet dress, it left a big bare patch as if some cricket eleven had played a five-day test on her midriff! On with excoriation – U. of Cal., U. of Iowa – ceramics – Horizon – PMLA – Evergreen Review – sociologists studying Judaism – mobiles in the living room – old kitchens – Danish modern – wedding rings made by artist friends – "

"You mean like Angus Cary and Harry Bale – "

" – three children – taking an interest in architecture – VWs – obviously loving one's spouse – marinas – belles with extravagant overbites majoring in Slavonics seduced by European exchange students – "

"She wasn't worthy of you, M, you have Serena now – "

" – Poetry about jazz musicians – poems about Dylan

Thomas and Rilke – quotations from Dante – John Cage – Karlheinz Stockhausen – Ingmar Bergman – "

"Oh no, not Ingmar Bergman! He wanted to give me a part in *Summer with Monika*!"

"He did? What happened?"

"I got in a fist-fight with the head of the studios. Over his waif."

"Waif or wife. It's the story of your life. On with excoriation – Ingrid Bergman – Audrey Hepburn – Marilyn Monroe as 'sensitive actress' – Club Nine – College Board exams – Adlai Stevenson – driftwood sculpture – guitar-playing folksingers – Charlie Parker – in a word, Barney Rosset. Note that I did not mention beards."

D had been wondering when M's list would reach Beards.

It's difficult to recall in 1998 what fury beards aroused in the usual onlooker in 1961. The usual cleanshaven or naturally beardless persons who came and went about their civic business in Vancouver then. Passing motorists would wind down their windows and shout "Hey, Fidel!" at D or M walking down the street. It was not meant to be a friendly greeting. Old ladies (old, and thus presumably beyond the sexually predatory orbit of these barbarians) at bus stops who would take the trouble to cluck deprecatingly and say, "What a pity you cover up your face that way. We can't see how good-looking you might be." Random thugs who wanted to smash in your face who didn't know why and didn't care to. "Hey, beatnik!" What could the subtext be, D wondered, years ahead of that term. Were they reminded, with an unpleasant shock, of "hairs less in sight, or any hairs but these"?

Mind you, there were beards and beards. M's – couldn't G see this? – had fled his scalp to flourish on his cheeks and chin. It was luxuriant. D 's was sparser. During his brief courtship of Frederica Henry, D was sitting one evening having a brew with Mr. Henry, a superintending sort of chap and man of few words. Eventually he spoke. "It's like a forest where the underbrush has been cleared," he told D. "Do away with it. My daughter comes with a substantial dowry, but not to a beard like that."

G had once said to D, "If I couldn't grow a better beard than that, I wouldn't grow one." And he never did.

But DHL had worn a beard, and EP, and WW, and RC, and AG. By stopping shaving, D had announced himself of their lineage. But it was a growth in part of a Bohemian gesture and therefore meriting the mindless hostility of those it was meant to shock. Decades later, pins in the tongue would constitute the same contradiction – or a gorgeous teenage head of heavy honeyblonde hair streaked frightful red, if somebody's teenage daughter's reading this.

Loggers, however, though of the square world, were allowed to go bearded and untaunted. Sea captains, Sikhs – though not untaunted for their headgear. Rum, that…

"Treatise on Beards. (Are you listening, Broadbent?) Beards are physically beautiful. Beards are spiritually beautiful. Beards are practical. These arguments will, I think, be found overwhelming, against any counter whatsoever."

The penny dropped. D realized that M was trying out on him the essay he had promised D for the next issue of *Jackdaw*.

"On with excoriation: poets inevitably have the whitest underbellies, and the yellowest teeth. And it is tacit in the ranks of the seedy intelligentsia to ignore the sinister significance of this, and pretend that great gaping souls have a veracity apart from the bodies housing them. I can never understand why the sight of the gorgeous blonde with the glassy-eyed stare is necessarily more depressing than the totally scruffy mien of the little sparrow of Cader Idris. It's past time to drop the cult of the soul and react in favor of the glistening exterior."

"You are so prescient, M," D interpolated. "I too predict the era of poets as shiny, glittering creatures, upon whose bright surfaces one will obtain no purchase. And I see them glassy-eyed too. 'Come down to earth, you shiny things!' That will be the call. But their overflowing polysemy shall be all their answer."

"Now some few," M continued, clearing his throat menacingly, as to say, 'interrupt me again at your peril, you yellow-toothed loon,' "Now some few have had sufficiently cool vision to be antipoetry, but they have let this manifest itself in the insane form of *further* literary mags –"

"*Hits*," D breathed.

" – thus by Dogman's Law (to discuss, even for the purpose of rejecting, the shoddy is to commit a shoddy act) adding to – "

"Where does Dogman's Law leave us?"

" – adding to the miasmal abundance. We must stop producing literature until everyone has a chance to read all the books existing now and discuss them with everyone else. As things stand one can't in a normal lifetime – "

"M, you will never, never have a normal lifetime! You – "*

" – in a normal lifetime read even the bibliography to a given subject. Try it. Take any subject of your choice: – 'fish' 'the English novel in the 14th century' 'trepanning' 'Wilhelm Gorgy' 'struttin' pomposity as measured in a representative sampling of Deans of Applied Science at the Canadian Universities' – you'll see that I do not exaggerate.

"*One* solid little journal devoted to both new fiction and poetry and to critical material, of one hundred pages, published quarterly in French, German and Latin, would do very nicely. We have instead a great belching, sneering glut of verbiage, soggy with concept, devoid of saving sensuality. This phlegm, this loathsome smear, this gutwrenching, fatuous dribble, this maleficent ooze, this pululating whey, this reeking and screeching flux of gelid neurotica surges across a landscape littered with the half-eaten corpses of the monolithic scriveners of antiquity – Homer, Dante, Shakespeare, Donald Culross Peattie. Why cannot we let the bones of these great men rest easy beneath the tennis courts of Goucher college? Surely it's clear now that cognition will never survive verbiage,

---

*v. Gifford, B., *Francis Goes to the Seashore*, 1982, p. 125.

that whereas 430 words might convey some crude message 4,3000,000,000,000,000,000,000,000,001,700,000,020 words can only mean confusion and heartache.

"The writer is the most dispensable man in any civilization worthy of the name. As his craft offers continual opportunity for the use of his inmost bestialities, he is not ever likely to be a very considerable human being.

"Let's have an end to his writhing and clacking."

"I'll take it," D said excitedly. "It'll fill a full three pages in *Jackdaw*. There's a satirical poem titled 'after a literary reception for a contemporary poet' that can precede your essay, and I can put an essay by G after it."

"Why would you put ANYTHING after it?" M wanted to know. "Don't you think it must be the Last Word?"

"G already paid me, uh, that is, um, persuaded me, that he should have the last place. Anyway, let him have a hard act to follow. His essay is about being dead so it'll fit in like postmortem effects following your destruction of literature for our time."

"How does his go?" M wanted to know, well aware of D's photographic memory.

"'There was one thing that bothered me that year when I was thirteen going on fourteen, and that was what it meant to be – '"

"So you really like my essay?" said M, who had stopped listening as soon as D had begun his recitation.

D was about to reassure M, but they were interrupted. Two village lasses of more than usual pulchritude and with that mix of shyness and boldness D found charming, who were walking the seawall in the other direction, spoke to our lads.

"Aren't you Wendell Corey behind that beard?" The bolder said to M.

"Aren't you Michael Wilding behind that, uh, beard?" The second blorted in D's direction.

They were chewing on Nanaimo Bars. Nanaimo Bars are

made with half a cup of butter, quarter cup of white sugar, and three tablespoons of cocoa. These ingredients are stirred together in a double boiler until smooth. Then a second layer is added, consisting of a quarter cup of butter and two cups of icing sugar, mixed into a kind of cream, to which are added (until smooth) two tablespoons of custard powder, three tablespoons of boiling water. Or sometimes only two. This is then spread over the first layer.

There is a third layer, made of two squares of unsweetened chocolate and two tablespoons of butter. This layer, melted, is spread to be a top to the bar. The whole bar is then chilled.

"Well nice talking to you," said one.

"Ta-ta," said the other.

"?" said D to M, as the girls sloped off.

"That *was* their big thrill, D," M assured him. "Let me explain something to you about Nanaimo. You will become well-known as a writer. You will read in the World Poetry Festival at Harbourfront in Toronto, accommodated in a hotel that is made for corporate chiefs, wined and dined in a different restaurant every night for a week. Phyllis Webb will be your table-mate. You will be flown to Paris to read at the Museum of the City of Paris on Woodrow Wilson Avenue. Your writings will be translated into Italian and published in a journal so avant-garde its cover will resemble a packing box while its pages will feel like silk. The Canadian government, on behalf of its taxpayers, will give you chunks of money, and will fly you back and forth and up and down this mighty continent to carry your version of culture to the masses. Not to be outdone, the United States government will also squeeze a little largesse upon you and your poetic productions."

He broke off here to spot-kick a dead gull into the briny. The two chums had hopped down from the seawall to walk the beach proper, crunching evidence of their seashell existence as they went.

"A consortium of the thirteen western United States," M resumed, his handsome teeth flashing within his luxuriant beard, "will choose your selected poems for their prestigious award, and as a consequence, you will be flown to New York City, to the Hawaiian islands, to Anaheim even, where you will be put up in a hotel with a view of Disneyland. You will be fêted at a billionaire's mansion in Newport Beach, in a room with two grand pianos with dead animals on each, while the three-piece Creole band plays 'Banana Boat Song' following and followed by 'Yellow Bird'."

Here D interrupted. "When is this particular musical event going to happen?"

"Twenty, thirty years from today," M said, indifferently. "Depends on the outcome of the Cuban Missile Crisis."

"Well my dear M," D laughed, flashing him his most winsome look, clear sign he was enjoying this glimpse into his future and hoped to avoid abrupting it by such small correction as he now felt impelled to offer, " I expect there will be other songs by then. We cannot expect this calypso craze to continue. Why, some friends recently returned from England speak of 'a Liverpool Beat.' Who can say what songs new tunesmiths will have provided by that time?"

"No," M responded, firmly, "It will be as I say: 'Banana Boat Song' following and followed by 'Yellow Bird'. " To emphasize the finality of this judgement, he stooped to take up a piece of driftwood, which he then began to smash on a nearby rock, meanwhile screaming, "Thus perish all fetishes! Japanese fishnet ceiling draperies! Conversation-pits! Pipestem pants!"

"But M," D protested, "You're wearing pipestem pants yourself!"

"However," M resumed, as though his little fit had never been, "You will not win all the prizes. You will unaccountably be left out of several important anthologies. But those in the know will quickly figure out what petty jealousies and disgraceful self-serving resentments were the cause of these anomalous exclusions. They will remember whom you reviewed with brilliant malice, and how they or their friends decided to pay you back. No, D," M concluded, becoming stentorian so as to indicate the end was nigh, "Your fate shall be even as I say. The rewards, while puny compared to what you might make in a dedicated lifetime of real estate dealings, will be immense compared to the common lot in these matters. When publishing becomes extortion – sometime in the late 80s, I imagine – you will be required to pay less than most authors, to get your work into print and – ha! – distributed. Someone will actually try to get admitted to UWO by announcing he intends to do a PHD dissertation on your oeuvre. He will be denied admission, naturally. Someone else – "

"Huh?" said D, who had almost ceased to listen; overindulgence was catching up with him again; he had begun pretending to be the Consul in his garden at Cuernavaca: "Huh? I'll get admitted to a UFO shaped like an egg in French? How's that?"

"Even though you will become more famous at writing than any of our generation at UBC save for G – "

"Save for G?" D interceded, dismayed.

"G will be published by Penguin Books," M said, smiling fatly. "G will win three Governor General's Awards. His works will be made into movies. He will be flown to the Antipodes. He will live in Cleveland."

"What's any of this, M, have to do with Nanai-im-i-o?" D spoke from his position in the sand of Vancouver Island.

"Just this," replied M, magisterially: "After this long and distinguished career, you will suggest to a college teacher in Nanaimo that you be given a fee to read at his college. And he will report back to you, D, that you are tiny tubers in Nanaimo. That is all I know, and all ye need to know, about Nanaimo: tiny tubers." A crazed grin blazed across his hirsute countenance as he spread his arms wide like a Roman consul approving a crucifixion or a German goalie anticipating a penalty kick. "And," he ended, "I shall make this paradise my home!"

CHAPTER TWENTY

Every once in a while G found himself sitting in a chair in a classroom while a professor tried to interest a room full of poorly-dressed youth in some ideas he had jotted down for a class a few years ago. G was jotting notes himself, sometimes some pearly information about the structure of the Department of External Affairs, and sometimes about fist and stomach experiences closer to home. Closer to the Vancouver Public Safety Building than to home. What is home anyway, he jotted, making a question mark that looked like an unknown script on a brewery wall or the newest stain on D's favourite and only tie.

He was a young man in his twenties. He often thought things like this: what is home, anyway? Erstwhile classmates back in Lawrence, BC would have been impressed, had they escaped the orchard for the coast and the uni on the ocean. "Shut your face, asshole," they would have exclaimed in their admiration.

G was not happy that he had signed up for this course in Political Science. He had to take something outside his major, and he did not fancy Physics or Fish Farming 101. So Political Science it was – Ottawa in the International Community. There was really only one reason he had settled on Polysigh, and that was A. A had signed up for the course, and at the time that the school year had started, while the last tennis plocks of the summer/fall were to be heard, G was still a swain, not an accomplishment. He longed for A. He craved her from afar. As was his habit, he had been craving her for almost a year. After seven months he had managed to croak a stupid remark to her, one he regretted all that night while he tried to read an Eighteenth century novel. After twelve months he was prepared for drastic action – he enrolled in Polysigh 445.

A week into class he got the nerve to borrow two sheets of lined paper from her.

Three weeks later she got impatient with all this waiting and maneuvered him into his own bed. She managed over the next month to do this three more times. On the fourth occasion she persuaded him that she would not hate the sound of his name for all time if he put his poor shy thing right there. Yes, there. Okay, now hold still, I'll show you something.

And so on. It was not long till G was walking around with a smirk on his face. Got me a special, he was thinking. I am the man with a high feathered hat. Don't get in my way.

Till a few months later he found himself in his striped pyjamas on the Upper Levels Highway. A was at home correcting his essay on Eighteenth century fiction.

What the heck was he doing in this PS class while the world was on fire? Well, part of the world was on fire. D's tie was covered with barbecue sauce.

Now this was a very boring class because A was not attending. G tried to remember how to ogle women. There was a dark-haired, honey-eared beauty next to the window, but he could not ogle. He rolled his near eye. No use. He looked at the expanse of smooth dark skin between her short skirt and her white boot. Nothing. He needed A. The very thought of A and what she had done with the four rawhide belts stirred him. He uncrossed his legs. The short fat man with the white moustaches that seemed to emerge from his nostrils was explaining what he used to think about the post-Korea era. There was a knock at the door.

You usually didn't get knocks at classroom doors. You got students skulking in or out with a squeak. But not a formal knock at the front door. The man with the nostril moustaches did not know what to do. A petite creature with a bun of brown atop her skull got up, and without straightening to a stand-up, sidled over and opened the door. A man in an overcoat without a stain asked for G.

Happens all the time.

G walked to the back door and out into the hall. There

were now three overcoats, not a mark on them.

"What's this all about? You boys from External Affairs?"

"Shut up," was all the information he could pry from them as they walked, as if by agreement, toward the east stairs of the Gorp Building.

"I should warn you guys that I have a blue belt in Wing Ho."

Halfway down the stairs one of the men in black belted G across the back of the neck with the back of his fingers. This induced G to make his own way to the ground floor, on his knees. He managed to hold onto his notebook and the liquid in his stomach. Here we go again, he thought. At least this time I will have my regular clothes on the highway.

His regular clothes would have made a mother weep.

But they did not want him to go motoring with them. They had just wanted him to get the message.

"We've got A," said the one who had come to the door.

"Will you spell that?" asked G.

Fingers on the bridge of his nose.

"If you want to see her in one piece, be at the Sylvia Hotel at eight o'clock tonight. Come alone."

"Where in the Sylvia?"

"The bar, asshole. You think we rented you a room?"

"Where is A?" he asked, feeling for blood on his nose.

"She's with Louie," said one of the natty trio.

Then they were gone. He tried to follow them but they were experienced movers and he was just a Political Science student. It was five hours till eight o'clock.

He could go to the police. That would be the intelligent thing to do. He decided to try to contact D and M.

Where was M?

That wasn't hard to figure out. This was Wednesday afternoon, and on Thursday morning the campus newspaper, *The Bad Seed* would regale the fortunate and casual reader with the latest effulgences from the mind and memory of M, most acerb and genial critic of his generation. The deadline for his copy was five of the clock on Wednesday afternoon. At a little after three he would be at the Seed offices, sprawled in one of the old spilling leather chairs with a young female journalist placed in his care in the experimental apprenticeship programme created by Donald McDonald, editor in chief.

There wasn't anything carnal about the entwined figures in the chair. M was due to pounce upon an Underwood in half an hour or so. What he was doing in the chair, this time with the afore(a long time afore)mentioned Miss Take (at least that had been her name in dramatic-fictive life in yon Seattle) was what he called "warming up," or sometimes "priming the pump." Miss Take had the end of her tongue in M's left ear, but this was only a symbolic gesture, her tongue meant to suggest the spoken word brought to its greatest acuity, and M's ear the intelligence honed by his verbal skills. Miss Take had her right hand resting upon his groin, but there was nothing of crudity in this disposition. She was, as instructed by literary minds more trained than hers, representing the grip on essentials that M would attempt to exhibit in the quick words he would be typing in less than half an hour. The columnist and his apprentice lay quietly curled on the old upholstery, the picture of dedication, the anticipation of fiery creativity. At the moment that G entered the dank below-ground office, the apprentice was heard to offer some pre-linguistic sounds, and G knew that his old buddy would convert those sounds into wisdom, bashing out seven hundred and fifty words that would etch the feathers of the Winged Victory of Samothrace.

"On your feet, scribe," said G. "We have some saving to do. The bad guys have A."

M would get to his feet eventually. At the moment he was engaged in cataloguing the body parts of veteran newsman and tyress.

"Your descriptive efforts are succinct, but at the price of elegance," said M, attempting to dry his ear with his sleeve.

"I'll hold that," said G. "You get your column done, and then off we go."

But Miss Take only looked at him as if he were a broadcast journalist. She pouted, then sneered, then picked up her briefcase and climbed the circular staircase.

M pounded the Underwood while G tried to get D on the phone.

"I'm sorry," said the sweet voice on the line. "That is a number for which you have to dial long distance."

"Impossible. D lives in a coach house in the hoitsy-toitsy district right here in town."

"Do you want long distance?" asked the voice.

"I want my sanity," said G.

"I only work here," said the voice.

G hung up. The phone rang. It was D.

"We are in serious trouble, old chep," said D.

"Where are you calling from?"

"I'm calling long distance, so I can't talk long," said D. "Can you and M make it to the Cecil Hotel at eight o'clock tonight?"

"We have to be at the *Sylvia* Hotel at eight," said G. "They've got A."

"I said the Sylvia Hotel," said D. "*Who* has A?"

"I distinctly heard you say the *Cecil* Hotel," said G. He was trying to reach a rather long cigarette butt in a brass ashtray on the desk he was leaning on.

"This is long distance," said D, his voice beginning to sound peevish. "I don't have time to argue about hotels."

M stopped bashing the Underwood long enough to listen to half of the conversation.

"Where are you calling from?" asked G. "Can you make it to the Cecil by eight o'clock?"

"Not the Cecil. The Cecil is where all the Caribbean poets and actors drink. I am talking about the Sylvia Hotel. Over by the water."

"Well, just about any Vancouver hotel you can name is pretty near the water," said G.

"Let me talk to him," said M. "You finish my column. Mention Jean Paul Sartre."

"I'm not that crazy about Jean Paul Sartre," said G. "What about Samuel Beckett?"

He sat himself in front of the Underwood. He could hardly understand the dark letters on the scruffy paper in front of him. M was not a meticulous typist.

"Hello? Is that D?" is what M shouted into the cracked black bakelite.

"Is that M?" came the reply, thin and long distancy.

"Just the sort of question I was addressing in my column before you interrupted," said M. "What is all this about the Cecil Hotel?"

"Sylvia! Sylvia! Sylvia!" It was as if D had decided that the constraints of long distance called for one-word sentences.

"What is all this stuff about being and dung?" asked G, turning the platen and squinting at the yellow paper with the random-looking dark marks.

"Being and *doing*, you dolt."

"Sylvia! Have you got that?" asked the voice on the phone.

"Who is she?" asked M, his eyes rolling with delight.

"No, *what* is she," said D. "Who is Sylvia, what is she?"

"Who is who?" asked G, typing all the while. "Tell D that we have to save A from someone. Got to be at the Sylvia at eight p.m." He typed a period, hit the backspace, and hit the apostrophe. Someday they were going to have to make typewriters with exclamation marks already on them. The future belonged to exclamation marks.

M was listening to D shout the name of a hotel, and looking over G's shoulder as the latter typed faster and louder. Seven hundred and fifty words were far back on the side of the road.

"Frustum? What the hell is a frustum? There's no such word," he said.

"Ask D. He's an Englishman. He has a large vocabulary," said G.

"Hey, D? Have you ever heard of a frustum?" said M into the bakelite.

There was a Beckettian pause on the telephone. Then D was heard to say: "A frustum, my dear chep, is what would remain were I to saw off the topmost part of your head. I know that you have been quite sensitive about that part of your anatomy of late – "

"That just goes to show how much you know, Mr. Smarty English Remittance Man," said M, with an insincere smile in his voice. "Not a half hour ago the topmost part of my head was being held in the long hairless arms of an apprentice reporter."

"In any case, I can't stay on the line, because I am speaking long distance," said D.

"Where are you?"

"Where, indeed. I was mulling that very question not more than an hour ago. Where are we all? Where is Sylvia, what is she?"

"She's a hotel," said M.

"No, my Arctic-born acolyte," said D in his Christopher Plummer voice. "You will some day learn that Leonard Cohen, the young Montreal poet and actor, is a hotel. Sylvia is simply the name of the woman on my lap. Say hello to M, my dear."

"Hello, M." It was the kind of voice that could strip words from the page.

"Make sure that she comes to the Sylvia with you. Apparently we are meeting there for drinks tonight."

"-30-!" shouted G, and ripped tomorrow's column from the Underwood.

CHAPTER TWENTY-ONE

"Get your tongue out of my ear, your hand from off my groin.
For thou and I must make words fly, before they'll let us foin."

Thus M to Miss Take as his friend G lumbered out of the Sports Department of The Bad Seed and, alternatively waving his long arms and clutching to the bridge of the nose his spatulate fingers, cried Havoc and Where's Our Dogs of War, the Bad Guys have A, we must call D, where is my sanity. He grabbed the telephone.

M grabbed the typewriter, an Underwood. He wished it were a Remington, but Perry Southam, Bron Cornstead, and Pat Mawldunk, the general news reporters of *The Seed*, always hogged the Remingtons, (bunch of Remington stealers, D had remarked) and had hold of them now, writing sober and reporterly accounts of campus doings and issues. "Golliwog Wins Cakewalk" and "Riot on Lower Mall; Chinks Routed by Engineers" said the Seed, employing the language particular to that time at the university. *Portrait of the Artist as a Mad Dog* was a loose confederation of movie, book or theatre reviews interspersed with quotations or pseudoquotations from whatever Jacobean dramatist M currently favoured. This column, largely sophomoric wind, was cherished by D, the editor of The Critics' Page where it appeared. From an editor's point of view, M was reliable. He wrote, rewrote, revised and redecorated endlessly his bellowing, brazen, rococoo, ululant too-clever-by-halfings, but every Wednesday afternoon he came in and produced them, unfailing. (Failure he reserved for his performances on final examinations in Second-year Russian. His signal achievement here was an exam paper that weighed in at seven marks out of a possible hundred and fifty. It had taken him three tries at the subject to reach this level, starting at forty-eight marks and moving inexorably downward each year as he attended ever fewer classes and remembered ever fewer of the rules of the language picked up in his first year. The seven Russian émigrés and one Canadian spinster [a male, be it noted] who composed the Slavonics Department toasted M in flavourless Alberta vodka at their annual end-of-year party. ("Iss an inspirashunal depth of knowing nudding, a Kasbian zee uff eegnorance, eefen vor a Kanaddian stoo-dent.")

At the telephone, G was gibbering, his off-arm sawing the air in an artless rodomontade that suggested he had not paid much attention to Hamlet's advice to the players, an impression confirmed whenever he took to the stage, even in such a minor role as the elm tree in Maeterlinck's impressionist epic, *The Forest of Guliann*. G was announcing, apparently to D, something about meeting at the Cecil at eight o'clock.

M grabbed the phone from G, who sat himself in front of the Underwood and stared in wonder at the buff copy paper on which was limned the first part of M's theatre review, entirely and extravagantly scathing except for some ga-ga gurglings about "the comely thighs" of the juvenile lead of *The Forest of Guliann*.

"Is that M?" shouted D on the phone. "And if it is, why is it M?"

"Just the sort of question I was addressing in my column before you interrupted," replied M. "What's all this about the Cecil Hotel?"

"Sylvia! Sylvia! Sylvia!" shouted D. "Sylvia who comes with the north wind in her hair! Sylvia who brings on her enveloping wings the scent of northern forests, the scent of pine needles, moss and forest loam! Sylvia the eldritch queen of the herring chokers!"

D had spent a summer haying in Sweden. It was a part of the ill-conceived practicum of the agricultural college to which his parents, at a loss for how best to harness his young energies, had sent him. He'd spent as much time that summer pitching woo as pitching hay. Or doing both at the same time. The girls very gradually assembled to watch the skinny aristocratic-looking English boy, who would by-and-by stand leaning on his fork, panting a little. Sad brown eyes.

"Heavy work for a little fellow like me," he said softly in his over-enunciated Swedish. "Where do you girls work? What's it like there? Do they need any more hands?"

At the edge of the farm stood seven birches, as perfect and silver-fawn-green as the Great Artificer promised us they would be in all our dreams of Sweden. By nightfall D had a new job, an easier one running a machine, and quarters upstairs next to the girls' dormitory. Late in the night, his education continued, giggling. Light young legs endlessly moving, twining. The birches trilled and murmured, their limbs phosphorescent by moonlight. By the time his shifty eyes gazed over the rail of the MV *Bursk* in Göteborg harbour at the start of his journey home in September, three amiable young Svenskas were in the family way with little D's and Deas. One of these girls was indeed named Sylvia. She would have had a daughter with shifty, sad, brown eyes, also named Sylvia perhaps, but these were schoolgirls after all, and their mistakes were corrected, a few weeks after D's leaving, in a state clinic in Skovde which specialized in such errors.

"What is all this stuff about being and dung?" asked G.

"Being *undone*, you dolt!"

"Sylvia! Have you got that?" asked D, adding "And don't get confused about this, because it's certainly a life-and-death matter. Eight o'clock. And at all costs keep G on a short leash. Muzzle the lad! For if he goes shrieking about the place like a trumpeter swan, as he's all too likely to do, the game's up and they're warned. In particular, Diana will be warned!"

"Who is she?" asked M, his eyes rolling with delight.

"*What* is she?" corrected D. His voice became thinner and harder, more clipped than ever, as confidential as Liam Chutney's. "Diana is a code name."

"Who is who?" shouted G from the Underwood. "Tell D we have to be at the Sylvia at eight p.m." He typed a blizzard of words or near-words, including a sentence which included "his long, agyle fringers delicatelli fringring her frustum." Reading G, one never knew how much to blame on haste and overconfidence, how much to credit to inborn genius and wisdom.

"D? Have you ever heard of a frustum?" said M into the bakelite.

"Look here," said D. "You must understand that our friend G, because he is losing the deevine A to dark forces we all wish and fear to comprehend, is at this time experiencing a state known to medical science as perdition of the marbles, permanent – PMP for short. It follows that he will blunder at the Underwood even more than he usually does. In any case, I can't stay on the line, because I'm speaking long distance."

"Where are you?"

"Where, indeed. I am a distance considerably south of you and G, in a spot rather more infamous and more mythic than virtual. Here I am watched at all times by authorities whose purposes are fell, and whose standards of civility fall somewhat short of what we're used to in the British Commonwealth of Nations. I am surrounded by Americans, by Chesterfield cigarettes, Walgreen drugstores, and chicken-fried steak. I am amongst people the depth of whose love of liberty is exceeded only by the shallowness of their perceptions of good and bad, which childish terms are the entirety of their metaphysics. I crawl parched through Mencken's Sahara of the Bozart. But then, considering what a pee-green boat of a world we're all – Yanks, Canucks, and woggish what-have-yous–living in, where are we all? And where is Sylvia?"

M had bought cheap cotton dacron slacks from Fred Asher on the promise that they were "American-styled." They had been dyed in sort of woadish blue, and that woad was now coming off on his hands, which, unusually large and dangling far down, nearly to his knees, looked like those of the monster with the bolt stuck horizontally through his head. Stained dimly blue and confused by the sinisterly hissed farrago coming from the telephone, M was also feeling and thinking like Frankenstein's monster. D rasping in one ear and G clacking at the other made him want to dash their heads together, as John Wayne did in the movies. And it wasn't the first time. Where was that apprentice reporter? Perhaps she'd gone off to fetch him a stirrup cup, something to uplift and sustain him through the long evening of early summer, sunshot and cloud-raddled, gathering itself outside the narrow basement windows of The Bad Seed.

The pause having now become nearly Pinteresque, M muttered into the phone, "We're due at the Sylvia at eight p.m. A stands in danger there, or nearabouts."

Suddenly reverting to his normal voice, plummy and purry, all edge of urgency gone, D responded, "My dear chep, who is Sylvia?"

"She's a hotel."

"No, M," said D in his Plummery voice. "Thou brutish slave and sullen wretch, thou shalt some day learn that little Leonard Cohen, mocked as both actor and poet manqué, and generally seen to be about as handsome as a vampire bat, and no less pale, tiny, and caped, is, in no less august estimation than his very own, an hotel. Sylvia is simply the name of the woman on my lap. Say hello to M, my dear."

"Hello, M." It was the kind of voice that could strip words from the page, or lift varnish from the woodwork, rouse a dead man's member, waken Jordan's Chaucer class from slumber at 8:30 in the morning, Monday, Wednesday, Friday, Buchanan 118, settle the cooing dove in its roost, knock the top off a Sherman tank, raise the Marine Building, Vancouver's tallest, out of its foundations, spin Sir Philip Sidney in his grave, rouse the Greeks against Islam, the Israelites against Egypt, settle the furious brannigans of Eire, hail Bonnie Charlie back from Skye, erect a mighty plinth to which the gods might descend, arrest the Jordan River in its rolling, lull the earthworms of Luna with blue and silver lullabies, rouse jaded Jesus from Plato's sleep, raise a mighty army against the Usurper, meet him on the beach, fight him in the fields and ditches, carry off his head in triumph, and bring the boys back home.

"All is dross that is not Sylvia," resumed D's voice now. "I will be Paris, and for love of her instead of Troy shall

Wittenberg be sacked. And I will combat with weak Menelaus and wear her colours on my plumed crest. Yea, I will wound Achilles in the heel, and then return to Sylvia for a kiss. She's fairer than the evening's air, clad in the beauty of a thousand stars."

"Well," gasped M, "you'd better bring her along to the Sylvia with you, then."

"-30-!" shouted G., ripping the sheet from the Underwood. He handed M this and several more sheets.

M stared at the melee of dark letters, into which G had randomly flung every special character, from ampersand to @, on the keyboard, as well as others usually found only in the land of ASCII. "G!" he cried "this is gibberish! You'll ruin my reputation!"

G smiled fatly. "Unlax. This is postmodernism. It'll be the making of you."

Cloud, showers, and thunderous anticipation of more and harder rain followed G and M downtown on the Number Eight bus and along Beach Avenue toward the Sylvia Hotel.

As they left the bus on Beach, an Oldsmobile 98, modishly black with white sidewall tires and chrome Buck Rogers miniports followed them, and Agent John Ames McDonald slipped the Hydramatic Drive lever into low. Beside him sat Top Agent Roy Daniells, eyes hard and teeth clenched on his brier. In the back seat, Agent Clyde Gilmour peered from under his slate-blue fedora at the raffish West-End street life and the two tall young men gesticulating their way toward the hotel. It was Gilmour who cranked down the street-side window and called.

"Hey! You men!"

G turned first. "Jesus, M, those guys..." He shot for the heavy oak and glass door that led to the beverage room of the Sylvia, M right at his heels.

Just off the DOT. marker buoy at the entrance to Burrard Inlet, the thirty-two-foot *Topham Island* slowed to eight knots and coasted into English Bay, sliding over light chop toward the beach. The Sylvia Hotel, wavering, bobbing in the windscreen, rose just above the beach.

"How's she doing back there?" The twang was that mysterious amalgam of Northern England and East London that calls itself Strine. The speaker sounded nervous, but grasped and arced the steering wheel with assurance.

"She's talking that stuff again, that language." The second voice was Canadian.

"Yih?"

"Yieh."

CHAPTER TWENTY-TWO

The Omniscient Narrator strolled down Robson Strasse, envying the narrow dead-end lives around hemhir. At the same time, shey was strolling down everywhere, anywhere. Therefore shey was also strolling down the Main Mall (not a shopping centre, campers!) at the University of British Columbia, which would one day grant an Hon D Litt to G – shouldn't that be an Hon G Litt, to D? – So anyway, the O.N. was envying the narrow dead-end lives passing him by on campus, too. So as one particular insouciant young man came abreast of him, the O.N. spiked him with the tip of that redundancy, his Omniscient Umbrella. "Ouch, asshole" muttered D, who kept on going. It stung for a moment and then was forgotten, to do its deadly work in the dark.

D strolled by the Freddy Wood Theatre. The door was open. He peeked in. He had once found a wife here, disguised as an Ugly Sister. He had found a friend at the same time, disguised as Prince Charming. So he peeked again, to see what he might find.

He found G Delsing, dressed in a white floor length dress and wearing bright orange lipstick and a white lace mantilla. He was surrounded by Dekes. The Dekes, the dorkiest frat on campus, had rented the theatre and were rehearsing their spring follies. D knew that G was no Deke – he must have taken money from them to play this role.

G, besides looking absurdly, disturbingly beautiful, was singing to an instrumental version on tape of *I Went to Your Wedding*. But the words he was singing had been written by D himself some months ago at a drunken party.

> Your mother was boozin'
> Your father was boozin'
> And I was boozin' too

> And why were we boozin'?
> Because we were losin' /You.

> You walked down the aisle
> Wearin' only a smile
> A vision of loveliness
> You tripped and you fell
> You bellowed Oh hell
> Drunk as a skunk I guess

> Yer brother was usin'
> His boyfriend was usin'
> And [up two octaves] I was usin' too
> And why were we usin'?
> Because we were losin' / You.

D resumed his stroll. But the melody had ahold of his mind now and he could get no peace. He recalled the ensuing verses, even though he could no longer hear his friend's surprisingly accomplished falsetto:

> The vicar made speeches
> I shit in my breeches
> And Dean C – was shittin' too
> And why were we shittin'?
> Because we were gittin'/ Flu.

D fancied now that the words were coming, not from the orange-encircled *bouche* of his long chum G, but from the darker *embouchure* of the dulcet-toned Damata Jo, who recorded this song in '52:

> Yer taxidermist was swannin'
> Yer taxi was runnin'
> Yer taxman was connin' / You
> (ONE two three ONE two three)
> Yer toxics were leechin'

Yer tuxedo had come un/Glued

Lovely; lovely, lovely, lovely. What power music hath! D had walked all the way from the Freddy Wood to the Caf without once thinking of how G had snatched A from him, of how G had stolen his song and sold it to the Dekes, of what the CIA gangsters had promised/threatened him with, of what Beth had said to him concerning his manhood that morning, or of what K had said Tom told him concerning his marital state the night before. And even on the very brink of further distraction, on the very top step of the descent to Caf Hell, where a place awaited him at the AH's table, the melody still suffused his poor brain, so much so that he needed nothing else to sustain his being, so that he about-faced and went on his way, headed toward true North, with new and yet newer phrases popping into his consciousness on the waves of the sickening tune:

> D, M & G
> Before they could pee
> Saw an amazing flash
> It lit up the night
> With its staggering sight
> From the Burrard Street/ Brash
>
> And next on the wall
> In front of them all
> A vision of mystery
> Some hieroglyphs stood
> Meaning no good
> On the wall of the brewery

D's spontaneous non-bop prosody composition had so preoccupied him that he had walked clear off campus – had damn near toppled off a cliff into the Straits of Georgia. Come to his senses, he found himself in a wooded region steeply banked, which, he now recalled, led down to the Point

Grey beach. The time of year being April (although other people might have other impressions as to the season, not to say the year), and the week being exam week, the dizzy trail revealed sporadic knots of "cliff-jumpers," students gone clean out of their gourds with the pressure of cramming after a wastrel winter, scrambling down to put into practice the sentiment, "But best of all, a drunken sleep on the beach." (Rimbaud or Baudelaire? Quick!)

D was on a walking jag. His legs moved of their own accord. His feet automatically found where to walk. They carried the bemused poet while his cranium kept cranking out verses.

> Imposters, poseurs
> These men friends of hers
> And A would be one too
> Told true fakes from false
> (This is a waltz)
> Felt the pebble inside her / Shoe.

> But no more of that
> –M 'n D's plans went splat!
> D was kidnapped by blackcoated goons
> They warn him "Shut up!"
> Enforce it with slpas
> And dialogue out of car/ Toons.

> G gets the funnies
> The a.m is Sunday's
> The same goons grab him too
> How can this be?
> I think we agree
> It's fiction, it must be/ True.

D had arrived at the beach. Washed-up logs and washed-up students occupied the sandy strip in like numbers. The sweet, sickly smell of marijuana assailed D's flaring nostrils, but it would be years before D would be able to identify it. So whose is *this* point-of-view?

D did recognize the beer bottles and the packs of cigarettes, and began to scan the figures that weren't logs, looking for a friend, or an acquaintance, or even an enemy, to bum stuff off. But the only person he knew was some yards out in the water, being attacked by a large dog. It was Eduardo Viejo Pink-Meadow-Pink, a large creature himself, but barely a match for the slavering hound at his throat. D plunged in fully clothed and splashed closer.

"Hello, Brahms," said Pink-Meadow, who liked to say that D resembled the Nineteenth century composer. "Come to frolic with us then, have you?" And one arm went above his head and its hand curled inward above the head in a characteristic gesture.

"This is play, Ed?" D sounded querulous. His pants were wet.

Pink-Meadow had by now struggled to his feet, and laid his other hand upon the dog's muzzle. "This is D-d-d-dog!" he told D. "D-d-d-dog is my new friend. "

"With friends like that, who needs enemies? Goll-ee, Eddie, he fair bid to drown you!"

The friends splashed out of the Straits of Georgia and picked a log to sit on. "He's the kind of dog that has to save people," Pink-Meadow explained. "I can't swim because he's always trying to save me. Would you mind holding him while I go back in?"

D agreed, with some misgiving about his ability to restrain the animal. But D-d-d-dog had had enough for now. He put his head on his stretched-out front paws and rolled a cloudy brown eye up at D.

Pink-Meadow reappeared, and stood shaking his massive, doggy form so that drops of cold, cold water flang themselves all over D. "Wonderfully stimulating, Brahms," he cried loonily, pirouetting with that singular gesture, arm bent up above head, "Why not go in yourself? – You might as well, you're pretty wet already," he added annoyingly.

"You're interrupting my composing," D sniffed huffily.

"Composing? Well, it's better than decomposing. I have some bonehead students from Engineers English down here with me – that's them over there, burning livestock. Mmm, wouldn't I just love to get my tongue on *that* little one there," he added wistfully drooling. "I love them when they have all those spots on their angelic faces. I suppose if you would sing your latest verses to them, they would beat the living daylights out of you. Too bad. They seem to quite like me, Artsman though I may be."

"You haven't given them their grades yet. Wait till next week."

"Ah, yes, well, I'll be over on the Island by next week. Why don't you come, Brahms. Pick strawbs as you did those many years ago, with that delicious friend of yours, whatsisname? Is he still around? Have him come too."

The sciencemen had given up on the sheep or goat – or Arts and Humanities Professor – they had roasted on a makeshift spit till it was an inedible black mass. Now they were manipulating some largish sheet of shiny metal whose purpose D could not glean. Pink-Meadow was none the wiser, and he was three sheets to the wind. D inadvisably let him know he was setting doggerel to "I Went to Your Wedding."

"Brahms! How splendid!! But you shouldn't reshtrict yourshelf to one song. There are so many others."

"That's why I restrict myself," D said, mordantly.

"How about something for D-d-d-dog? How about (and he sang it) 'How Much is that Doggy in the Window'? How about 'Daddy Wouldn't Buy Me A Bow-Wow'?? How about – "

"No, Ed, frkkzzakes don't! Don't plant another tune in my head. I'm three quarters done and I want to ride the same vehicle throughout!"

But Pink-Meadow had ceased to listen – if he had ever really begun. He was now shouting and waving at someone on a natty little cruiser offshore. His greetings were returned.

"Brahms, that's Read Only on that boat! We'll shimply swim out and he'll give us drinkies."

D didn't think this was any great shakes as an idea. The cabin cruiser looked to be at least one hundred yards out. However, activity nearby changed his mind.

The scienceapes, while not letting go of their huge piece of tin, had caught the accents of a Professor of Bonehead English and were drunk enough to assault him *before* he had graded their finals. Besides, wasn't that DB, that loathsome dilettante who edited the Critics' Page, standing next to the big faggot? Faggot himself, most like. Fucken eh! Let's get their trousers off for starters!

Picking up the general drift of things, D plunged into the ocean in tandem with his chum. Soon enough, they were being helped into the cruiser by Read Only himself, the anthropologist from North Borneo and Seattle. Read wrapped D in a blanket and set him in the sun with a highly sophisticated cocktail.

Then he and Pink-Meadow went below to smoke some funny stuff. D didn't smoke funny stuff. Funny, eh.

D watched the beach. The Apes of Engineering had given up their quest for Artsman flesh and gone back to their dinkering with the sheet of tin. D hadn't realized that these simians had that much ability to focus. His own mind was wandering once more.

> D, G, M and A
> were on the TV
> Ready to talk about sex
> Love: Different Things
> to Different Genders
> Was the topic announced for their/ Text.

> "How much is that fellow in the window?
> The one with the waggly – tail?
> How much is that fellow in the window?
> O I do hope that isn't a tail!"

But now what was happening to the boat?!

D was living in the present now, at last – leastwise, in the *recent* past.

"Eduardo!"

The big guy came ponderously up the ladder that led below. D was handed at his request the ship-to-shore phone. The cruiser without any helmsman had turned in a big circle and was now headed south, towards the mouths of the Fraser River. Read Only, alerted, took the wheel. D dialed.

D was sitting at a table *outside*, drinking *liquor*, and it was legal because at Read's suggestion they had dropped anchor at Point Roberts, a geographical and political anomaly dear to D's heart. On his fifth vodka and orange (for D was ever-mindful of his health) he was becoming expansive. Unfortunately for his companions, however, he had also regressed:

> I saw an explosion
> Of light o'er the ocean
> And G and M were there
> We've been painfully muzzled
> while Molson's we guzzled
> Though I did tell on the /Air.
>
> I never balled Byrna
> She only balls Werner
> Who creates lampshades out of paste
> And M never reached me
> Altho' he beseeched me
> M's mind is a terrible / Waste.

D's audience was agog. "Get on with it, man!" His neo-discursiveness was the blunt instrument of suspense. It was Read's turn to treat.

M's fanciful scene
From "Duck Soup," I ween
Scrambled in M's mighty mind
We see what drinkin'
Does to your thinking
 – O thank you, Read, you're too/ Kind.

It's six-ten already
I'm slightly unsteady
But must get to English Bay
So Read, rent a chopper
We all three can hoppa/ Board.

CHAPTER TWENTY-THREE

Who are they? What are they, A was thinking, not just these ones who were merely representative, but all of them. The Sylvia question was merely concerned with the mystery of sex – all those stars and magical symbols they plastered over a woman's skirts – as if she owned the answer to the secret and was not caught in its mystery as much as they. A didn't know either who or what Sylvia was, but she was scared. The sky was dark and lashed with rain and the three hummocked slicker-covered shapes in the front of the boat were unknown to her. Speed, bonny boat, she thought. "Raptus," she said, "to be carried away." In a rapture of terror she thought anywhere for harbour. "O wynde of wynde the wedder gynneth clere," then realized, when the others turned, that she had spoken out loud. *Suomen leinnen tutte*, she said, her grandmother's words. "Little Finnish girl." The others looked distinctly nervous. A wept and longed for the sweet green place on the island, where she'd been born. "The sisters of mercy, they are not departed and gone," she shrieked. "Polymorphous perversity of the dialogical imagination," she warmed up, suspecting that her survival might depend on pretending to be crazy. She knelt on the bottom of the boat and made the conventional sign. Prostrating herself before her amazed captors, arms outstretched, she kissed the bottom of the boat, gagged and vomited neatly over the side as brackish sea water rose in her gorge. The boat had obviously been standing in water for some time. Not only that, but it was slowly filling with water. It was not a seaworthy vessel, A realized. Or was it a vessel at all? Nearly as suddenly as it had begun, the squall subsided and as A gazed about her, she understood that this was not a boat. It was a tub, outfitted as a motorboat.

Meanwhile a completely inebriated D was fighting for

what he thought were the controls of a Bell helicopter, not realizing that in truth if not fact he was aboard a white cabin cruiser, and what he was fighting for, was the untimely erection being sported by a large friendly dog named D-d-d-dog. D-d-d-dog suffered, if that indeed is the word, a condition known in his land of origin as "Dooba-twickism," an affliction whose victims have hard-ons except when they are rescuing people who are in danger of drowning. D had no knowledge of medicine. He grabbed for the canine phallus.

Pink-Meadow grabbed for D, seeking to protect his old drinking buddy from the consequences only he knew.

But Read Only, who was holding the wheel of the cabin cruiser in one hand and a Singapore Sling in the other, saw only that his crew appeared headed for an altercation, and grabbed for Pink-Meadow, letting go of the wheel but not of the tall pink drink with its perfect little umbrella.

The cabin cruiser jigged.

Read jogged, over the side and into the American chuck. He bobbed to the surface, but the umbrella was gone. He took a sip of the Sling and grimaced his approval.

But Pink-Meadow had already jagged. He landed like an Orca atop the salinated cocktail.

And before Pink-Meadow could resurface, D-d-d-dog lost his tumescence while making a lovely doggy-dive into the dangerous element, where he splashed on his unimmersing master.

D wracked his spirits-filled brain for the right word. The music of "I went to your wedding" had disappeared thence the moment the doggy was no longer in the window. "Aha!" he shouted into the slight breeze, but he knew that was wrong. The cabin cruiser performed a circle about the two water-treaders and the one dog paddler. "Oho!" tried D. He saw Read sipping from the tall glass. "Ahab!" shouted D.

Now the desired word slid into D's brain, as if typed there by G on a big dull Underwood. "Ahoy!" he shouted, in an accent usually assigned to mariners in The Bight and northern East Anglia.

The cabin cruiser circled in its own wake. The two sailors and their dog in the water turned their bodies to keep it in sight.

"How does a chep steer this thing?" shouted D. "I mean in this instance a chep who knows not how to control an automobile."

"I cannot hear you," asserted Read. "It's either your accent or the combination of wind and motor. There is no hope of understanding anything more than a single word, or perhaps two in these circumstances."

But now D-d-d-dog had his canine teeth firmly in Pink-Meadow's half-Eton collar and was swimming toward the saloon on the beach. Read threw his empty glass out to sea and prepared to follow them. He turned and shouted instructions to D. Unfortunately D was unable to hear them.

But he knew that D-d-d-dog would do his duty. He also knew now that this water craft was not a helicopter. He remembered the shore-to-ship phone call and the earlier one. For a moment he wondered what had happened to the lissome Sylvia, but with A to be rescued and G and M to be joined, there was no time in his thoughts for an S. He hissed when the thought elbowed its way past the mind-altering chemicals in his cranial lobes. Now there were more important things at hand. Such as the method whereby one guides a sea-going vessel toward a bay that seemed less and less English all the while.

For the first time in his creative life, D was having trouble handling his craft. But he fought the wheel and that other thing, some kind of vertical stick, all the way around each headland. Other small boats veered out of the way as their passengers espied his eccentric approach. Otters scattered. Herons took to the skies like gossamer pterodactyls. Canada Customs stayed in the shed. Loose logs floated out of the way. His Byronic hair flying behind him, D stood at the helm and sang into the salt air.

My old chum went swimmin'

> The skipper went swimmin'
> And D-d-d-dog went swimming' too
> In Canadian waters
> Along with the otters
> I can't find the god-damned/ Loo!

The verse may not have amounted to much in terms of the furtherance of plot, but at last he had got the scansion aright.

Miraculously the powerful boat made its way around the beautiful Point Grey, and in a moment that would beggar belief, D saw the west wall of the Freddy Wood Theatre at the university. Then it disappeared behind some trees, and D looked into the maw of English Bay. There has to be a way to slow this sloop's forward progress, he mused, and began to push and pull things. The Evinrude engines responded with a surge of power, and the bow of the vessel lifted from the water. As it did, D saw a pillar of fire and water just this side of what he did not recognize as the Burrard Bridge. Had he looked away from the pillar of fire and water he might have seen to its right the tall yellow wall of the brewery, and to its left the creeper-covered walls of the Sylvia Hotel.

"*Mein Gott*! What have I done?" asked D, who was holding on to the wheel with whitened fingers.

"One: you haven't done anything," came a voice in the roar of the Evinrudes. "And two: I am not your *Gott*. Your *Gott* is Fame." (Big G – knew how to project).

Pieces of the Bathtub *Topham Island* fell into the water beside him, as the pointed end of his boat fell back into the sea and the cabin cruiser slowed nearly to a stop, having consumed all its purple fuel. D looked at the fragments of the unfortunate thirty-two-footer that floated about him.

"They look like forlorn pages of a jerry-built novel," mused D, his hair still sticking out straight behind him, though Read's boat was only floating shoreward on the waves.

"My recent sentiments, exactly," said a good-natured Finno-Canadian voice behind him.

He had not even noticed a tipping of the boat as she had

climbed the ladder affixed to its side. But it was A, indeed, her hair and clothing clinging to her frame.

For a moment he was filled with regretful affection, but he was made of stern stuff. His parents had conceived him at the very back of the Calais ferry. Perhaps the instinct for driving a boat had been born with him.

"Where is Sylvia?" asked A.

"The nose of your rescue ship has just nudged the sand a hundred yards from her beverage room portal," he replied. "Where that large Oldsmobile is idling at the curb."

CHAPTER TWENTY-FOUR

M and G sprinted past big brass ashtrays full of sand and up the marble stairs to the Sylvia's second floor. As if magic had come to aid them, an elevator door opened and there did stand D, smiling his smile, a rather thin thing, but the only smile he owned. "Look, you cheps," he said, "I'll just run down to the lobby and get some ciggies and meet you in the room."

Scarcely breaking stride, G pushed D back into the elevator and followed, M too. G pushed the button for the sixth floor. "But I haven't any cigarets at all, G," cried D. "I think that A stole them. And then three men in suits, the leader of whom wore, like the head of the UBC English Department, an Andy Gump moustache, stole A! They grabbed her the minute we stepped onto the beach!"

G's face contorted to a fierce question.

"I don't know where they took her; I just ran like hell up the beach, across the street, and in here. Without any ciggies. Look, G, I must break it to you that A didn't look all that unhappy to see those Guys. There's something going on there."

"Well," allowed G, "whatever they're doing they were right behind us on the street and they're in the hotel by now. If we don't get up there, they'll beat us to the room."

"How do you know the room?" said M.

"It's room 614," muttered G. "The room always has a six and a one in it."

"Oh yes," said D. "Remember, M, at the Roundtowner, the room that the body was in?"

M just gaped. His friends were hip; he was laggard.

On the sixth floor they followed the corridor west toward the water. Room 614 turned out to be in the ell of the northwest corner. Its door, painted a hideous Chinese orange, was open.

G boldly advanced into the hall; 614 was a suite with a separate bedroom and a large kitchen off a hall beyond the main room, furnished for sitting. All seemed deserted. M stepped into the kitchen and looked in the refrigerator. "There's food in the fridge!" he called. "Someone's staying here." He withdrew consideringly a small, stout pie. "This, by its height, its girth and its scent, is a Melton Mowbray pork pie," he announced. "Wouldn't ya think 'twould be a marvel in the mouth as in the eye? Yet it is not a marvel; it is a chunky, congealed thing that doesn't take to being heated, that refuses to get moist and brown and rich and loving. It's just a damned grey, gelid, obdurate cold duchess of a thing that belies its divine ingredients. Though I am catholic in my tastes, I cannot worship at this shrine," he concluded, putting the pie back into the fridge.

"Well, there's nothing in the bedroom," said D.

"There's nothing in the bathroom," announced G, "except tiny paper-wrapped Palmolive soaps."

The three turned as one toward the large main room. It was no longer empty; two men who looked like monks in movies and comic books sat against one wall on the plain leatherette-seated chairs. Commandingly in the middle of the room, in a striped armchair, sat a third man, also in robish clothing, of lapels and layers. His face was plain, ascetic, with large eyes, pleasant. His hair, even for 1961, was cut extremely short.

The three young men walked to him and simply stared. Whatever the explanation for these ecclesiastical-appearing figures, clearly something special had been laid on.

"My name," announced the man, "is Nicholas Breakspear." His voice was British, but accented in a way that fell strangely on the ears.

"I have come to you this evening," the man continued, "because some mysteries must have an end and an explanation, because young men must get moving in their lives, not remain youths forever, and because when the callow vanity and idle pranks of youth grow near to overwhelming the world, time itself cries for an intervention. Even an intervention that mocks the laws of time."

M thought, is this one of G's literary persons? Another Corno Emblemado, Patrick O'Groin, Anselm Hoohaw?

There was a muffled shout somewhere in the hall outside, and some thumping, lurching sounds along the hall, coming nearer to the room. There came one large thump against the door to the suite, which popped open. Three figures in dark overcoats huddled over a huge canvas sack and thrust it into the room. The figures receded into the hall; Agent McDonald's red face was seen briefly at the edge of the door as he closed it. Six men stared at a struggling, shapeless, dun-coloured thing on the floor. Pale fists split the zipper of the sack from inside, and out stepped A, wearing freshly short, straight hair and a toggled duffel coat.

"Christ, what I've been through," she muttered. Then she saw the man who had introduced himself as Nicholas Breakspear. A turned to G and grabbed the lapel of G's salt and pepper fleck sportcoat.

"G!" she exclaimed, "Do you know who this man is?"

"This is Nicholas Breakspear, A," said D.

"Yeah, I know it's Nicholas Breakspear. But do you people know what that means?" said A.

"No," said D, "I don't."

"Nope," said G.

Breakspear smiled widely and gently from the striped chair.

"Well," he said pleasantly. "You are all here now. I can tell you of myself and of my reason for being here with you."

"I was born in England, at Abbott's Langley, on a farm, as most people were in my time. My family was a large one. I had three brothers, with myself the third boy born. I had five or six sisters, and I cannot know how many really, for two had left the family, married and gone off to live elsewhere by the time I was old enough to have any conception of what my family was. I had two sisters near my own age, one older who died of a fever when I was six or seven years old, and one younger."

Breakspear now turned his mild but direct gaze for a moment on G, then on M. "You two do not have sisters," he said. "It is a misfortune for you."

G looked for a moment as if he would set the record straight, then looked as if he would keep the correct information in reserve, just in case it might become an asset of some sort, for a change.

"As I grew up," the seated figure continued, "I found myself more and more, though happy in the life of growing, reaping, and tending fowl, drawn to the life of our church, and, to make the story short, I took orders for a holy mission at the monastery at Verulamium.

"From the sixteenth year and ever afterward, my life was one of service. Whether in the monastery or in the churches and courts of Europe, mine was, I may hazard, a more simple and more rigorous life than you could dream of. It was very exact, yet with very few rules written down, though a very great many understood, and understood as quite absolute and beyond appeal or cavil."

"Sounds like Robertson Davies," said G, who had some knowledge of the literature of the Dominion of Canada.

"It was somewhat as Robertson Davies pictures it," said Nicholas Breakspear, "but I warn you not to depend on such an author for an understanding of my period of history. Too melodramatic, for one thing. But above all you must realize that an author who is false to his own time and place, as Robertson Davies is, will be false to all the world, to any part of history that he seeks to convey to us."

Breakspear continued. "Encouraged in my spiritual life and in my worship by the fostering influence of Verulamium, I pursued an ecclesiastical life, and such was my fortune and blessing that I achieved honours that allowed me much travel, and for some years a life away from England, in Europe, in Scandinavia, in France and Italy. Your books of history will tell you of some events in which I had a part. Not all of them, indeed, events I could wish to remember. I had Arnold hanged, burnt, and thrown in the river. I wished to see Frederick thrown sideways through Hell. But I did as my faith counselled me to do, and as my church required."

"What has this got to do with us, sir?" said M in the subdued, almost polite tone that he had learned in the private school his parents had seen as the only alternative to reform school.

"You three almost by chance were selected," said Breakspear, "for the sort of missionary work that is always going on in the world, in all ages. This work is a commerce between realms, whereby ours seeks to influence yours, which scarcely wits that it has called out to ours for help."

"You're not seizing us to go to Utah and collect pamphlets and wear suits, are you?" asked G, who had fled desert places, and wanted no more to do with them.

"Really, I have no more to do than to give you the words of a Dutch uncle. We wished to signal quietly to you. We hoped not to have to use such masquerade and ceremony as we have employed this evening. We sent you a sign; it was the flash in the mountains that has puzzled you these last few weeks."

"How did you do that?" said G.

"We simply exploded an electrical transformer: in Lynn Vale, I believe the place is named."

"But the flash – it was way bigger than that would be," said M.

"Oh, yes," said Breakspear. "We enlarged it, of course. And the hieroglyphics that you and indeed the rest of your city saw on the wall of the brewery were simple enough also. They were done in the same manner as signs, whether on walls or in the air, have always been done."

"The sign was Assyrian, ancient Assyrian," said M.

Breakspear nodded. "Yes, we provided, on the yellow brick wall of your imposing modern palace, a passage from the ancient story of Gilgamesh. A passage in which the young and heedless prince is told of the limits of mortal power, warned that he must heed those limits and that he must fear and acknowledge death. 'On the bed of fate he lies; he will not rise again.'"

Breakspear now looked with some sadness at the three students. "When the reader is ready, the sign is made. Though you three were ready to see the signs, you have been slow to consider them seriously, or to put aside the fretful fevers of youth, to conduct yourselves toward sobriety and duty." Breakspear paused, looking at D. "We thought we had better go further and speak to you directly."

"But damn it, sir!" exploded D. "There's been all this other cloak and dagger stuff, all these cheps in dark suits running after us, kidnappings, thuggery, muggery, buggery. . . we've been treated pretty roughly!"

"Oh, yes," answered Breakspear. "We threw into the masquerade a few touches suggested by the mythologies of your time, a few playful. . . love-taps, let's call them. These men in dark clothing have always been for hire, you know, for a few florins, in any city in the world, anywhere in history."

D thought of the distinguished professor, the distinguished hunt-and-pecker, moonlighting as a gunsel, a footpad. And what that suggested of the propriety of Sixteenth-century verse forms practised in the latter half of the Twentieth century. He smiled.

"Where am I in this?" demanded A. She had fired up a Matinee cigarette, and jetted smoke from the corner of her mouth as, ignoring D's long questing fingers, she plunged the pack into her coat pocket.

"Oh, you are most usefully influential on all of these young men," said Breakspear. "But not enough to take them on a clear course through the confusion of roaring, tailor-worship, penis envy, and braggadocio that now mars their progress."

"But you're saying this is their story?" persisted A. "I'm just an influence? I don't play a leading role?"

Breakspear smiled again his soft smile. "Perhaps you have a power of creation beyond any such power that these have."

"I will not be consigned to motherhood," said A, with intensity.

Breakspear's reply was a quizzical look, cheerful and ambiguous.

The room was a moment silent, except for a buzz of consternation in the heads of the young people and a short "genk" from the radiator. On the broad brick window ledge could be seen one large and three small raccoons. This family had ascended by means of the Virginia Creeper which flourished on the Sylvia's north side. On the thick stems and branches of this wondrous vine Feather McFiddle-dee-dee and Peaches Dobell also had ascended, and now peered from the foliage into the room. Nicholas Breakspear continued.

"I want to tell you of how I came to find my way in life. As a boy, younger than you in years, I had trees to climb. I had, G, an orchard, an English orchard of pear trees and cherry trees and apple trees, with sweet apples that tasted like cherries at the core. In a field near the Breakspear home was a sycamore tree, sixty feet high. I often climbed that tree, for the sheer sport and joy of pulling myself up its grainy, friendly bark, and the poles and struts, regular almost as a ladder, of its branches. And I felt wonderfully vantaged when I looked out and down at Abbott's Langley from a place near the top of the sycamore. I felt in command, in some way, of the scene I looked upon. That group of cottages, with a smithy and a bakeshop and a tithe barn just beyond them seemed almost a world to me, a kingdom. And I knew that far beyond them, down the road that curved up the hill toward the London road, was a greater world, of cities that I had seen drawn on maps, and those cities always were seen from a vantage of height that the map-maker took for his eye and his pen. The maps showed the cities, London, Paris, Tours, Lyons, Bologna, Rome, always as if each city had been drawn from a huge tree at its outskirts. Of course the mapmakers had in truth looked at their towns from the tops of towers or walls, or castellos. While looking at my own small village world from the height of my sycamore tree, I conceived, over weeks or months, and without putting it very directly to myself or to anyone else at all, that I might one day be an author of causes. I knew that I must one day reach some place in affairs – for me, of course, affairs meant the church and its enterprises, both ecclesiastical and civil – where I could manage and shape, in the great world beyond my home village, the peace, order and good purpose that I now saw beneath me in my village. Those views from my tree were the signs that were put in my life to guide me. You three likewise need to find your callings, find how you will make harmonies in your world. You would not have paused on that bridge had our flash not arrested you. You would not have sent that poem, G, to the *Tamarack Review* if we had not given you the first important word of it on that envelope. The one word in your own language that was mixed in with the Assyrian characters.

"So you do work in poetry!" cried D. "You do use the power of rime!"

"We use," said Breakspear, "whatever tropes will speak to those whom we seek. We work, you know, in many places, among many sorts of people. Some of those people suppose us to be spirits; some think us demons; some give us Greek or Hebrew names. We make these journeys not infrequently, yet it is a privilege to receive our visits. I hope that you will consider with care and (may I say) piety this visit and the counsel I have urged on you.

"For my part I must take my leave, hoping that my explanations of the mysteries in your lives recently have helped you."

He stood, and extended a hand to D, who stood nearest him. "I hope," he said, "that you will each give me your hand, and will not be bothered that my hand is a cold one. My best wishes are nonetheless warmly meant."

The young men in turn shook Breakspear's hand; as did A. Nicholas Breakspear spoke again. "What you must do, above everything, is bring the birds back to your new world here."

"?" said G, with his eyebrows, thinking of an osprey sailing over Skaha Lake.

"Eh?" said D, thinking of the zoo in Regents' Park.

"Birds?" said M, not thinking at all.

"That's what you haven't got, don't you see? You haven't got the birds, not the birds such as we used to have in Britain before the cities, nor the birds that you once had in this country before you started burning coal and gas, and making these big towns and cities. You've got nothing here" – Breakspear gestured at the window with English Bay and Stanley Park out beyond it – "nothing but some crows, and some dirty-looking seagulls. A remnant of the birds you had here once! You must get back those birds. Much of what has been lost between my time and yours can never come back to this earth and this place in it, but some things can come back. My church has always stood for the rejuvenation of our natural world. You can help in this."

Breakspear looked hard at each of the four young people. Then he slightly turned and walked out through the Chinese-red door, followed by the two other men in robes. If this made any sound it was no more than the phantom sound of cloth moving over carpet.

The four people in the room looked, each, about two feet in front of their noses.

"Birds?" said D.

"Birds," said G, smiling.

"Birds," said M, smiling a little.

"Birds," said A.

CHAPTER TWENTY-FIVE

"Truth is a banquet where everyone is drunk on the same wine"
– Hegel

Breakspear & Co had left the door ajar. The door gratefully tippled from it. "Can't beat that corn likker from Abbotsford," Door said, wiping the back of its hand across its door-y mouth, before setting the jar back in its rightful place in the semantic chain. The Hotel Sylvia surrounded it. Exegesis might commence.

Impervious to this S.J. Perelman surrealistic sideshow, which was not for all eyes after all, D trained his attention down the fairway of Breakspear's track. What he now witnessed stunned him. He was very stunned, and could only repeat the mindless "Birds?" phrase so popular at the close of the previous chapter. For the elegant and lordly Breakspear was now covered by a large net. It was held in place by the two monklike attendants and by the three thuglike intruders, who must have been waiting in the corridor.

As he struggled to escape, Breakspear began to chirrup. "Thus perish all *Dei Ex Machina*," D murmured, a touch unsure of his Latin. He gestured to his alphabetical fellows, who came to stand side by side slackjawed at this latest development. G's was the slackest, D figured, glancing along the row that formed on his left. Of course, M's mighty beard – what might it not conceal?

Birdsong interrupted or realized this thought. But such birdsong as had seldom graced the living air. It continued to emanate from the enmeshed guru. Looking up from their difficult task, one of the attendants smiled apologetically at the four A- students, and their hangers-on, who were by now peering over their shoulders – their own, or MAGD'S, according to their builds.

"Wanted to spare both him and you this embarrassment. Hoped he'd come quietly. It was good of you to humour him. We'll have him back in Essondale before you can say Adrian Leverkuehn."

The entire crew vanished around the bend, net and all.

A was the first to speak.

"I'm f-f-fucken f-f-freezing you j-j-jerks. And, this isn't the r-right r-room."

M looked puzzled.

"But, but, 6, 1, "

G looked mortified.

"Hey, A, take those wet things off!"

He began to help her.

"Take your public hands off me, you loony. I'll find something when we get to the right spot. Room 5-5-522. F-F-Follow me."

They took the stairs. The Management demanded their immediate return.

"Fire code," they said, shortly. But the action had already moved a floor lower.

"Keep your rotten old stairs," G told them. Then "But Hey, A, you can't just barge right in there. What if someone's checked in?"

"No one will have checked in, but someone might have checked *out*," A replied, with grimly humorous emphasis.

She took a key from her reticule and inserted it in the lock. The door sprang open. She was right. The suite was empty. Everyone crowded in. D beat M to the refrigerator.

"It's gone," A wailed. She pointed to the north wall of the sitting room-cum-master bedroom, to the corner behind the small round table. All looked (except D, who had his head in the fridge). A was right: there was nothing there.

"The Osborne Ray Machine. It stood right there!"

Ham Meatfist and Jack Strop and Nels Nailbender drew up and parked on Gilford. They had heard it on the grapevine that Feather McFiddle-dee-dee and Peaches Dobell had been seen shinning up the Virginia Creeper whose main stem next the north wall winds thick as Hunk Hogan's biceps to the Dine in the Sky atop the fair Sylvia. Party, they had chanted at one another. McFiddle-dee-dee and Dobell were members of the sorority that belonged to their fraternity. The three dufusses – dufi? the Coming of the Dufi? – began their huffing puffing ascent.

"But Read," Eduardo Pink-Meadow was saying, as the pair hurried along Beach, "Brahms might not want us there. He might want to handle this alone. What say we sit in the beer parlour with a couple of beers until he happens by?"

"Hee's risponseebl fur thi wreck uv thi Hisperas," Only replied, alluding to his late yacht.

Pink-Meadow wasn't sure whether the boat was still in good shape and was christened *The Wreck of the Hesperus*, just as Hopkins's poem is titled *The Wreck of the Deutschland*, or whether the boat was now a late boat, and had been titled "The Hesperus." If the former, he thought, muzzy with drink, why, remarkably prescient of Read! Jolly good fellow, Read. Let every man dance attendance on Read Only, he thought. Excellent thought! – He tried it out loud.

"Let every damn man's son tend ants at Freedonia." It had sounded better when, like Keats's unsung melodies, it... his inner monologue vanished inside a tunnel. He followed red-haired Read Only into the lobby of the Sylvia, and began pushing buttons beside the elevator door.

Fee McMannic was slumming. He was out with the cousin of a future Prime Minister of Eire, and the son of a Vancouver high school principal. The reason Fee was out with them? They were the outgoing (in both senses) editors of the campus litmag, *Jackdaw*, and Fee's poem had won the Poetry Prize.

His prizewinning poem, *The Truck Farmers of Dewdney*, was disarmingly simple. "The truck farmers of Dewdney/ How yellow in the snow/ I am pale/ My famous tan raincoat is torn at the shoulder/ When we meet/ You will take my disgust/ And pour it over your fields."

"The editors like your work," the two had written, "for its announcement of Minimalism, a movement in which all the 'i's sound the same." But they did not know the poem would be more famous one day thanks to Leonard Cohen plagiarizing – and misquoting – its longest line. The editors had handed Fee the fifty dollar cheque that afternoon; now they were sticking with him till it was all spent.

If he must drink with jerks, Fee figured, he would at least avoid the embarrassment of being seen with them in his favourite haunts. Thus it was that these three, who otherwise never ventured bayward of the Dev (and then only when someone they owed money to was already in the G), prepared to enter the *terra incognita* of the Sylvia beer parlour at the precise moment McFiddle-dee-dee and Dobell were ascending the vine. McMannic, checking the sky for portents (his famous tan raincoat *was* torn at the shoulder, and elsewhere besides), glimpsing them from directly beneath, recognized both at once. They were the women who had posed as ex-cons in the house by the golf course.

Hmm, thought Fee. Another three or four brew, another ten Black Cats, and he would look further into this.

Montgomery Incline drove down Denman in his bug. The passenger seat had been removed to make space for props. He procured props for the local TV station. This meant that his passenger had to sit in back. His passenger today was Tamara Nevers. Turning round to talk to her in an uninterruptible spate of phrases, Incline scattered denizens to right and left. Smoking, looking boredly out the window, his companion ignored the mayhem. Suddenly she spotted the Sylvia. She had an impulse.

"Drinkies."

The distinguished members of the English Department panted over the logs on Sylvia Beach while reassuring one another of the complete propriety of their prurient interest in the doings of the Alphabet Four.

" Shouldn't that be the dongs," G put in.

" Impossible," A pointed out.

But this was in the Utopia of the Text, while we have a story to complete.

"Owe it to the young people to check up on them," said Dr. Lyons.

"Absolutely. We have a reputation to be worried about already." Thus Dr. Tyger.

"Today's students have started taking drugs," added their junior, the callow Mr. Bearass. "I don't know where they get them. But I intend to find out."

"I'm just here for the fun," giggled Wystan Buckett, to the disgust of the others. Except possibly, Mr. Bearass.

They disappeared into the Hotel Sylvia.

Mary Beth Hansen batted her big blues at Soyez Mysterieuse.

"I wonder where Fee is this evening," she mused.

Her midnight-brunette friend (whom Mary Beth had recently rescued from a suicide attempt in the Roundtowner Motel) cancelled her instinctive scowl (Fee was using Mary Beth as a subject for his undergraduate thesis, *A Comparison of Brassiere Sizes Among Aryan-Looking Sophomores at the University of British Columbia in 1960-1*) and smiled sweetly back, thinking "I owe her one."

"I heard there's a boat-wreck just offshore Sylvia Beach. Fee's bound to be down there scavenging."

The mothers of the future took some quick pulls on a pint of Jim Beam as Soyez cut some tight corners in the car D alluded to as her MGM. Shortly, the towering edifice that was The Sylvia loomed above them.

Romany Intense was barefoot, her sandals having finally disintegrated in the course of her hike over the seaweed and the oyster shells. A tall building loomed before her. Naturally, she went in. There were bound to be people she could offend.

Marianne McLuster had completed an unusually taxing paper. She stretched and yawned. Her phone, the bill still unpaid, hadn't, of course, rung. A little intercourse would be welcome – or a lot, actually. It felt like days since the last incident. She recalled a lively desk-clerk who'd wanted to exchange, among other information, DNA. But what was the name of that hotel? She stabbed into a phone directory at random. Her firm finger probed the name "Sylvia." Having no phone, she set off down the street like one of her ancestors striding the heather, singing *a capella*, something about feeling pretty, o so pretty. . .

"Handsome rather than pretty," observed Barry Noir, a teenager vacationing in Vancouver that week.

"Wellset jello on springs," commented Gordon Jordan, his companion.

"If I could get three like her a day," Barry replied. "Just three, that's all."

Pablo d'Oliviera was in town with his high school R-n-B band from Palos Muy Altos, California. Their bus was stuck in traffic on Denman.

"Sumthin shakin here, bro," Pablo told the driver, a certain Rey Charles from Seattle. "Reckon we'll go take a look-see." Turning towards the back of the bus, he called out to his musicians, "Hey! I know you'd be a fool to trust me, after what's been done to you – but I don't think this is gonna be somethin' we'll want to miss!"

Instruments slung over their shoulders, the unruly ninth-graders piled off the bus and into The Sylvia.

Another ninth-grader, Ray Rockaway from Brooklyn, NY, at fifteen already wearing a full, russet beard, slipped his hands out of the hands of his vacationing parents and darted into the venerable pile. Entering, he collided with d'Oliviera.

"Hey, watch it, Buster," Pablo told him.

"Be sure you know my name before you reprimand me," Rockaway sauced back. "Or it won't be long before you say 'Oi Weh'!"

D'Oliviera roared with laughter. Encouraged, Rockaway continued to speak as the band stood there pressing buttons for both elevators. "So you're from Palos Muy Altos," he said, reading their jackets. "Where the palm trees touch the skies? And a thousand Pee Aitch Dees are asking 'Why?'"

"These are the words that confuse what we feel we are," the band-leader told him. "I guess love just comes by surprise."

They took a chance on the South elevator.

Other, less attractive, less savory types were closing in on the Sylvia too. But as they drew near, they shrank back. An invisible radiance beamed from that site, more good than bad, and it rendered them into shadows, arms crabbedly aloft as though to ward off these benign rays. They stopped, rooted to the spot, then began to fade back into the encroaching night.

They watched with stony hearts as five men bundled a sixth into a van with "Essondale Hospital" painted on the side. It was the kind of thing they saw. The kind of thing we were born to report.

Lorraine Tartan had to investigate a complaint that the West End's most noted hotel was paying above union scale. That's what brought her to the Sylvia, where she bumped (Ooff!) into a lot of people she knew, and rode up with them to Room 522.

One of these persons was Beth. Returning from her afternoon with Phyllis Only, she had found news in the mail that D had been awarded a fellowship so that he could go to graduate school. She had been wondering where D could be. She knew he would be pleased by the news, and she wanted to share this pleasure with him. Then on the radio that evening she had learned of the wreck of *The Hesperus*. Of the somehow-connected-with-this (the newscaster was vague) gathering at the Sylvia.

Outside the Sylvia, she ran into Arthur Maguey, who was trailing his customary garland of stage-struck handmaids.

"Incline just went into the Sylvia," he told her. "In fact, there's quite a lot of people inside there now. I suppose it's one of Ink's non-events?"

"I'm looking for D," Beth told him, with that uncustomary impatience for which she was actually quite well known by longterm acquaintances. Screw *you*! But she kept smiling. It was a Velvet Steamroller.

"So is D," quipped Maguey. "He thinks he's the worm at the bottom of the bottle."

"I'm going in there."

"Why not?" Maguey purred. And so that little lot went into the hotel too.

Prester John loped up Gilford. He was late. He had been sitting too long in his UBC office advising Amanda Tunefork and now was late for a cocktail party at the flat he shared with his spouse not three blocks from the Sylvia.

As he passed that establishment he spotted one of his better students, Romany Intense. She was prancing barefoot up the steps and into the lobby. Acting on a poetic intuition, he followed.

Jacques Derrida strode broodingly down Beach Street. All this deferment and delay was no mystery to him. It was inscribed in the code. An ugly brick cube stood in his way. He went around it and on into the Park to feed the black squirrels. He was surprised by the raccoons.

D inspected the inside of the refrigerator. A square gray box of what looked to be generic cereal was its only content. What a racket there was in the other room! A was going on about having been a spy for the federal government which had been conducting experiments with a secret weapon, the Osborne Ray, in the course of which it had been directed at

D, G and M, and about how she had been told to study its effects on them, but how she had fallen in love with G and switched sides. No, Breakspear wasn't a spy, he was someone she had run into one night at the Blackstone where she had fallen somewhat under his unlikely spell and had allowed him to keep buying her drinks while he told her about the birds, how they were mysterious messengers from the other world, and how we would perish when they disappeared.

"Well," D could hear her saying defensively to the people in the other room, of whom there seemed to be more every minute, "I owed him a tale too, so I told him the tale of all of you. That's how come he knows what he knows about us. But he's nothing to do with the plot."

"Mmm," D thought. "This stuff tastes good." He continued to eat it with his hands, shovelling it in and chewing. Meanwhile, he wandered back into the other room. Some fifteen or twenty people were gathered there. A was in the center, naked beneath a blanket she kept forgetting was all she had on. Well, she had to gesture. It was vehement information. The duffel coat had been appropriated by M, always one with a quick eye for fashion. No doubt he was doing the gentlemanly thing, for A must have been sodden when the coat was wrapped around her by the mental hospital attendants, and the coat must have quickly become wet also. M stood there steaming with chivalry.

But now A's series of disclosures had hit a wall. She could come unravelled no further.

"What about the hieroglyphs?" G wanted to know.

"What about D having Fee's sexual experiences?" asked M.

This raised the mutter-level among the uninitiate in the room.

A could only gesture helplessly, raising her hands in the air. G retrieved the blanket.

A reporter from *The Vancouver Bun* barked his question. "If you had a penis for a day, what would you do with it?"

"I'd show it to all my friends," A responded.

D realised he himself was quite wet. He began to disrobe.

And as he disrobed, he began to speak.

Who was this glamorous woman seated on the thwarts of this beat-up old boat moored in Coal Harbour, doing three crossword puzzles at once while discoursing on Wittgenstein, listening to Stan Getz on the beat-up old turntable and meanwhile beating Paxton Coppersworth at Scrabble? Sophia Loren, surely! But no, she was Deirdre Fuller, she whose genius-class mind had been further shaped, long arm of coincidence, when she was still named Deirdre Littlewood (no relative of the ex-Mrs D), by highschool teacher Percy Delsing, G's progenitor.

Game over, Paxton – he whose fund of anecdotes concerning one Swatow Smith, entrepreneur of the South China Sea, could hold listeners spellbound at a table in the "G" for hours – found himself uncharacteristically tongue-tied. So he suggested taking a little cruise.

"In this thing? No thanks. I have a brilliant career ahead of me."

"How about a little spin in the windowcleanermobile, then?" Paxton squared his already square jaw against further rejection: his van, faded apple-green where paint remained, lacked a muffler, and rattled even in Park. But Deirdre thought this was a risk worth taking: better odds.

So it was that they came to be passing by The Sylvia when the crush to enter the hotel was at its greatest. Like the man of action he so ably simulated, Coppersworth laid his ladders against the north wall, and the couple shinnied up and through the window of 522, just as Fee came through the door.

Douglas Faun and Dundee France went up the ladder a minute later. At first confused as to the location of the hotel ("Is a beach a street? Is a street a ford? Is a man, even a dun man, a thoroughfare?" queried the habitually looped Faun; and, told by Dundee "*Den*-man, *Den*-man!" responded "What is it dow, chick?"), the skinny linguist and the voluptuous librarian – neither known to have missed a party since arriving at UBC – leaned in the window like – the light behind them – satyr and nymph in D's now whacky vision. D began to slip into his *fin-de-siecle* mode.

And those attending marvelled at the transformation in D's bearing and appearance. Later, they were to say it was as though the Holy Spirit had descended from Heaven to touch him with its fire. Well, Barton Martlett said that. Others had more secular explanations to offer. But all agreed that they had witnessed a miracle. Room 522 filled with the charisma.

The poison of all-knowingness from the Omniscient Narrator's Bulgarian umbrella was coming on, but so was the "oatmeal," and D naturally confused the cause of these effects. D of a sudden could know what everyone present was thinking. This alone would have made it impossible to speak with any coherence, except that he could also edit and extrapolate in some extraordinary way. A golden glow burned all over his skin. Waves of energy pulsed through his what were then called loins and are still called armpits.

"Then this is the explanation which I am at this moment eating," he began. "This stuff in this box must have been inadvertently left behind when the Feds cleaned up and cleared out. One of them had earlier given some to A, telling her it was loaded with vitamins and to give it to her friends so they'd get better grades, have better sex, write better poems."

("Far fucken out," asided A. "How'd he know that?")

"The rime part had nothing to do with it. False conclusion. Merely coincidental. Fee's sexual escapade? An extreme case of my uncanny ability to 'get inside' another person, to get them on my wavelength and let the river answer."

("I don't know why he puts 'get inside' in quotes," sniffed several of those present.)

"As for Brian Stewart and friend, G and I pumped them in The Georgia and concluded they were hapless victims of the class-war. They had heard us on "Youthless" and wanted so badly to see some middleclass, beatnik phenomena of their own, that they projected it – I speak of psychological dynamics, not Incline-tricks – onto some harmless graffiti, scrawled on the Hastings Street walls by that downtown poet, Gerhardt Gildart." (Gildart giggled.) "The engineers on the beach with their sheet of tin were likewise responding to our appearance on "Youthless". They were attempting to simulate the Great White Flash.

"When the Feds trained the Osborne Ray on the Burrard St Bridge as we crossed it, we faced directly into it. Although it was only a narrow band, seeing it head-on that way made it look like an atomic detonation.

"It threw our shadows on the brewery wall."

D virtually sang this sentence. Dan Danielson began to play his ukulele. Pablo d'Oliviera unslung his guitar. Harmonicas were produced by Barry Gary and, astonishingly, Prester John. Ray Rockaway opened a drawer, stole a sheet of paper that said "Hotel Sylvia" across the top, and folded it over the business end of his rat-tailed comb. Hans Geiselglobe came in with his bongos. Barton Martlett produced an amazingly large portable organ and began to finger it, to everyone's entertainment.

But before they could do more than tune up, D concluded.

"But at the very instant when the ray of light struck us, a flock of birds started up, startled out of their roosts beneath the bridge by the unwonted illumination.

"These birds shattered our reflections, no, shadows, no, uh, yes, shadows, into the hieroglyphs of Sicks."

Everyone began to chatter to his and her neighbour, the volume rose, the excitement increased. The band began to play. People began to dance, a new kind of dancing, the kind of dancing you can do while removing your clothes.

It wasn't always pretty at first, but it was real.

D, divested of clothing, an Etruscan in the mind of DH Lawrence, kept right on talk-singing, but nobody was listening any longer.

"It has been our own shadows, broken by contingency,

we have been struggling to decode throughout this episode in our young lives! Breakspear was wrong, but he was right too! What can madness signify to us, but divine rightness? He was gloriously right! And what's more, stylistically right! And Yes and I said Yes and Yes I said Yes Yes Yes Yes Yes Yes Yes Yes Yes!"

The noise reached a crescendo, and then another, and another. The contact high from the Government oatmeal foretold lysurging acid as it sped through the crowd; but in addition, the oatmeal D had not eaten was being eaten now, had been being eaten for some little while. People were *blending* – merging and moving through boundaries become shimmery and opalescent, in couples, triples, quadruples, quintuples – taking on colour and form from one another – sexier than the most abandoned of merely physical orgies. It was Eleusis come again. The entire gathering began to move in this strange new dance.

G danced with A. M danced with Serena Rapt. Romany Intense merged and emerged with and from the Downtown Poets. One of them got off his bicycle…

Use your imagination! You know their names by now. And you've seen your share of orgies. Well, this wasn't like that. This was in another league. Its like shall ne'er be seen again. The Government "lost" the formula. Oh, maybe in Massey Hall…

Peaches Dobell found the corpse of Pat Boone in a closet and polka'd around the carpet with it. It quickly came alive, like Bernie in the second "Weekend at Bernie's" movie when the Reggae strikes up. And Pat Boone turned out to be a marvelous dancer! Too bad these were post-mortem effects…

"Let it rip, citizens!" cried the indistinguishable and unattendable D. "This is the last party of your youth! This is our final Hurrah! Tomorrow, diapers and diaspora!"

The assembly heard this last phrase and took it up in an eerie chant as the band hit a heavy rock beat:

DIAPERS N DIASPORA DIAPERS N DIASPORA

What beauty in that gracious room – what tsunami

energy! Then an amazing voice said, "Hi. I'm Sylvia!" Everyone's head was turned. The gathering was entering eternity.

Then every single damned light. Went out.

"-30-!" came G's voice out of the darkness.

Typeset in Minion
printed at Coach House Printing on bpNichol Lane
the text paper is 60 lb. Williamsburg.

The first 150 of this first edtion are bound in boards.

To order or read online versions of this
or other Coach House Books titles,
please visit http://www.chbooks.com

To be added to the emailing list, write
mail@chbooks.com

For more traditional interaction, contact Coach House Books at 401 Huron
on bpNichol Lane, Toronto, ON
M5S 2G5
or call 1 800 367-6360